"Aren't you going to invite me in?"

They'd reached her front door and Ellen panicked at the thought. "You wouldn't like it in there. It's cold, remember?"

Simon leaned closer. "We could warm it up."

She opened the screen door to scoot inside, but he held it. "I just thought it was customary to invite your date in."

"Oh, I'm afraid I break with custom on a lot of things," Ellen hedged.

Simon smiled. "Even time-tested dating rituals like this?" In one motion his lips claimed hers, and his body pinned her against the door. Instantly she was dizzy with desire, and she could feel the same response in him. If she wanted, she could open the door and invite—

The television! She heard it and gasped. She most certainly could *not* invite Simon Miller in. Not when her dead husband was watching sitcoms in her living room!

Dear Reader,

This month a new "Rising Star" comes out to shine, as American Romance continues its search for the best talent...the best stories.

Let me introduce you to Liz Ireland. The author of a handful of historical, contemporary and young-adult romances, this Texan makes her American Romance debut. She's been a fan of ghost stories ever since seeing "The Ghost and Mrs. Muir" as a child, so she's delighted that her first American Romance is a woman's choice between a dark-eyed charmer and a devilish ghost with an attitude!

So turn the page and catch a "Rising Star"! I know you'll love Liz's wit and humor. She had me laughing my whole way through!

Regards,

Debra Matteucci
Senior Editor & Editorial Coordinator
Harlequin Books
300 E. 42nd St.
New York, NY 10017

Liz Ireland

HEAVEN-SENT
HUSBAND

Harlequin Books

TORONTO • NEW YORK • LONDON
AMSTERDAM • PARIS • SYDNEY • HAMBURG
STOCKHOLM • ATHENS • TOKYO • MILAN
MADRID • WARSAW • BUDAPEST • AUCKLAND

For Meg Ruley. Many, many thanks!

ISBN 0-373-16639-7

HEAVEN-SENT HUSBAND

Copyright © 1996 by Elizabeth Bass.

Prologue

> Gorgeous young widow of a brilliant aspiring writer wishes to correspond with man of substance. Must be intelligent, self-supporting, have a warm sense of humor and an artistic spirit. Good looks a +! Sincere inquiries only. Send photo and well-written and entertaining letter addressed to P.O. Box...

Abel Lantry lay sprawled on a puffy white cloud, thumping his gold fountain pen against his temple, deep in thought. Writing this thing was turning out to be harder than he'd expected. But he had to keep at it, for Ellen's sake, and his own.

Oh, he'd seen plenty of raised eyebrows from these cherub types around here over his wife's behavior. She had practically put her life on hold. Back in school, eternal love had always made for great poems, but up here angels in the know had told him that for a raw recruit like himself, it looked bad. Like *he* was being selfish, and somehow not letting her get on with her life.

Yeah, right. Like he was sending vibes down below that were causing his wife to have the social life of a hermit crab.

Man, what a mess. Didn't anything ever work out right? He'd thought that once he'd gotten up here, afterlife would be a breeze. Not so, apparently. As a not very productive graduate student back on earth, he hadn't racked up the kind of credentials that won the big halos around this place. And then there was the whole business about Ellen . . .

Well, he was just going to have to fix things the best he could.

He gave his handiwork a critical once-over and felt a smile twist his lips. Not bad, if he did say so himself. Oh, maybe a man coming across this ad in the personals might think Ellen a little immodest for referring to herself as gorgeous, but . . . well, wasn't it the truth? Besides, he wanted results. He couldn't announce that the woman was so reclusive that the heavens were frowning on her. He needed to get his wife some dates.

"And this might just do it," he said to himself, pleased with his effort. "Man, you haven't lost your touch."

No, it wasn't bad at all, he decided. By far the best thing he'd written since dying. Now, the only hard part left would be trying to find out how to get a P.O. box in heaven.

Chapter One

Two months later...

"I don't think fifty million is too much to spend, do you?"

Ellen Lantry clenched the phone receiver in her hand and gulped. She'd known Vern Samuelson was one of the richest men in San Antonio, but... "Not if you have it, I guess."

"Oh, I've got it, all right."

And the dear old cranky man intended to spend it all on a memorial for his late wife... much to the distress of the many long-lost relatives who kept popping out of the woodwork. As the assistant to the Austin attorney in charge of Mr. Samuelson's fortune, Ellen had endured enough angry conversations with these relatives to know the extent of their distress, though she, a widow herself, thought it was wonderful that a man could be so dedicated to his wife that he was willing to devote everything he had to her memory.

"I've hired a big-shot architect to design the park. You might have heard of her—that lady who designed the Vietnam War Memorial."

Heard of her? "I've seen her work," Ellen said.

"Well, I'll send the plans up to Harlan when I get them," Vern promised.

Harlan Smith, the senior partner of Smith, Levin and Smith—just plain "Smith" to its employees—was Ellen's boss. "We'll look forward to seeing how the Louise Samuelson Memorial Park is coming along," she said.

After hanging up, Ellen leaned back in her chair and listened to "Eleanor Rigby" being butchered by one hundred and one violins. Yolanda, Smith's receptionist, referred to this as "night of the living lawyers" music, and it was only one of the lesser changes their boss had instigated recently. When Ellen came on years before, the firm had a reputation as being one of the stuffiest in Austin. And things had poked along that way until Harlan Smith had suffered a heart attack three months ago.

Everyone had expected him to retire after his bypass. Instead, he had come back with a vengeance. His hair might have turned a silvery white overnight, but the rest of him was completely rejuvenated. He had begun a revamp of the office, too. The chilly silence of old was out; Muzak was in. Every afternoon the whole office congregated for a healthful quarter hour of stretching. He hired a new younger lawyer and was always trying to recruit more. And Harlan was in the middle of renovating the old somber decor of the office, which had already been through one thorough paint job, with more doubtless on the way. Some of the older partners—stuffy ones who were happy with their clogging arteries—didn't appreciate the Big Bird yellow Harlan in his new, brighter mood had chosen.

"What are you still doing here?" Harlan said, peeking around the corner of her cubicle. He was wearing a bright blue sweat suit, high-top sneakers and a disapproving frown.

Ellen looked up, mystified. "It's ten till five."

"It's also your birthday. Go home!"

He darted away before she could respond. How had he known? She'd never made a big deal of this day—perhaps because it always seemed so sad to her now. So many memories. Abel had loved birthdays. Four years ago, on her twenty-third birthday, he had proposed marriage....

Ellen sighed, got up and threw the plastic cover over her computer. Maybe Harlan had looked it up in the personnel files. He really was a sweet man. He just didn't realize that on today of all days she'd rather be here, working, than at home, brooding. Nevertheless, she would follow his orders. She'd never be productive now that she'd started thinking about Abel.

Slowly, she gathered her things and made her way out to the reception area, which, thanks to its new yellow paint job, had to be one of the most blinding spots on the planet.

"Message for you, Ellen," Yolanda said as Ellen punched the button for the elevators. "He called while your line was busy."

Ellen stared a moment at the pink message slip in her slot on the reception desk's message carousel.

"Looking forward to tonight!"

The enthusiastic message was signed simply "Joe," but Ellen didn't know a Joe. She frowned, then turned to Yolanda, whose speculative gaze was glued on her. "Didn't leave a number," she said before Ellen could ask. "With a message like that, I assumed you'd know it."

Ellen smiled limply. Maybe this was some kind of joke. "Did this, uh, Joe ask for me by name?"

Yolanda rolled her big brown eyes toward the ceiling in her most long-suffering manner. *"Honey,* if your name is still Ellen Lantry, then let's just say it sounded to me as if your dream boat has just docked at a pier with your name on it."

Ellen took that for a yes. She swallowed, feeling even more uneasy. "You mean his voice was—" she lowered her voice "—sexy?"

"The man gave me goose pimples—and I hear a lot of voices."

"Hmm."

"I can't believe you've had somebody in the wings and haven't told me about it," she scolded. "It's about time you found somebody."

Ellen felt herself freeze, as she always did when conversations took a turn down the "you've-been-grieving-too-long" route. If she tried to argue, she would no doubt be reminded how long it had been since Abel died. Four years. As if she could ever forget. People didn't understand that grief wasn't something you could turn on and off like a faucet.

"I want the details Monday," Yolanda demanded, "and I mean a.m., understand?"

"I doubt there will be much to tell." Ignoring Yolanda's skeptical gaze, she stepped onto an elevator, glancing down at the pink slip again and again, as if the answer to the puzzling message would come clear if only she read it over enough.

A fluky mistake—that had to be the explanation. Joe was probably trying to reach an entirely different Ellen Lantry. Ellen was a common-enough name, as was Lantry. Perhaps she should take cold comfort in the fact that somewhere out there, a person named Ellen Lantry actually had a life.

She put on her sunglasses as the elevator approached the ground floor, preparing herself for the Texas sun's assault. It was early summer, the days were long, the mercury was already beginning its long but inevitable climb toward the century mark, and there was enough humidity hanging in the air to send her long strawberry blond hair into an instant frizz. As always, she tried to concentrate on getting her body from the air-conditioned building to her air-conditioned car, while keeping the sweat factor to a minimum. She strode in long, easy steps toward the parking lot, which was to the side of the building, down a foliage-lined sidewalk.

She had nearly reached the parking lot when, to her left, she heard a bush rustle. Surprised, she turned, expecting to see a squirrel darting out, or a cat. Instead, a full-grown man hopped out in front of her path.

She let out a startled yell, nearly dropping her soft-sided briefcase.

Simon Miller, Smith's newest associate, skidded to a stop in front of her, a devilish grin spread across his handsome face. From behind his back, he pulled out a huge cellophane-wrapped pile of long-stemmed red roses.

"Happy birthday," he said, handing them to her.

"For me?" Sheepishly, Ellen lifted her glasses to the top of her head. Ever since he had walked into Smith two months ago, Simon had set many hearts aflutter—including her own. He was Harlan Smith's second act of office rejuvenation, one much nicer than the Muzak. His tall, lean build, healthy tanned skin and deep brown eyes, which were usually sparkling as if enjoying some private joke, created an irresistible package.

"This *is* your birthday, isn't it?"

Her brows knit together quickly. "Yes, but how did you know?"

"I have my ways," he said with a sly grin. "Never fear—" He winked and leaned in closer, his thousand-watt smile shining on her full blast. "Your secret's safe with me."

Ellen tamped down the butterflies that smile sent flapping around her insides. "Thanks," she said, awkwardly trying to balance purse, briefcase and flowers.

"I hope I haven't upset you," he said.

She nearly let out a mirthful hoot. Just having Simon smile at her caused her heart to skip; having him hand her flowers made her dreary day. Even if he was only being nice—which she was certain was the case. "These roses are beautiful, Simon. Thank you."

The words were intended as a conversation ender, but he wasn't about to let that happen. His hesitant but slightly aggressive stance sent a jolt of recognition bubbling up from somewhere deep in the recesses of Ellen's memory. That stance meant more than nice. It meant *date*. Warning bells jangled. She knew she had to bolt away, fast, before something awkward happened, but her feet were suddenly encased in cement boots that locked her in place. And the intensity in Simon's dreamy brown eyes served the same purpose—an intensity that was heating up something unfamiliar inside her.

In a split second, though, she had a name for the feeling. Lust! The realization was enough to send her rocketing out of her cement boots.

Yet before she could move, Simon sidled quickly to put himself between her and the parking lot. "How about dinner?" he asked, the anticipated words coming out in a rush.

Ellen attempted to gasp in a breath. To her horror, a bashful flush washed over her, and she glanced away toward her car, her watch, then a twittering bird in a nearby tree—anywhere but into Simon's eyes, which she was sure would have melted her resolve like butter.

How could this be happening to her? She wasn't looking for any complications in her life right now, wasn't ready to jump back into the swing of things. Especially not tonight of all nights.

She'd been so good about avoiding this kind of situation. The only man who had asked her out in four years was Larry Lambert, an ex-football player turned divorce attorney and the resident office lothario. He tried to date every woman who crossed his path, so it hadn't been difficult to turn him down.

But Simon wasn't Larry. She just couldn't imagine going out with Simon—without falling head over heels for him. There was something about the man, besides his exceptional looks, that she found wildly attractive. She'd always thought she'd been drawn to moody, temperamental types. Like Abel. Simon had charisma, but it was more that of a man who took things in stride and approached life with grace.

"Hesitant because of work?" he asked. "Believe me, I'm Mr. Discreet."

For a moment, she was torn. It had been so long since she'd let herself be wined and dined, and the romantic rumblings Simon set off inside her had a powerful pull. But that didn't make it any less problematic to get involved with a co-worker.... Then again, his exuberance was hard to resist. She sensed he had a romantic streak a mile wide.

Ironically, that quality was what made up her mind. She had a romantic streak, too. But she could never have a romance with another man like the one she had had with Abel, and right now she wasn't ready to settle for less. She looked once more at Simon's handsome face. He deserved a woman who was ready to fall for him head-over-heels.

"Oh, well," he said, guessing her response from her expression. "I just thought it might be fun."

"I'm sorry," Ellen said. "It's just—" She bit off her words.

Simon put a hand on her shoulder. "I understand."

The contact affected her more than she might have expected. Her knees wobbled. "You do?"

Simon's bright brown eyes zoomed in on her. "I've heard about your husband. He was a writer, wasn't he?"

His words shocked her. No one talked to her about Abel anymore; they just lectured her. "He wanted to be. Actually, he was a graduate student while we were married."

And she had started working at Smith to pay the bills, putting off momentarily her own dreams of going to law school. After Abel's motorcycle accident, she had applied to school, and was accepted, but she just couldn't get worked up to face three grueling years of law school. So each year since she'd filled out a deferment.

"It must be hard for you, especially on days like today. That's why I thought you might like to do something."

The sympathy surprised her; she felt ashamed, as if she'd asked for it. Then shame turned to a sharp pang of disappointment. Was she the only one feeling wobbly here? His flowers and dinner treatment seemed to be all about pity now. She didn't know why that bothered her so, since she definitely preferred friendly concern to any kind of sexual interest on his part.

Nevertheless, she found herself resisting being regarded as a charity case in his eyes. "Actually, I have plans," she lied. Well . . . it wasn't *exactly* a lie.

He watched her silently—and then that hand on her shoulder squeezed a little tighter. "C'mon, I'll walk you to your car."

He placed his hand below her elbow and strolled easily beside her. As they passed under the shade of a tree, he sighed and admitted, "I was going to take you to this restaurant that has the greatest French food you can imagine. Everything the chef cooks up is an absolute masterpiece."

Ellen nodded. Her stomach, already in knots from Simon's light but electric touch at her elbow, growled.

"This man can whip up mousses that you would just not believe!" He looked at her apologetically. "But you're probably going to have birthday cake or something, right?"

She thought of the pound cake in her freezer. Her lips twisted into a limp smile.

"Oh, well." He shrugged genially. "I'll take a rain check. That bottle of champagne will keep for some other time."

"Champagne?" Ellen asked. Her footsteps slowed reluctantly as they approached her Toyota.

"Of course," Simon answered, smiling as he tugged her forward. "You didn't think I was going to skimp on your birthday, did you?"

It had been ages since she'd drunk champagne, or really anything beyond the glass of red wine at her parents' Christmas dinner. It had been so long since she'd let go. Since she'd found herself actually wanting to go out with a man.

He opened her car door for her. "Well, anyway, I hope you have a good time. It'll probably be more fun than dancing."

She dug in her heels before he could push her inside. "Dancing?"

"Okay, you caught me." He bent closer. "By the water cooler the other day, I heard you admit that you hadn't been dancing since..."

"Since Abel died." Actually, it had been since before she met Abel, who hadn't been much of a dancer. He'd always been more of a lounger than a mover, and to avoid making waves, she'd submerged the toe-tapper in her personality while they were going out. She sank, frowning, onto the velour of her front seat. "My, you're all ears."

"Ears and feet, you might say." When she looked up at him questioningly, he went on, "Arthur Murray was my savior in law school. If I hadn't learned to dance after the first semester, I'd probably still be in that law library, a calcified one-L."

Ellen laughed at the vision of a crazed, overworked first-year law student taking out his frustrations in a tango. "A legal eagle with twinkle toes," she mused.

"I'm always on the lookout for a partner."

Ellen's smile faded as those brown eyes fastened on to her, and she felt a wave of heat spill into her cheeks. How would it be to be this man's "partner"? Usually, her own tall, lanky frame towered over men; she and Abel had been the same height. But Simon was slightly taller, just right. She felt dizzy just imagining being swept into his arms for a romantic waltz.

"Oh, well," he said, "maybe some other time."

"I can't, Simon," Ellen replied quickly. There was no sense putting off making a decision. Nothing had changed. Simon was handsome and charming, every woman's dream—but there had to be a catch somewhere. That's why Ellen wasn't interested in going out with anyone. She had experienced one perfect love, and though her marriage had been tragically brief, she wasn't interested in taking the risk of getting involved again. Not yet. Maybe not ever.

"Please don't take this the wr—"

He silenced her with a killer smile, leaning down so that she got a close-up of it. "Didn't I tell you? I intend to keep asking you out until you accept."

She looked up at him quizzically. "Oh?"

"Weekly," he assured her.

He bent down, his tall frame casting a shadow into the front seat of her car. At first Ellen was confused. What was he doing, checking her mileage? Then—too late—she realized that it wasn't her odometer he was focused on, it was her lips! Before she could speak, pull away or protest, Simon placed his mouth against hers.

Ellen sucked in a shocked breath. He was kissing her! She was being kissed—right here in her Toyota!

And it wasn't just a quickie, see-ya-later kind of kiss, either. Not if the floppy feeling in her stomach was any indication. His lips molded perfectly to hers, exerting only the slightest pressure. Still, she was as captivated by the feel of them against her own lips as if they had been joined by a tube of Super Glue. He held her arms gently but firmly, and pulled her ever so closer to him.

A wave of heat that had nothing to do with the sticky June temperature washed over her, and she suddenly panicked. She was trapped in a bucket seat, one hand on the steering wheel, the other on Simon's arm—how had it gotten there? She had a lapful of flowers and no idea what to do to stop this madness. Only one thought raced through her mind in the endless moment that his warm lips remained fastened on to hers. *Kissing was even better than she remembered!*

HE HADN'T INTENDED to do this . . .

Nor had he intended to ask her out. In fact, when he woke up this morning, Simon hadn't even known today was Ellen Lantry's birthday. But once he had found out, ideas just started snowballing, words came out of his mouth, and it seemed so natural just to take her into his arms and give her a birthday kiss to remember him by.

Her lips, so soft, so yielding—he hadn't expected that. Especially after she'd turned him down for dinner. The sharp fragrance of the roses filled the hot interior of the Toyota, mixing with the vestiges of her perfume. The heady smell nearly knocked him out. *Ellen* nearly knocked him out.

Ever since he'd started working at Smith two months before, he had wanted to do this. To kiss her. He had held back, not wanting to be perceived as some office lech, like Larry Lambert. And everyone knew about Ellen. Her widowhood was a fortress few people had overcome, even in a friendly way. So Simon had attempted to stay in the background, giving her time, carefully planning how he could launch an assault against those barricades of hers.

And what had all his patience come to? This—hopping out of a bush and kissing her in a parking lot! *Smooth, very smooth.* Just what was it about this woman that drew him like a magnet draws paper clips?

Now all his good intentions would fly out the window. After this unguarded moment, Ellen would probably avoid him like the plague, unless he could figure out some way to recover the situation, make it seem like this was just a casual little birthday kiss.

Summoning the will he wasn't sure existed inside him, he forced himself to pull away. He heard her give out a light gasp of surprise, and had to stifle a disappointed groan himself. He could have kissed her forever.

"Have a happy birthday, Ellen," he said, his voice slightly gravelly.

"Oh..."

Her eyes widened in surprise as he straightened and carefully closed her car door for her without another word. What more could he have said? *I know we've hardly spoken in two months, but I think I'm falling in love with you...?*

Somehow, as Ellen finally turned over her engine and peeled out of the parking lot as though the very devil were nipping at her wheels, he doubted those were the words she wanted to hear.

ANNIE DUNCAN, WHO LIVED in the adjoining apartment in Ellen's duplex, was out front in the yard when Ellen pulled onto their street. Annie, who was about Ellen's age and single, had been religiously tending the beds in front of the house since breaking up with her boyfriend four months earlier. Tonight she was watering the pink coleus plants that bordered the walkway.

Looking up from the nozzle at the end of her watering hose, she took a gander at the flowers Ellen was juggling along with her usual load and let out a low whistle. "What happened? Did you win a beauty pageant?"

For the first time in the past fifteen seconds, Ellen thought of Simon and fought back a blush. "Oh, I . . . I got these on the way home."

Annie laughed. "Thought you might have hooked yourself a live one. As you can tell, it's another thrilling Friday night of swinging singledom for me."

Ellen remembered Simon, his romantic evening itinerary, and his teasing kiss. Maybe she should have gone out with him, she thought, her resolve waffling. But it was too late to change her mind now. "Me, too," she commiserated.

Briefly, she considered telling her neighbor about her birthday. Annie was the closest thing to a friend she had these days. When she'd taken her own apartment in the bleak days after Abel's death, Annie was already installed next door. They shared a front porch and a small wood-plank back patio, and often when they came home in the evening, teetering tiredly on their heels, they would swap war stories from the business day. Or Annie, whose feelers were always out for the elusive hunk of her dreams, would bemoan their single status and the lack of available men in the world.

And Ellen had to admit, she hadn't met anyone new and interesting in a coon's age herself.

Except Simon. Her chest rose and fell in a sigh. How would it have felt to dance in those arms of his?

She put the thought out of her mind, as well as the idea of telling Annie about her birthday. She was just being self-pitying.

"Got anything going tonight?" Annie asked.

"My VCR, probably."

Annie barked out a laugh, and her bobbed hair danced around her jaw. "I forgot to tell you, I have a date with Tom Cruise."

"Oh, really?"

"Picked him up on my way home."

Ellen laughed and mounted the steps of the porch their entrances shared and let herself into her apartment. It was time to give herself some birthday TLC.

Two hours later, after having devoured a microwave meal fit for a queen, complete with a glass of red wine and served on real live china, she popped her favorite old movie into the VCR and settled down on the couch. She'd changed into her favorite nightgown, a ruffly white cotton affair whose thick weave after years of washing had softened like fine down. With her matching robe wrapped around her, she felt thoroughly swathed. During the opening credits for *Casablanca,* her cat, Hawthorne, jumped into her lap. The yellow tabby purred loudly as he settled onto Ellen's tummy.

This was what she had passed off as "plans" to Simon—watching an old movie with her cat. For entertainment value, it couldn't be beat. But for companionship...well, much as she liked Hawthorne, something was definitely missing from this picture.

What really worried her was that none of this usually mattered to her. She and Hawthorne had been watching the VCR for years without feeling lonely. Until today. Until Simon had jumped out of that bush. Until he'd kissed her.

On the television, Humphrey Bogart and Peter Lorre were in Rick's Café having their secretive conversation about letters of transit. Distracted as she was by her own thoughts, Ellen barely heard the familiar words, and didn't see the two characters at all. Nor did she take note of another character. A newcomer was sitting at the roulette wheel, surreptitiously watching not Bogart and Lorre, but Ellen....

That kiss had consumed all her attention for hours now, Ellen realized. But what kind of kiss had it been?

A hot, lazy kiss, she thought, smiling as she remembered the pressure of his lips against hers, the urge she'd had to throw her arms around his neck and move against him. Thank heavens she'd shown some restraint!

After all, to Simon that kiss was probably little more than an innocent peck. She feared, because of her general isolation these past few years, that she had lost some of her powers of perception when it came to males. In fact, it seemed her sexual antennae had been down for so long that she was no longer picking up signals.

The doorbell rang, nearly scaring Ellen out of her wits. She jumped, knocking Hawthorne off his resting place on her knee. He stretched his back and glared at her resentfully as she straightened her robe. Who would be coming to visit her?

Ellen turned down the sound on the television, padded to the door and opened it cautiously. What she saw on the other side of the screen nearly took her breath away.

A man, a great-looking movie star of a male, smiled at her. He had long golden blond hair, a Hollywood tan, blue eyes and white, white teeth. Ellen's mouth dropped open. Then she saw what he had in his arms—long-stemmed red roses just like the ones she'd put in a vase on her dining table, a package and a huge cellophane-covered box of candy. The package especially caught her eye, since it was wrapped in bright, festive paper.

"Happy birthday, Ellen."

She stared at the handsome man, straining her memory. But it was hopeless. His wasn't a face she would forget. She'd never seen this person in her life.

But he knew her name. And that today was her birthday. She began to panic.

"Ellen?"

She gave herself a mental shake and tried to compose herself. If the man was a loony, the phone was just behind her to call 911. The screen was latched, so she wasn't in danger—unless the man was toting a gun, which by no means was unheard of in these parts. But even if he was, his arms were so full of junk that it would take him forever to reach for it.

Besides, he didn't look like a wacko. In his dark suit, he looked more like a hip accountant. Ellen peered around the man's head toward the street. A Volvo was parked at the foot of her walkway. Did psychopaths drive Volvos?

"Ellen, are you all right?" The man craned his neck to inspect her more carefully.

She stepped back almost instinctively. "How do you know my name?"

He let out a nervous laugh. "Are you kidding me?"

He seemed pretty sure of himself, whoever he was. "This is no joke. I don't know who you are."

The man's smile faded abruptly. "I'm Joe, remember? We had a date."

Joe! She'd completely forgotten about him. "But...I don't know you...."

He huffed out a breath. "Look, Ellen, if you've gotten cold feet at the last minute, I understand. But please don't lie. You look exactly like the picture you sent, except maybe a little older."

"*I* sent *you* a picture? Of myself?"

He rolled his eyes in exasperation. "Two months ago, remember? When we first started writing?"

Now she knew she was going crazy—or that this Joe person was truly certifiable. "I'm sorry, I don't know what you're talking about."

Joe's patience was at an end. His baby blues narrowed on her and his jaw sawed back and forth before he spoke. "*You* were the one who put the ad in the paper, not me," he said, pointing to the roses at her accusingly. "'Gorgeous widow,' remember? If you didn't want to see me, you should have said so."

"But I swear, I don't know you."

He fixed her with an icy glare. "Fine," he said, his hands shaking as he leaned the roses against the door. "These aren't returnable, so keep them. This *is* your birthday, isn't it?"

Ellen nodded glumly.

"Have the candy, too." He dropped it unceremoniously on the porch, turned and strode toward his Volvo. "Happy birthday!" he yelled at her angrily before roaring off.

Ellen slumped against the screen door with a mixture of relief and bafflement. What was going on?

Just as she heard the Volvo peeling down a side street, Annie burst through her front door. She had changed from her work clothes to a pair of stretch pants and a T-shirt. "*What* was that!" she exclaimed in wonder.

Ellen was still in shock. "I have no idea."

Annie turned back to her, arms akimbo. "Ellen Lantry, don't be a ditz. That was a hunk in a Volvo, and you just kicked him off your porch!"

"I didn't know him," Ellen said defensively.

"But he even brought you birthday presents." She slapped her hand over her mouth—too late. "Well, anyway," Annie defended herself, "you didn't tell *me* it was your birthday!"

Ellen flipped the latch on the screen door and stepped outside to pick up the "gifts." The box of chocolates had been banged up in its fall. Ellen tore the cellophane off and offered her neighbor a candy.

"Thanks," Annie said. "You seriously don't know that guy?"

Ellen shook her head. "I've never seen him before in my life."

"I should be so lucky," Annie moaned, biting into a cherry cordial. "Mmm, good chocolates, too. How do you suppose he found you?"

Ellen shrugged as she chewed on a peanut cluster. Now that she looked at the second batch of red roses she'd received that day, she found the whole situation a little scary. Especially after that "gorgeous widow" business he'd been ranting about. Did that mean *her?* "I have no idea."

"Hmm." Annie obviously was searching for something comforting to say—and coming up woefully blank. "Okay, so maybe he's telepathic."

Ellen raised her eyebrows skeptically. "Then why did he say that I had written to him?"

"Yeah, that did sound kinda strange." Annie shook her head. "Maybe it's like sleepwalking—except that in your sleep, *you* write to good-looking men and invite them out on your birthday."

"Have another chocolate, Freud," Ellen answered with a laugh. "I'm going in."

Annie took two chocolates for her troubles. "If he comes around again, don't be so quick to kick him off the porch. If I'm fast enough, I might be able to catch him on the rebound before he makes it to the steps." She winked, then ducked back inside.

In her dark apartment, Ellen latched and locked her door carefully, then tripped over to the table to deposit the roses. The room's only light was the eerie blue glow from the television. Hawthorne darted nervously between her legs, frightening her. In her mind she pictured Joe, her rebuffed birthday date, stalking her house. Maybe she *should* call the police, just in case anything strange happened later. She reached for the phone.

"Don't do that," a voice from behind her said.

Ellen's spine stiffened just like Hawthorne's sometimes did...when he was very, very scared. She froze in place, not breathing, feeling her eyes bugging in their sockets.

Abel's voice! He was telling her not to call the police.

Now she knew she was going insane. *Get a grip, Ellen. Abel died in a motorcycle accident, remember?* She wasn't the type to be easily spooked, or fooled. Not once in her life had she consulted a psychic or even a Ouija board, and she certainly didn't believe in voices from the beyond.

But Abel's voice...it had sounded so real!

Suddenly, the only way to get a grip on reality was to turn on every bright light in the house. She rushed to the switch on the nearest wall and flipped it. Hawthorne hissed at her quick movement. Startled, Ellen pivoted.

On the couch, where she herself had been sitting just minutes before, lay Abel. Her husband, dead these four years. He was even wearing the same jeans and flannel shirt she'd last seen him in!

He grinned coyly and waved. "Hey, babe. Happy birthday."

The room went black as Ellen fainted dead away.

Chapter Two

Simon threw his foot on the brake to avoid the speeding Volvo careening through the four-way stop. His Jeep stopped just in the nick of time, the "happy birthday" Mylar balloons tied down in the back bumping together and squeaking in protest. The other car honked as it ran the stop sign and angrily darted away down a side street without so much as even slowing down.

Must be a lunatic, Simon thought hotly as he drove on.

Of course, at this point, he wasn't sure he could vouch for his own sanity, either. As he wound through the tree-lined, curving streets of Ellen's neighborhood, Simon felt as if he could have found her house by some kind of intuitive navigation that only the lovelorn could understand. His attraction to her was so elemental that directions seemed unnecessary.

If that wasn't crazy, what was? He barely knew Ellen—now in the course of one day he found he was unable to leave her alone.

Actually, for two months, Ellen Lantry was about all he had thought about. Oh, he'd done his best to acclimatize himself to a new town and job. Really, he was still coming to grips with why he suddenly had the restless urge to pick up and move to Austin, when he'd had a fine job, a nice house and plenty of friends back in Dallas.

Maybe, after nearly a year, he still wasn't completely over Jennifer. She was a woman he'd known since law school, a good friend until her husband left her. Then their relationship had shifted. Simon had naturally lent his ear to Jennifer's woes, whether it was over lunch, at a happy hour or even sometimes late night over the phone. Which somehow turned to late at night in person. And then they'd fallen into something...he still wasn't certain it was love. More like an emotional roller coaster whose final twisty curve came when Jennifer reunited with her ex.

Simon was all for keeping families together. Still, the whole experience had left him with a bitter taste in his mouth. All he'd wanted to do was go somewhere new and throw himself into his work.

That changed when he walked into Smith...and saw Ellen. Ever since, he'd barely given a thought to his old life in Dallas, or Jennifer, or practically anything else besides her. Not only did she have a spectacular natural beauty that he found entirely appealing all on its own, but she also possessed a slightly self-effacing humor he savored whenever he was around her. Winsome, reserved Ellen drew him to her like a dizzy moth to a silent, flickering flame.

She made him feel impetuous, protective, light-headed—made him want to sweep her into his arms and waltz off into the sunset, a combination Roy Rogers-Fred Astaire number. There was just no pegging down all the things she made him feel, or what he was likely to do around her. Like this afternoon. That brief kiss had only been a hint of what he actually wanted. Yet, unsatisfied as it had left him, their kiss had shown him something he would have paid money to find out—that Ellen, at least on some level, was attracted to him, too. Otherwise she would have slammed the car door in his face.

Wouldn't she?

Simon slowed as he pulled onto her street, checking the address written in ink on his palm to make sure it was the right one. He ducked his head furtively as he drove. It was hard to appear inconspicuous in an open Jeep, especially with eight bright silver balloons bobbing in back of him, but that's what he was trying to do. Maybe he should park a little farther down the street from her house, he thought, considering.

Instead, when he came to a stop, his vehicle hugged the curb in front of Ellen's duplex—practically in her front yard. The location gave him a good view, but unfortunately, there was nothing to see. The house was dark except for a faint glow from the front windows. Was she watching television?

She might not even be home, he thought. He'd meant to park, march up to her front door and leave the balloons, instead of spying on her like an amateur flatfoot. But what if she came to the door? Then he'd have to explain how he found the address to her house, which wasn't listed in the phone book. And he didn't think she'd like the answer to that.

The whole situation made him feel rather foolish. He'd never been reduced to spying on a woman before! Simon didn't consider himself an Adonis by any stretch of the imagination, but he'd never had trouble convincing women to go out with him until this afternoon. Until Ellen.

He should just drop off the balloons and leave, he thought. Obviously she wasn't home—hadn't she said she had plans?

Still, he didn't reach for the door handle. His eyes remained glued on the miniblinds on her windows for a minute, alert for any sign of movement inside. Then the lights in the front room suddenly flashed on.

The shadowy movements of two people—a man and a woman—were visible. Then the two shadows merged, and it appeared that the man was carrying the woman across the room. After that they disappeared.

As he sat, still staring at the window, Simon's heart sank. So...Ellen Lantry wasn't such a lonely widow, after all. Strange, he cared enough about this woman to be happy for her even at his own expense. Why hadn't she simply told him that she was dating someone?

Then again, that obviously wasn't his business. Except that she hadn't reacted to his kiss on the lips this afternoon like a lady who was madly in love with someone else. Yet that appeared to be the case.

With a sigh worthy of the most lovesick of bachelors, he reached for the key, turned it and pulled slowly down the street. All during the long, melancholy drive home, with his festive balloons trailing behind him, one question nagged at him.

Who was the widow Lantry's mystery lover?

"ELLEN, WAKE UP. It's me."

Hearing the familiar voice, Ellen kept her eyes squeezed shut. If she opened them and Abel was there, she was certain she would faint again. But if he wasn't, she wasn't sure she could handle the disappointment.

Disappointment? Because the husband whose funeral you attended four years ago isn't alive?

None of this made any sense. Except that when her hands brushed over the material of the couch, she remembered she'd fallen on the hardwood floor. Someone had moved her; she was too numb to have made the trip across the room by herself. That someone could only have been ...*Abel?*

No way. Things like that couldn't happen. Couldn't.

Slowly, very slowly, she allowed her lids to open a fraction. She saw his eyes. Brown eyes—she'd always been a sucker for them. Abel's were a light brown, the color of oak, but bright and intense. An artist's eyes. And they were staring straight at her with obvious concern.

"Hey," he asked, his voice as it had always been, "are you okay?"

She bolted upright, breathing in quick, painful gulps. He was here, talking to her! But he *couldn't* be. She wanted to touch him, to be sure, yet she was afraid.

"It's me, Ellen," he repeated in his unmistakable voice. How many times had she dreamed of hearing that voice, of having him tell her that it had all been a terrible mix-up?

That's what this meant, right? Abel couldn't have died and then come back. Things like that just didn't happen!

"Abel, what's going on? Can I touch you?"

In answer, he smiled. His lips parted in that lopsided grin that showed his beautiful white teeth, even the crooked incisor he'd never bothered to straighten. Seeing that snaggly tooth made her want to howl with joy.

Abel was here, in the flesh!

She launched herself at him and cried out in happiness when she came smack against the hard muscles of his chest. Tears poured down her cheeks.

She couldn't believe she was in his arms again—arms she'd dreamed of, yearned for, for so long. He gave her a gentle squeeze and pulled her closer, his throat emitting a surprised "hmm" that Ellen remembered meant that something had caught him off guard. Memory sent a thrill down her spine. Or was that edginess she felt? Something about the way Abel was holding her felt different—it wasn't, well, wholehearted enough. And why would he be surprised by the feel of her in his arms?

"Abel," she said, still hugging him to her, smelling his familiar scent. Refusing to let him go completely but needing to see his face, she pulled away slightly. Her hands held tightly to his arms. "Where have you been?" she asked, searching his face for signs of change.

But there was no change. In the back of her mind, she thought of the difference four years could make in a man—especially since Abel would now be her age. *Had* to be. And yet, he still looked a youthful twenty-three.

And that shirt! The years had also been good to that cheap cotton flannel shirt.

There was overwhelming tenderness in those eyes of his, mixed with pity. "I'm sorry, Ellen."

With those words it felt as if her chest deflated.

"I'm dreaming, aren't I." She knew it had seemed too good to be true. Tears spilled down her cheeks, and she didn't even bother to dash them away. "Either I'm dreaming, or the men in white coats are going to haul me away."

"No," Abel said. She looked up at him hopefully, and he smiled. "But I might have a hard time making you understand where I've been."

"Try me," she said.

He cast his eyes up toward the ceiling. "Would you believe...heaven?"

Ellen let out an exasperated breath. She'd forgotten how difficult Abel could be at times, how boyish. "This is no time for joking, Abel. Where have you been?"

"I've been in heaven, Ellen," he said seriously. Their eyes met, and she felt something go cold inside her as he grinned at her skepticism. "I thought you'd be relieved to know that—for my sake. Or maybe you had more faith in me than I did."

"B-but..." Her mind whirled in confusion. It was inconceivable, impossible... Yes, impossible. She laughed, tossing herself against his chest once again. "You lunatic," she said, punching him playfully. "You almost had me fooled! It's like that time on our honeymoon, remember? At the hotel you told the desk clerk—"

He stiffened, stopping her words cold. Reluctantly but with a resolution that seemed alien to him, he pushed Ellen a proper distance away. Proper, that is, if they had been on a first date. In 1895. Ellen looked at him questioningly.

"I don't think it's appropriate for us to talk about our honeymoon now."

"What do you mean now?"

"Now that I'm..." He swallowed. "I'm an angel."

Only for the briefest of moments did she consider that *Abel* might be the one who needed psychiatric assistance. The words were spoken too reluctantly... and in dead earnest.

"Angel?" Ellen repeated a queasy feeling bubbling in her stomach.

"Almost," he replied, too matter-of-factly to be doubted. "At any rate, I've just come from heaven."

"Then you're really..." She punched his chest. But he felt so real!

He nodded. Ellen felt faint again.

"Heaven," she repeated, her voice wispy and thin. "You say it as though you'd spent two years in Albuquerque. You've actually been in heaven!"

"Well, I've also spent some time in your TV set."

Her eyes looked pleadingly at him. "Please don't kid me, Abel. I'm having a hard-enough time believing this isn't a dream already."

"I'm not. I've been sitting in Rick's Café, waiting for you to watch *Casablanca* on your birthday."

She cocked her head. "How did you know I would?"

"Because you do every year." He laughed. "Poor Hawthorne. He might like routine as much as you do, but I bet he wishes you'd change the birthday movie every few years or so."

Hearing his name spoken by his old master's voice, the large yellow tabby meowed loudly in return, then ran over to rub himself against Abel's leg.

Perhaps her life would seem routine to a celestial onlooker, Ellen realized. She felt a bit embarrassed—until she remembered who she was talking to. "How dare you criticize! You left—died," she corrected herself. "I've been so lonely and..."

Unbidden tears spilled down her cheeks, stopping her words. She couldn't believe she was arguing with Abel. She didn't care if he'd spent the past two years in Bora Bora, he was back now and she wasn't about to ruin their reunion by fighting.

"I've missed you so much," she said, hugging him again.

Though his arms didn't relax when they went around her, they were soothing. The kind of hug a concerned friend would give. "Tell me about it," he said, his tone one of gentle reproof.

Ellen looked anxiously into his face. "Is there something wrong with missing you?"

His jaw sawed back and forth, and he reached up a hand to rub it. "Well...it just *looks* bad, Ellen."

"Looks bad? To whom?"

Abel cleared his throat. "You know..." At her look of complete bewilderment, he rolled his eyes. "Shall we just call him the Big Man?"

Understanding dawned with a jolt. Ellen's eyes grew wide. He'd been to heaven—what had she expected?

"You can't grieve forever, Ellen."

She looked up at him, blinking. "I didn't intend to."

"Then why did you send Joe away?"

Her eyes narrowed in suspicion. "Do you know Joe?"

"Know him!" Abel let out a snort. "I've been writing him love letters for two months!"

Ellen's mouth dropped open. "*You've* been writing to him? In my name?"

"Of course, what did you think?"

"Didn't it occur to you that I might not figure out why a stranger would appear on my doorstep with flowers and candy?"

Abel rolled his eyes again. "Yeah, but I didn't think you'd just throw him off the porch."

He sounded like Annie. "Abel, please! I didn't know him. And I'm not looking for another relationship—especially now."

He froze. "What do you mean by that?"

Ellen shrugged. "Well . . . you're back."

"Hey, wait a minute." He put his hands firmly on her shoulders. "Ellen, I'm not . . . alive."

Disappointment shot through her to hear him say it so bluntly, although she'd expected it. But somehow, his being flesh-and-blood human didn't matter to her. Flesh-and-blood ghost was enough for her. As long as she had Abel, she didn't need anybody else.

"Do you understand, Ellen?" Abel shook his head. "I guess I didn't make myself clear. I'm only here for a short time."

Ellen swallowed hard. Oh, not again—she couldn't go through losing him a second time! There had to be a way to keep him with her. "How long?" she asked feebly.

"I'm not really sure. See, I've been having some problems . . . you know, I didn't have much time down here. Some folks up there think I've got to do more to earn full angel privileges. Know what I mean?"

"I'm trying," she said. She really was.

"Look, being an angel's not so easy. It's not all wings and harps, you know. You've got to have done things. . . ."

Ellen gave his old outfit of plaid flannel shirt, ripped jeans and army surplus boots a quick once-over. Poor Abel. He'd become a slacker angel. "You mean you have a . . . a good deed deficit?" she asked, trying to phrase it diplomatically.

"Yeah, I guess you could put it that way." He let out a little sigh of frustration. "So I've got to work that out. And on top of that, I can't go back until you're not lonely anymore."

Ellen's mouth dropped open. She seemed rather secondary in this scenario! "Not lonely, as in married?"

"Or on your way."

"That's the craziest thing I've ever heard of!" Ellen cried. "I can't believe this is *you* talking, Abel. You punched a man out for hitting on me in a bar once."

He shook his head. "Things were different then."

She couldn't argue with that. Back then, she'd felt sane. "Look," she argued, trying a different tack, "you can't expect me to marry some guy I don't know just so you can get . . . wings." It sounded so preposterous!

Not, apparently, to Abel. He picked up a manila envelope from the coffee table. "That's the beauty of it," he told her with a trace of enthusiasm. He put a stack of five different folders that he'd pulled from the envelope on the coffee table. "You won't be marrying just anyone—I've weeded through some prospects for you. These are your choices."

Each folder contained a snapshot stapled on the cover with two months of correspondence inside—letters that, by merit of their wit and warmth, were supposed to win Ellen's heart. But what caught her eye was the picture of herself that fell out loose from one of the envelopes. It was an eight-by-ten studio portrait that had been taken right after her high school graduation.

"That picture used to be on my parents' piano," Ellen said, inspecting it. She'd always liked it—her first grown-up photo.

Abel nodded. "I had to steal it to send to the correspondents. I told them you were a gorgeous widow. After two months of writing to them, I had to prove it."

"You've been writing love letters to all these men for two months?" she asked in amazement. "And you sent them *this?*" She waved the picture in astonishment. Was he crazy? She was only eighteen in that picture! "No way am I going along with this, Abel."

He blinked, uncomprehending. "Why not?"

"Because you're my husband—"

"Were," he corrected her.

She sputtered unhappily. "Th-that's weird enough. But these people are complete strangers. It's outrageous!"

"They're all dying to meet us," he argued, then amended, "I mean, you."

She sat up straight, her hands on her hips. "And where do you plan on being while I'm out dating these guys you've rustled up?"

He shrugged. "I thought I could crash here."

Aha.

The news that Abel was planning to stay for a while calmed her somewhat. *As long as he was with her...* Maybe this setup could work to her advantage. Ellen leaned back close to his chest as they perused the photos. He felt awfully lifelike for a ghost. Or maybe it was just that shirt. It was so soft, so familiar, so Abel.

He launched into a discussion of the pros and cons of the different sweethearts he'd picked out for her besides Joe. The others, a music professor, a dentist, a judge and a painter, seemed an eclectic group to Ellen, but Abel spouted off about their virtues at length.

Meanwhile, a little plan hatched in Ellen's mind. All she wanted was for Abel to stay with her. And if he intended to stay as long as it took her to find a husband, then what could be the harm in her taking a very, very long time to find one? After all, what was the rush? Knowing Abel, it was going to take a while for him to get his butt in gear and do some good deeds. This was the man who had never turned in a paper on time. Frustrating as that characteristic had been once, it might work well for her now. She was sorry if her grief made him look bad in the great beyond. But surely a man with eternity yawning before him could spare a measly lifetime for her.

Abel snapped his fingers. "Earth to Ellen!" She jerked her head up from the photos. "Are you paying attention?"

She nodded vigorously, her plan solidifying. As long as she kept being unlucky in love, Abel would be bound to stay with her. Perfect!

She looked down at the pictures. What difference did it make who she picked? The best-looking man in the world—to her eyes, at least—was seated right next to her. There was only one man who even compared . . .

A thought suddenly occurred to her. "Abel, have you been writing to someone named Simon Miller?" That would explain Simon's sudden interest—and how he had found out when her birthday was.

Abel frowned in thought. "I don't think so. I was writing to a lot of people for a while, but I weeded them down to these five. Now four," he added bitterly, thinking of Joe.

Ellen looked back down at the men and felt a stab of guilt. These poor guys, thinking they were finding true love when they were actually corresponding with a ghost. And not even a female one! She supposed she would have to go out with at least one of them, and probably all of them, if she was going to keep Abel with her. It hardly mattered which.

"I'll try that one." She pointed randomly at one of the photos.

"Really?" Abel asked, shocked. Nevertheless, he became excited. "That's Martin Mayhew, the dentist. I thought he'd be a real long shot...but I guess you never can tell."

"Jealous?" Ellen asked. She'd hardly given the man a thought, but now that she looked at his picture, she saw that the dentist was pale, with what appeared to be light brown hair and a receding hairline. Mousy. *This* was who Abel wanted her to spend the rest of her life with?

"I'm not jealous," Abel said. "I guess I can see the attraction. And hey, he likes old movies."

She laughed to herself at the idea of Abel giving her a sales pitch for another man. The old Abel had been on the possessive side, but maybe that had just been his youth showing. Or his aliveness.

"He writes poetry, too," Abel added. "He's a very sentimental dentist."

"I'm sure he'll do just fine," Ellen said, turning away from the folders and into Abel's arms. "So I guess you can't tell me who killed JFK, can you?"

Abel shook his head.

"Or what happened to Marilyn Monroe?"

"Ellen..." He shot her a warning look, then weakened. "I might be able to arrange an introduction, though."

Ellen sucked in a shocked breath. "*You* know...?"

"Society is a little more democratic where I come from."

"I guess so," she said, trying hard to digest this new information.

In the end, they snuggled down on the couch and did watch *Casablanca,* but for the second time that evening, Ellen's mind wasn't on the movie. She couldn't stop thinking about the miraculous second chance she'd just received. Now all she had to do was see how long she could outsmart an angel at his own game.

TOO EASY, ABEL THOUGHT. Too easy and too hard.

Though Ellen had acquiesced to his scheme, she had been busy all weekend playing the happy housewife. Now she was preparing Sunday breakfast as if she were still twenty-three and nothing had ever changed. And it was tempting for him to play along with this make-believe.

She came into the room bearing a serving plate. "Have another Pop-Tart."

Remembering that he'd had a weakness for toaster pastries, Ellen had gone out and stocked up. The cabinets were now jammed with a six months' supply. Did she think he'd be here that long?

"Hey, babe..." he began, but she cut him off by hopping in his lap and throwing her arms around him. Something she did frequently. Though it was almost summer, she was wrapped in a sweater against the air-conditioning, since Abel was accustomed to a colder climate now. She snuggled close to him, her red hair pressing against his cheek.

Holding her was agony. Physically, Ellen's jumping in his lap didn't have the effect on him that it used to, but unfortunately, he discovered quickly that he had a crystal-clear memory. While he hadn't exercised it much during his time in heaven, it came swiftly back into perfect working order whenever he held Ellen this way. Or she held him. He tried not to encourage this kind of thing. Doing so brought decidedly unangelic thoughts to his mind.

He hadn't expected this to happen. Coming from the beyond, he'd naturally thought he was beyond such mortal thoughts. And he'd also never expected to feel covetous. But as the weekend wore on, and the work week approached, he wondered what he would do without her company.

"I can't get over how real you feel."

"I'm a real angel," he told her, reaching forward to grab a Pop-Tart. Unlike his libido, his taste buds seemed to be stronger than ever, which was some compensation, he supposed.

Ellen laughed—a sparkly, sweet sound he had also forgotten about. "You're going to be a real fat angel once I get through with you."

Abel shook his head and swallowed. "Doesn't affect me," he said.

Her green eyes rounded at this news. "Angels don't gain weight? Ever?"

"Nope."

She shook her head in wonder. "You can eat all you want, hop from picture to picture, disappear if you have to and recline on clouds all day long—it sounds perfect!"

Abel's smile froze as he looked at her crystal-clear green eyes, her beautiful face. "Perfect." *Except that you aren't there with me...*

He shook off the thought guiltily. Back in heaven he'd never had thoughts like that, hadn't dwelled on what he'd lost. Instead, he'd been glad that Ellen still had a life ahead of her—until he had realized she intended to hide away from it in grief.

"What do you want to do today?" Ellen asked.

He sighed. "I think I'll watch television."

"Again?"

He steeled himself against the disappointment in her voice. He wasn't here to entertain Ellen—he was here to get her married. Television was one way to get his mind off the memory of desire she kicked up in him, especially if he watched shows she didn't like. Yesterday he'd tried sports, which she had sat through for his sake. Today he would try something else. Would she be able to stomach twelve hours of cartoons?

Would he?

He couldn't wait for Friday to get here, and for Ellen to go out with Martin Mayhew, the dentist. Maybe they would hit it off. Then he could go home again....

Before home started seeming as though it should be here...with Ellen.

ELLEN LANTRY WAS disgustingly chipper.

While Simon looked on silently, her toes tapped out a happy rhythm on the ladder in the law library as she reached for the volume she'd been hunting. She hummed another bar of that infernal tune she'd been humming all week and smiled, staring at the rows and rows of floor-to-ceiling law books as if they were colored with paisleys and polka dots. When she reached out to grab a book, her plain navy dress hugged her slender back and bottom and accentuated her long, shapely legs in a way that reminded Simon that no woman in the world looked as good in drab office clothes as Ellen.

Not that he needed a reminder of anything about her. She hadn't been out of his thoughts in days, ever since he'd driven by her house.

"Finding everything you need?" Simon moved forward quickly, forcing a smile into place.

She swung around on the ladder, her green eyes round, her mouth a red O of surprise. Simon's head was even with her knees, his hand rested inches away from her navy blue pumps, giving him an up-close and personal view of those drop-dead gorgeous legs of hers.

"Oh, it's you!" she said, giggling. Along with toe-tapping and humming, she'd been giggling a lot lately.

She hadn't even heard him coming, he thought a little peevishly. But how could she, when her mind was so obviously filled with romantic music and happy memories?

He glanced around the mahogany-paneled library, empty except for them. "Don't you know it's against the rules to be amused in this room? The firm can charge two hundred dollars a chuckle."

She laughed again. "I don't know what's wrong with me—too much legal mumbo jumbo crowding my brain, I guess."

In one easy movement, Simon swung himself up onto the ladder next to her. Her perfume hung in the air around them. "I bet you have beautiful gray matter, Miss Lantry."

Their gazes met and locked, and for a moment he remembered what it had been like to pull her into his arms, to hear her little gasp of surprise.

Ellen flushed and quickly looked away. "Did they teach you to leap like that at Arthur Murray, too?" She edged past him and scrambled back down to the floor.

"Absolutely not," Simon answered, taking mock offense. He made a conscious decision not to trail after her—just yet—and sat himself down on one of the rungs, watching her flip anxiously through a stack of papers. "I haven't failed to notice *your* bouncy step since the weekend. Or that goofy grin plastered across your face. Or the fact that you've been humming 'As Time Goes By' for three days straight."

"Does my good mood annoy you, Simon?" she asked, apparently amused by the petulant bite to his voice.

"Of course not," he said, drumming his fingers. He watched her searchingly. "It's just..." *It's just that I'm dying to know who that shadow was I saw you with Friday night.*

"Just what?" She glanced warily at him, and her fingers grasped the end of the oak conference table nervously as she awaited his answer.

He couldn't help himself. He had to say something about her secret romance. Maybe if they got it out in the open, she would be able to tell him he was wrong. Maybe he would discover that their quick parking lot kiss wouldn't necessarily be their last.

"I know, Ellen," he told her.

Her mouth fell open, then shut quickly. "Know? Know what?"

"That you've found someone," he said, his voice dropping a notch. He couldn't keep the gravelly, more than slightly jealous, bite out of his tone. "So who's the lucky guy?"

"Lucky guy?" Ellen blinked innocently, but the way she nervously darted her tongue over her ruby lips gave her away...and nearly pushed Simon over the edge at the memory of how sweet those red lips were.

"The one you've been looped about all week," he said.

Ellen stared into his face for a moment, her expression curious, pensive, as if she were weighing how much he could possibly know. "There's nobody."

It had to be a lie. Unless... Simon was torn. Maybe he'd been looking in the wrong window. Her house was a duplex, after all. Or perhaps what he'd seen had been completely innocent—a friend could have picked her up after she'd slipped and fallen. The scenario stretched credulity, but odder things had happened.

"Honestly?" he asked, stepping down from the ladder. He came to stand next to her, mirroring her guarded stance as she leaned against the table. He was close enough to smell her perfume again. The scent, something herby, natural— jasmine, maybe—worked a subtle sort of magic on him. He found himself wanting to forget all about Friday night and believe every word that she told him. Wanting to touch her, and not just in a co-workerly way.

Steady, boy... He gritted his teeth and decided to test her a little more. "I thought there must be some man behind so much chipperness."

A pert frown touched her lips. "Only a man would think that," she shot back. "Men find it impossible to believe that they aren't somehow connected with every emotion a woman feels. Can't a woman just be happy all on her own?"

Her words were spoken with such conviction that he had a hard time doubting her. He allowed himself to scoot another fraction closer, smiling. "Can't a guy try to make a happy woman just a little bit happier?"

She tilted her head and smiled back. Then, as their gazes met and held, her smile faded. He seemed to have that effect on her, which was the exact opposite of what he intended. He reached out and touched her arm, which made her stiffen. That wasn't what he wanted, either.

"I've got an idea," he said. "Dinner and a movie. Just a corny Friday night date."

The word Friday appeared to jolt something in her memory. Her mouth dropped open, then snapped closed again, and she worried her bottom lip slightly, looking away from him.

That delectable red lip sent his memory reeling again. Had their kiss only been last Friday? The too-brief moment had been pushed aside by subsequent events—but its impact hadn't. He hadn't been able to stop himself from leaning down and kissing her, just like he wanted to do now....

Ellen's eyes were dark green pools as she looked up at him; her cheeks glowed red as she took an uneven step backward. "I can't."

"Can't, or won't?" Simon asked.

Ellen sighed. "I'm afraid it's a little of both," she said with equal bluntness. "It may sound strange to you, but I'm still in love with Abel. My husband."

A feeling of disappointment flashed through him, followed by doubt. "So your heart's in the grave," he said, the memory of the silhouette in her window in his mind. Ellen tensed at his words, and he sounded a note of contrition. "I'm sorry, Ellen, but I find that hard to believe. You can't pine away for the rest of your life. Don't you want . . . well, to *live?*"

That, apparently, was the wrong thing to say. She crossed her arms and narrowed a sharp gaze on him. "Excuse me, but that's what I thought I've been doing, in my own mundane little way. Of course, you seem to think that a woman hasn't really lived until she's had the pleasure of your company."

He turned away, composing himself quickly. "Guess I did sound pretty conceited," he admitted soberly.

She harumphed her agreement.

His grin returned. "But isn't it the truth?" he asked, striking an innocent pose. If he couldn't get the facts out of her, he could at least have a little fun trying.

"You're impossible!" Ellen turned to pick up her stack of papers, plus the law book she'd pulled off the shelf, which proceeded to slip out of her hands and fall to the floor with a thud. She and Simon bent down simultaneously, practically bumping heads, and reached for the book. Her hand grasped the book, and his hand covered hers. The instant skin touched skin, both of them practically jumped in the air from the sensual jolt.

They surfaced again, still joined at the book. She swallowed anxiously, pulling her hand to wrest it and the book from him. Simon smiled. She obviously wasn't any more immune to his touch than he was to hers. "Hit a nerve, did I?" he asked. "Or does a woman with her heart in the grave have nerves like the rest of us?"

Pursing her lips, Ellen gave the tome a mighty tug and nearly fell backward when Simon let go. With obvious effort, she regained her balance and slammed the book against her chest. She clenched her jaw and lectured sternly, "This might strike you as odd, Simon, but some of us can achieve perfect mental health without the benefit of your advice."

"Maybe, but hey, it's free." He tucked his thumbs in his belt loops and swaggered over to her. "The date would be, too," he added, poking her in the ribs with his elbow. "I'm the old-fashioned kind."

"Well I'm the new-fashioned kind. I prefer TV dinners at home with my cat to *dating*." She pronounced the last word with a distinct air of distaste. "But thanks just the same."

He bowed good-naturedly. "If you change your mind, don't worry. I'll ask you out again next week."

"What a relief to know that," she quipped, backing out of the door with her load. It closed behind her, and Simon listened to her footsteps scurrying away down the hall.

His smile melted away. Maybe she was a modern woman, content to be on her own. And he could certainly believe that she still grieved for her husband. But those things aside, Ellen Lantry had something she was hiding from him. And she was clammed up so tight he wondered how he would ever find out what it was.

Chapter Three

"That stuff's poison," Martin Mayhew warned, nodding at the paper cup of cola in Ellen's hand. "Believe you me, if you'd seen as many abscesses as I have, you'd know what I mean."

Ellen nodded foggily, barely able to contain her boredom as she and the dentist stood in the lobby of the Paramount, Austin's oldest theater. It normally was used for stage shows, but occasionally in the summer they would feature classic old films. As luck would have it, Friday night they were showing a Bette Davis double feature. Bette Davis was Martin Mayhew's favorite.

Back when she was talking to him on the phone, setting up this sham of a date, Ellen had only briefly wondered about what kind of man loved old black-and-white weepies as much as Martin Mayhew proclaimed he did. But after a long dinner and the first feature, *Dark Victory,* his personality had come on like gangbusters. Martin Mayhew was a dentist right down to the dentist-drill whine of his voice.

A rather depressed dentist, as it turned out.

And where had those glasses come from? He hadn't been wearing the little round spectacles in his picture. Of course, she could hardly complain, since in the picture of her that

Abel had sent out she looked as young and fresh as a Doublemint twin.

"Those teeth of yours are going to look like Plaque City, Arizona," he warned. "Don't you know that carbonation works like battery acid?"

Ellen sucked on her straw.

"People don't listen to dentists," he droned sadly.

They still had twelve minutes until *Now, Voyager* started. Ellen didn't know if she was going to make it. She was beginning to wonder whether the poor guy wasn't a bit off. During the last feature, she could swear she had heard him sniffling during Bette Davis's death scene.

At any rate, she wouldn't want to be near him while he was wielding a drill.

"I still can't believe how tall you are," he said. "Kind of makes me feel like a Munchkin." The wounded look in his eyes as he stared up at her—as if he would hurl himself off her shoulders if he could climb that high—made Ellen grimace.

She would have tried to ditch out of the date, but she was sure Abel would have something to say about that. She had to at least appear to hold up her end of the bargain. Besides, for a fleeting moment, she'd thought she'd seen him spying on her from the marquee poster in the lobby.

"I think..." Ellen searched for something to say, but failed. All she could contemplate at the moment was escape. "I think I'll tag the ladies' room before the movie starts."

"Have a nice trip," Martin quipped.

Ellen made sure she was out of the dentist's sight before rolling her eyes. The rest rooms were on the second floor, and she sped toward the stairs. Turning the corner, she nearly flattened a passerby. "Excuse me," she mumbled, sidestepping around him.

"Ellen?"

The voice was unmistakable.

"Simon!" When she looked up into his smiling face, she felt like throwing her arms around him. It was wonderful to speak to someone who didn't talk at her as if she were reclined in a vinyl chair with a bib around her neck. Simon held out his hand to shake, and she grabbed it with the joy of a person who'd just been rescued from a root canal.

"Am I glad to see you!" she cried enthusiastically.

Simon appeared surprised by her warm reception, perhaps because their last conversation hadn't ended on a particularly chummy note. He hadn't spoken to her except to say hello since their meeting in the library. He wasn't speaking now, either. Just looking at her oddly.

She blinked, realizing that this was the first time she'd ever seen him in casual clothes—well-worn jeans that hugged him like a very kind old friend and a relaxed cotton shirt. He looked every bit as sexy in his play clothes as he did in his workaday suit-and-tie uniform. Just standing in front of him with her hand engulfed in his made her feel lightheaded.

"What a strange coincidence, our both coming here at the same time," she said a shade breathlessly, wondering why he wasn't saying anything. Or letting go of her hand.

"I'm beginning to think there's no such thing as coincidence when it comes to you and me." There was a smile on his lips, but his eyes were intent, serious.

Those eyes. They were a deeper shade of brown than Abel's, and she had to admit, they did crazy things to her. Like make her wish she had come here with Simon instead of...

"Are you here for the double feature?" he asked.

"Yes, I'm—" Ellen gulped, then glanced over at Martin, who had spotted them and was watching curiously. Oh, no, she thought, remembering her conversation with Simon in the library—when she'd insisted that she didn't date. Of all the times for Simon to pop up, why did it have to be now? "Uh, I'm a big Bette Davis fan."

She prayed Martin would have the decency to stay put.

"Not me," Simon said. "But I thought it would be interesting to see an old black-and-white movie on the big screen. I've never been to this theater."

Out of the corner of her eye, Ellen detected Martin Mayhew beginning to creep toward them cautiously. Her chest constricted with dread. Maybe, if she ran for it, she could make it up the stairs before he reached them.

"Then you're in for a real treat," she said quickly. What if Simon sat near her and Martin in the orchestra? "I suggest you try to get a good seat in the balcony. Enjoy the show!" She whirled to flee up the stairs to hide in the plush ladies' lounge, but a strong hand clamped down on her arm.

"What's your hurry?" Simon climbed a few steps after her.

Martin was almost upon them. Ellen looked frantically for some way out.

"It's almost as if you're running away from somebody," Simon mused.

That somebody stopped inches away and glared up at Simon. "Ellen, do you know this man?" Martin asked in a menacing tone.

Simon's friendly eyes turned frosty as he looked down at Mayhew. "Is this guy bothering you?" he asked Ellen.

"Me?" Martin asked.

"She certainly wasn't running from *me*," Simon shot back.

"Then why are you manhandling her?" Martin countered boldly.

Having reached a verbal impasse, the two men stared belligerently at each other, then turned in unison to Ellen for mediation.

"Oh, for heaven's sake," she said with a heavy sigh. She had no recourse but to make the introductions and hope for the best. "Simon, this is Martin Mayhew. Martin's a dentist," she put in, for lack of anything else to add.

Simon gave the man a thorough once-over, sizing him up. "You mean, *your* dentist?" he asked Ellen.

As if going out with one's dentist were a federal offense.

"No, I'm her *date,*" Martin clarified proudly.

Ellen winced at the word.

Simon looked at Ellen, then at Martin, then turned another incredulous gaze on her before breaking out into a wide smile. "*Date,* did you say?" The words were directed toward Martin, but Simon never took his eyes off Ellen.

"You heard him," she muttered back. If Simon's Cheshire cat grin was any indication, he wasn't going to let her off the hook on this one. And why should he, after she'd put him off in no uncertain terms mere days before?

"Now, *this* is interesting," Simon mused. He tugged Ellen down closer to Martin and made a show of relinquishing her arm to the other man. "I'm terribly sorry, Dr. Mayhew, for manhandling your escort. You see, I had no way of knowing you were her *date,* since Ellen has a reputation for *never* dating."

Ellen jerked her arm back from Martin and glared at Simon.

"That's okay," Martin answered in a conciliatory tone. "I understand completely. It's taken me two months just to get this far with Ellen."

The innocently spoken but loaded sentence hung in the air for what seemed like an eternity.

Simon smiled wickedly, barely able to contain himself. "And just how far is that?"

"It's our first date."

Ellen shuddered, then felt her face go beet red. Simon probably thought Martin Mayhew was the reason she'd been bouncing and humming all week.

"You don't say!" Simon exclaimed. "Your first date!" He looked back at her and scolded mockingly, "Ellen, you sly thing, why didn't you tell me I was interrupting such an intimate occasion? You made it sound as if he was just your dentist."

Ellen wrinkled her nose at his jocular tone. "He's not my dentist at all," she said in a last-ditch effort to wound him back. It was only fair. "I simply thought it would be fun to go out with a real red-blooded man."

"Me?" Martin asked disbelievingly. "I just thought you liked my letters!"

Simon's ears pricked up. "Letters?"

"Ellen and I met through a newspaper ad she took out two months ago."

Ellen cringed.

"An ad." Simon never moved his gaze from her. "That's very contemporary of you, Ellen. Although, frankly, I'm surprised."

"Why?" asked Martin. "It's pretty common these days."

Simon's expression grew misty and thoughtful as he turned to Martin. "Yes, but I'd always just assumed that Ellen's heart was in the—" he lowered his voice "—well, I don't want to say it, but you know."

Martin nodded vigorously, and added in a low, confidential voice, as though grief had made her hard of hearing, "Oh, yes, her husband. She wrote me all about him. He was a genius."

Ellen let out an exasperated huff. It figured that Abel wouldn't have failed to heap praises on himself in those letters.

"And on top of that," Simon went on, reminding her again of their prior conversation, "I just assumed that Ellen was one of those women who didn't need a man to be happy."

If she could just sink through the floor, she thought. Or tweak her nose and disappear like Samantha Stevens on "Bewitched." She felt humiliated, and as low as a worm, and disappointed. The last feeling disturbed her most—because she knew that Simon would write her off after this. Not that she had ever given any thought to taking him up on his weekly invitations, she assured herself. Still, she had to admit that his good-natured flirtatiousness was diverting. And flattering. And tempting.

"I was beginning to worry that Ellen was destined to walk alone through life." Simon patted Martin on the shoulder. "So you can imagine how I felt seeing you come along."

"I guess so," Martin said, missing the irony.

"Now, just what kind of letters did you two write during those months?" Simon asked Martin curiously.

The dentist blushed and shrugged. "You know..."

"As if that's any of your beeswax," Ellen interjected tartly.

He lifted his brows in alarm. "Oh, so they were *that* type of letter."

"No!"

"Oh, no!" Martin exclaimed nervously. "Not at all. Just plain old boring love letters."

"Boring?" Ellen threw in, amused. Abel would love that!

Thoroughly flustered, Martin looked from one to the other, and then cast his eyes down at the floor. "Well, I did write some poetry," he admitted shyly.

"Love poetry?" Simon asked.

Ellen froze like a stone on the red-carpeted stairs. *Please, please, please,* she thought, *don't let Martin Mayhew start reciting the awful poetry he'd written in those letters.*

Stubbing his toe sheepishly against the first stair's rise, Martin nodded. "Nothing . . . erotic, of course."

"Of course."

Ellen gulped, and yelped exultantly when the lobby lights started blinking, beckoning the audience back to their seats. Escape, and not a moment too soon. "Time for the movie!" she said in a happy singsong, hopping down a step.

"Weren't you going *up*stairs?" Simon asked.

Because he was still a step below her, they were almost nose to nose. His deep brown eyes fairly twinkled as they looked into hers, and she felt a familiar tightening in her chest.

"I don't know," she said. "Which way are you going?"

"Up, to the balcony. Somebody told me that was the preferred view."

"Too bad. We're going down."

She let out a light, breezy laugh as she dragged Martin away, and turned only briefly before disappearing into the theater. Simon was staring after her in speculation. Knowing that he was watching her gave her an unsettled feeling.

"He seemed like a nice fellow," Martin said.

"I guess," Ellen said with a sigh as she plopped into one of the seats. She took another sip of her soda and attempted to ignore her date's tongue clucking.

"Although I have to admit I was a bit jealous there for a minute," Martin said.

"Why?" But Ellen knew why. When Simon Miller wanted something, he didn't work too hard to conceal his interest.

"Well..." Martin looked her straight in the eye, then surprised her by saying, "Maybe because it's obvious that you've got a little crush on him."

"*I've* got a crush?" she practically shrieked. The lights dimmed, and a few of their neighbors turned in their seats to glare at her. Ellen lowered her voice. "That's ridiculous!"

"But the way you looked at him—it was just the way Bette Davis looks at Paul Henreid in *Now, Voyager.*"

"I don't believe it."

Someone threw her another look as the credits rolled, and she let the matter drop. But she was going to watch this movie—and the way the two leads looked at each other— very, very closely. She just couldn't afford even to *appear* to be in love with Simon. If Abel sensed she was, he would feel free to head straight back to heaven.

She would have to put a lid on Simon's interest—or at least shut him up. Otherwise, she would completely jeopardize her cozy little home life, which she couldn't allow. After all, men, even earthy tempting ones like Simon, were suddenly a dime a dozen. Angels, on the other hand, were always at a premium.

ABEL TURNED UP THE VOLUME on the television the moment he heard the car drive up. By the time Ellen's key turned in the lock, he was sprawled on the couch flat on his back, a study in nonchalance. Never mind that he'd spent the entire evening on pins and needles. Considering that this was his first time experiencing the odd sensation of having his wife go out on a date with another man, he thought he was doing pretty darn well.

Okay, so maybe he peeked in on her that once. Hiding in that marquee poster might not have been a very mature thing to do, but try as he might to stay away, he couldn't help himself. And he'd left the moment he'd made sure everything was going okay between Ellen and Martin. So maybe there weren't fireworks going off around them; he didn't necessarily want Ellen to have a grand passion. She was older now and needed to be practical. A dentist would be a good breadwinner.

But when she quickly stepped inside the door, her obvious relief at being home again told the whole sad story. Never mind fireworks—those two hadn't even worked up a single spark. Abel found himself torn between disappointment that his matchmaking hadn't worked out and complete, unadulterated joy.

He sat up, and Ellen dropped down on the couch next to him. Her brows knit together as she looked at the TV, and she folded her arms, trying to counteract the frigid air-conditioning. "What are you watching?"

"The Three Stooges," he answered. They were never one of Ellen's favorites—he was still trying to keep her at a distance, after all. "How did it go?"

She appeared distracted. "What?"

"Your date with Martin Mayhew!"

"Oh . . . fine," she said, never taking her eyes off the screen.

"Fine" after a date usually meant just the opposite. It sometimes even meant disaster. Abel felt as if he would bust if he didn't get some details. His practiced nonchalance went out the window. "Well, what happened?" he asked, practically hopping up and down with curiosity.

"Did you like The Three Stooges before?" Ellen questioned.

"Don't change the subject," he said.

She shook her head. "It's just a little hard to concentrate over the nyuck-nyuck-nyucks," she replied.

"I was asking about your date."

"What do you want to know?"

"Did he kiss you good-night?"

"Abel!" she cried, shocked. "Of course not!"

"That *is* what dates are supposed to do, remember?" But he couldn't honestly say that he was too disappointed with her answer. Reaching forward, he grabbed some M&M's off the candy dish on the table—actually, it was more like a candy platter—and popped a handful into his mouth. He'd really been scarfing down the sugar lately. But when they started talking about his wife kissing another man, what else could he do?

"Well, this date didn't," she told him. "Actually, I feel sort of bad for Martin. There was sort of a complication."

Uh-oh. He stared at her, a gob of chocolate in his cheek.

"You see," she explained, without his even having to ask, "this man showed up."

"What man?" he asked, alarmed. Shoot. He *knew* he should have stayed in that poster!

"Simon Miller, a lawyer at my office. I think—well, I know—he has a little crush on me."

"And you're pretty looped about him, is that it?" Abel asked, stunned at how hard the notion was to accept.

Her eyes rounded in something like horror. "No—oh, no!" she said. "It just created a sort of awkward situation. Anyway," she said, quickly turning back to their previous subject, "I think it's curtains for Martin. I'll set up a date with one of the others."

Abel shrugged. "Fine with me," he said, watching Moe bonk Larry on the head as if her dating life were positively none of his business. But inside, the wheels in his mind were spinning like mad. *Simon Miller.* She'd mentioned this guy before.

After a moment, Ellen sighed and settled back against the couch cushions. Abel tensed. "I'm just glad to be back with you again," she said. "But would you mind if we did something else—or at least watched something different?"

"No problem," he said, picking up the remote. He surfed through a few channels before stopping on one. "I could just watch this home shopping channel forever, couldn't you?"

Ellen's eyes glazed. "Sure," she lied, her voice listless. She reached forward and grabbed some chocolate.

Abel gave her thirty minutes of the shopping channel before she finally cried uncle and went to bed. He felt a little guilty for practicing this form of television torture, but Ellen was too much of a distraction. He needed time alone to think. Time to plan how exactly he could check out this Simon Miller.

Monday morning, Ellen arrived at work dead tired, with a runny nose and the sugar jitters. Keeping up with Abel's sleeping, eating and entertainment habits was a bit of a strain. And her house seemed more fit for a polar bear than a ghost.

As Ellen stretched, she discovered Simon's neat, angular handwriting staring up at her on a sheet torn from a legal pad. The paper had been placed smack in the center of her desk so she couldn't miss it.

> A kiss is just a kiss, but verse is for you,
> If I'd known that earlier,
> I'd have written poetry, like Martin Mayhew!

Ellen shot out of her chair, snatched up her empty coffee cup and stomped off to the coffeemaker. She had to put a stop to this sort of thing right now. The little office kitchen was just off the library, which fortunately was on the other side of the floor. Making the hike gave her a chance to work off steam.

Simon greeted her at the kitchen door. "You're here early," he commented. He looked well rested, well fed and worry free, and she hated him for it.

"Apparently not early enough to catch the worm," she shot back.

"I assume you're referring to the poetry worm."

Ellen poured herself a cup of coffee and dumped in a hefty portion of creamer. She couldn't let him ruffle her feathers. "I suppose he's like the tooth fairy," she said, "hard to catch."

Simon suavely rested his elbow on the microwave and leaned in close. "But worth the wait."

Ellen knew it was silly—they were talking about the poetry worm, after all—but the playful, husky sound of Simon's voice did something to her. Something disturbing. It was too early in the morning for thoughts like she was beginning to have. In fact, thoughts like that had no place in her life at all.

"Your nose is red," Simon observed.

Ellen dug a tissue out of her pocket. Here she was thinking how sexy he was, while she herself probably looked like she belonged on a cold medicine commercial.

Out in the office, someone was flipping on lights, and an extra-syrupy rendition of 'Moon River' floated in from the hallway. Pretty soon the kitchen would be in full morning rush hour swing. This was definitely not the place for what she had to discuss with Simon.

She swallowed, put away her tissue and looked up at him, but was disturbed to find his gaze had moved from her nose to her lips. "Stop that," she said. With a sheepish grin, he obeyed, moving his gaze up to meet hers. "I need to talk to you."

His eyebrows lifted in interest.

"In private," she added.

"Sounds intriguing." Simon searched her face for signs of what this might be about. "Guess we can go to my office."

Simon's office appeared the same as all new associates', a roomy box with a window. It was kept neat for clients, decorated with only tasteful prints and a graduation photo on a file cabinet in the corner.

"Have a seat," he said, shutting the door. He flipped on a lamp in the corner, as well as one of the fluorescent overheads. "What's on your mind?"

"I think you know," Ellen told him bluntly. She meant to be up-front about this. No getting sucked into his happy bantering, no forgetting what was at stake.

Somewhere along the line, she admitted frankly to herself, she'd developed a physical attraction for this man. Probably because she'd been lonely for so long and he'd seemed not only good-looking but good-hearted. But a simple attraction didn't mean—now that Abel was home and her life was back on track, sort of—that she had to lose sight of where her best interests lay.

"It's about the dentist," she said.

His lips quirked into one of his easy smiles as he seated himself across the desk from her. "Do you always refer to the men you go out with by their occupations?"

"Martin, then," she corrected herself. "I'm afraid he gave you the wrong impression at the movies."

"He gave me the impression that you hadn't been completely truthful with me."

Ellen let out a sigh. "I only went out with him . . . as a favor for a friend." That, at least, was the truth.

Simon perked up considerably, but he still bore a skeptical expression. "Did you write him love letters as a favor?"

Good question. "I didn't write love letters, he did."

"And you just strung him along."

Ellen had wondered why someone as nice as Simon had become a lawyer. Now she knew. The man was a shark at cross-examination. "I went out with him once, no more," she said. "So I see no reason why any gossip should be spread about it."

"You're absolutely right." Before Ellen could feel relief, Simon rose from his chair, placed his hands behind his back and began to pace. The move seemed calculated to put her on edge. "And I'm perfectly willing to put the whole thing behind us," he offered.

Us? Despite the ominous word, Ellen smiled.

"On one condition."

Her smile disappeared. "What's that?"

"That you go out with me."

"That's blackmail!" Ellen cried, rocketing out of her chair. She folded her arms across her chest and locked eyes with him.

"I know." He smiled.

Her mind whirred. How was she going to get out of this, and why hadn't she anticipated it?

Suddenly, a movement in the corner caught her eye. She peered over Simon's shoulder, to the graduation photo on the file cabinet. Behind the picture of Simon, whose hand was outstretched to receive his law degree, stood a row of professors in robes with hoods. One of the professors was waving at her.

The blond one with the ponytail.

Abel! What was he doing here—and what if Simon saw him? Feeling queasy, Ellen grasped Simon's arm for support.

"Ellen, what's wrong?" he asked. "Are you all right?"

"I think I need to sit down."

He led her back over to the chair she'd been in before. "Don't move, I'll get you some water. Would that help?"

Ellen nodded vigorously.

Simon dashed out like a shot, probably to the kitchen. That gave her only a minute. She jumped out of the chair and sped over to the picture.

"What are you doing?" she said under her breath.

Abel, diminutive in the photo, waved at her again. Despite the fact that he looked rather dashing in black, the ponytail and his high-top sneakers poking out beneath the academic gown lent him a comical, out-of-place appearance.

"I just wanted you to know it's okay with me," Abel said.

"What's okay?" Ellen asked.

"Simon—you can go out with him. He wouldn't have been *my* choice, of course.'.'

"You shouldn't be here," she admonished.

"Why not?" Abel asked. "In heaven I used to watch you all the time."

Ellen's jaw dropped. "You did?"

"Of course." His mouth moved back into a grim line. "It's harder for me to do that here. Everything's harder down here."

"No kidding," Ellen said. "How do you think I feel, seeing you pop up in pictures?"

"Sorry, babe. I just didn't want you to blow off a legit prospect just because I hadn't given him the thumbs up."

"You think Simon is . . . legit?"

He paused only for the slightest of seconds. "Sure, why not?"

Why not? Ellen tried to put aside the thought that Simon was too damned attractive to remain a platonic escort for long. In some ways, Abel's suggestion made sense. If she had to kill time going out with someone, who was more charming than Simon? Of course, she would have to keep the remaining three of Abel's correspondents on hold, as reserves. On the off chance she and Simon didn't get along.

But, of course, they would get along. It was going to take all her might to resist temptation. Yet, resist she would. She might have to go out with the man, and be subjected to his charm, but that didn't mean she had to enjoy it.

Too much.

SIMON FELT LIKE a lowdown cheat. He couldn't believe he was now stooping to blackmailing Ellen for a date.

What was the matter with him? The woman wasn't interested. Did he need to have that painful fact spelled out for him?

Of course, he still couldn't understand who the silhouette he'd seen her with in the window was, or why she was going out with the dentist, whom she clearly didn't like. And who was this friend she was doing favors for? And what kind of favors exactly was she doing? Surely Ellen didn't have some kind of wild secret life going on the side!

When he came back into his office, her back was to him, and she was staring intently at the graduation photo on his file cabinet. "Feeling better?"

Ellen gasped and whirled around. She was pale, almost green, and her limbs appeared shaky. Simon moved forward worriedly. "You look almost as if you'd just seen—"

"I'm much better," she said, cutting him off as she reached for the water. She gulped down the liquid and squashed the soggy cup in her fist. "Thanks."

"My pleasure." He cleared his throat regretfully. "About what I was saying before," he began. "About the date, I—"

"I'd love to go."

Simon's mouth was still open in midsentence when Ellen's words registered. Had he heard her correctly? He regarded her warily, not certain what to make of this sudden reversal. "Are you sure?" he asked. "I'm sorry if you thought I was blackm—"

"I'm sure," she said decisively.

"Well..." For once, Simon was at a loss for words. It all seemed too easy. Yet, he had to say something—Ellen was standing there in front of him, waiting. The odd thing was, it seemed as though she was trying to avoid looking into his eyes. As if she were resigned to going out with him but was determined not to have a good time.

Great, he thought. A reluctant date.

"How do you feel about Bach?" he asked, putting his mind back into a functioning gear.

"Love him," she said in a miserable monotone.

"Good..." He was nonplussed by her lack of enthusiasm. "There's a concert at the university Friday that we can go to."

Her shoulders rounded slightly. "Terrific."

"Terrific," Simon echoed, suddenly confused. This was terrible. The woman of his dreams had agreed to go out with him, but she was acting as though it was going to be sheer torture. "Look, if you change your m—"

"I won't," she bit out.

She forced a smile and turned to leave, and in desperation to salvage the situation, Simon caught her hand. Slowly, as their gazes locked, he turned her hand and lifted her palm to his lips. "I'm looking forward to it," he said in a low voice.

She closed her eyes as his lips made contact with the tender skin of her hand, and she nibbled on her red, full lip. Her body was tense, but then Simon felt a shudder move through her. That, at least, was reassuring. When he straightened and stood face-to-face with her once more, she looked the way he felt—unsteady.

"I'd better go," she said, her voice suddenly hoarse.

Simon sighed lightly. "Not a bad idea. The thoughts I'm having are completely out of place in an office."

Ellen headed for the door, opened it quickly and disappeared into the hall.

Simon moved around his desk and collapsed into his chair. Friday. It seemed too good to be true. And much too far away.

Chapter Four

"Is *that* what you're wearing?"

Ellen, in the middle of a final glance in front of the full-length mirror in her bedroom, looked up at the reflection of Abel leaning in the doorway behind her, his mouth squinched in a distasteful frown.

She glanced back at herself for a quick reassessment. Her long, curly hair was tamed into a tasteful French braid, and her face had received a dusting of makeup, lending her one of those "natural but actually too good to be natural" looks. The most fretful decision she'd made this evening was what dress to wear, but she'd finally settled on a simple solid black dress—of which she had many. This one was rough linen, and it had a scalloped, modest neckline that showed off nothing more titillating than her collarbones. Its short sleeves and length—to just above her knee—projected the image she was looking for. Nice, but not too nice. Appealing, but not too appealing. What could Abel object to? She certainly wasn't overdoing it.

"What's the matter?" she asked. He was looking at her shoes, plain black leather pumps that were nearly flats. They seemed perfectly fine to Ellen. They were comfortable, too.

Abel lifted his flannel-clad shoulders. "You look so, well . . . widowy!"

Her mouth pursed wryly. "There's a reason for that."

Abel ducked his head. "Okay, okay." She'd scolded him more than once in the past two weeks for not having been more careful on that motorcycle of his. "Hey, I like black. But you look so... plain."

"You mean you think I'm *under*doing it?" she asked. This was her husband talking!

"Couldn't you just jazz yourself up a little bit?" he pleaded anxiously.

"No!" Ellen protested. In fact, she wanted to stomp up and down and protest having to go out at all. She'd tried to hold her tongue, to be patient, but living with Abel under these circumstances was getting to her... as was the prospect of a whole evening alone with Simon. "This is so unfair! Why can't I stay home? We could order takeout and spend the evening together." This was where she belonged, where she was comfortable. Not traipsing around town with Simon, who definitely made her feel *un*comfortable.

For a moment, Abel looked as torn as she felt, and her heart surged with hope. She didn't want to go on this date. Just thinking about Simon made her knees wobbly.

So why didn't you cancel? a mocking voice in her head asked.

"I'm just trying to do what's best for both of us," Abel said, swallowing.

The stung tone of his words made her blush with shame. Naturally, a near-angel *would* be trying to do the right thing. "I'm sorry, Abel. I've just been out of it for so long. These dates give me the jitters."

The mixed emotion she thought she'd detected in her late husband's eyes was gone, replaced by a new determination to see her evening successfully launched. "Maybe if you could stick some jewelry on, or wear higher heels," he suggested. "You know, so you'd look ... sexier."

The last word came out little more than a mumble, but Ellen heard it loud and clear. Her face reddened to a hue a beet could be proud of. It wasn't very flattering to have her late husband so eager for her to entice Simon. "Absolutely not!"

"Well, that *is* the point of going out, isn't it?" Abel asked. "To make yourself... alluring?"

"Forget it," she said, snapping her velvet clutch handbag off the bureau. "I'm surprised at you! Don't people get jealous in heaven?"

"I'm not a people anymore."

"Ghosts, then," she said.

"I'm not jealous," he answered stiffly. "Why should I be?"

She had just one reason for that—Simon. But when she turned to inform her late husband of this, she discovered him on his hands and knees, sifting through the shoe rack on the floor of her closet. "What are you doing?" she cried in exasperation.

He picked out a pair of black stiletto heels she'd bought on sale the year before, a real whim purchase. "How about these?" he asked, holding one of the shoes up.

"Bunion City, Arizona," she said, echoing Abel's last Prince Charming.

"Oh, c'mon, Ellen, what'll it hurt to see how they look?"

"My feet!" she protested as he came at her with the torturous-looking things. But at the intensity on his face as he approached her feet, hunched over, eyes gleaming, hands ready to strike, looking for all the world like Quasimodo turned shoe salesman, she laughed and surrendered. "All right, you win," she said, collapsing on the bed and kicking off one pair in exchange for another.

They weren't too terrible, she thought moments later as she picked her way carefully back toward the full-length mirror—and they did make her look a little less frumpy. She turned to get a back view, and was accosted by Abel, who had been covertly raiding her jewelry box.

"These, I think," he said, nearly choking her with a short string of amber beads, the clasp of which he had closed before she could even protest. "And don't you have some matching earrings somewhere?"

Reluctantly, Ellen dug up the earrings and put them on, but protested bitterly when he grabbed for her hair.

"Abel, please!" she shouted in alarm.

"I won't hurt it," he promised.

But with a few quick tugs, he had dismantled the braid and liberated her curly red blond hair to its usual anarchic state.

"Aren't you overdoing it with the fairy-godmother routine?" she asked in frustration.

"Maybe, but just look at the results." He held up the mirror for her, and she sucked in a breath of surprise. "You're a knockout, babe."

Maybe *knockout* was an exaggeration, but for the first time in years, Ellen could honestly say she felt dolled up. Seeing her reflection, with Abel standing next to her, she couldn't help remembering old times, when they would go out to college parties, giddy at the prospect of an evening of play, high on the feeling of being young and carefree.

Abel was staring at her, too, completely still, transfixed, she was certain, by the same memories that were assaulting her. "Oh, Abel..."

She turned, ready to hurl herself into his arms, when a car door slammed shut outside.

"It's him!" they both cried at once.

Suddenly, Ellen's heart was beating double time. All at once she felt like a teenager on her first date—with Abel playing the part of her pesky little sister. Whatever tender moment had been about to occur was now broken. Ellen looked in the mirror, took in her long mess of hair and moaned.

Abel lifted his shoulders helplessly. "Oops, sorry."

She sighed in frustration as she hurriedly ran a brush through her unruly mane. Simon *would* have to be on time! She suddenly remembered the state of her cluttered living room and was thrown into a full-fledged panic. She ran out as fast as her shoes would allow and took inventory of the sea of chip bags and empty soda cans, evidence of Abel's couch potato presence.

"I can't let him come in here," she said, rushing for the door just as the bell rang.

"Don't forget your purse," Abel said, dashing behind her. She turned to take it and was hit with a heavy spray of perfume. Abel grinned mischievously as she coughed in surprise and flapped her arms in front of her to disperse the thick cloud of scent.

She grimaced unhappily as she snapped up her purse. "I'll be home by midnight," she said in a low whisper. She wasn't about to let Abel's last-minute efforts sidetrack her from her own private mission: to not have a good time. Or, more specifically, to not let Simon kiss her again.

"And you might consider tidying up while I'm gone," she added as a parting shot.

She opened the door just a crack and quickly slipped out of the house. Simon, standing outside the screen door, seemed intrigued by this method of leaving her home.

"Is something wrong with your door?"

"No, no," she said, making a show of locking up. "I, uh, just don't like to let the hot air in. I've got a high utility bill."

Simon nodded, seeming to accept her explanation. For the briefest of moments, they stood awkwardly on the porch. She gave him a quick inspection—and didn't like what she saw. In the waning summer light, his short dark hair looked soft and freshly washed. He wore a dark blue suit with a white shirt and a bright colored, splashy tie, like a guy who'd just stepped out of *GQ*. He looked good. Too tempting. She especially didn't like the look in his eye as he gave her his own inspection.

"You smell great!" he said, trying to break the ice.

Of course, the way Abel wielded that spray bottle, people could probably smell her clear over on the other side of town. "I had an accident," she explained.

"Don't tell me," he guessed, "you fell into a puddle of Chanel?"

"Not quite," she said evasively. Sensing that the only way to get the date over with was to get it under way, she pivoted on her stilty heels and began her treacherous descent down the porch steps.

"Here, let me help you," Simon said, taking her arm. When he touched her elbow, they both flinched—for entirely different reasons. Simon looked at her in shock. "No wonder that air-conditioning bill's so high. Your skin's ice cold!"

Ellen ducked her head, wishing she didn't feel so weak-kneed just because the man touched her. "We like it cold."

"We?" Simon asked, his brow knitting in puzzlement.

Her heart skittered anxiously. "My cat and I," she said, covering. "Hawthorne needs cold air. All that fur."

"You really should be careful, though," he warned as he escorted her to the passenger side of the Jeep. "I've noticed you've been sniffling a lot lately."

Too bad there wasn't a picture around so Abel could eavesdrop on *this* conversation, Ellen thought as Simon closed the door for her. Her late husband could take a few lessons on being conscientious from Simon.

Realizing that she had just compared Abel unfavorably to a man she barely knew, Ellen shook her head to get her thoughts back in line.

Simon situated himself in the driver's seat and turned the key in the ignition. "Ready?" he asked.

She turned away from his million-dollar smile, mentally bracing herself for all the many smiles and other charms he could throw her way in the evening ahead. "As ready as I'll ever be."

ELLEN MIGHT HAVE DECKED herself out in come-hither fashion for the evening, Simon decided during the concert, but she had unfortunately brought along her coolest keep-your-distance manners. Touching her seemed to trigger them. All night, if he so much as brushed her hand, she would stiffen perceptibly and keep herself at a safer distance from him. Now, in the concert hall, he could feel the tension in her ebb then return as they each shifted around their small theater seats, careful not to bump elbows or knees.

Lord knows, he was doing his best to show restraint—but she looked so damned good. He'd nearly been knocked off his feet when she'd slipped out her front door in that black dress and those sexy heels. Given the fact that she'd seemed to approach their date with about as much enthusiasm as one would for a date with a firing squad, he wouldn't have been surprised if she'd appeared in a flour sack instead of that black dress with the long zipper down the back that he could just imagine...

Whoa. Even though his physical desires were running rampant, he knew Ellen might need time to adjust to going out again. He just hoped she wasn't determined to live in grief for the rest of her life.

Because if that were the case, a little voice nagged, what had Martin Mayhew been all about? That's what Simon couldn't figure out, and he tried not to dwell on it. But if there was anything he believed, it was that relationships should be built on trust, and in return for that trust, openness. Just look at what happened with Jennifer. If she had been open with him and told him that she was still seeing her ex-husband and discussing a reconciliation—then perhaps he wouldn't have felt so deceived when the two of them had got back together.

Yet he couldn't allow his past to ruin his chances with Ellen. Suspicion could be just as dangerous as blind faith.

The pianist on the stage played the last notes of a concerto, ending to rapturous applause in the small but crammed concert hall. As the lights went up on the audience, Simon glanced over to Ellen for her reaction.

Her eyes were still on the stage, bright with appreciation for the music they'd just heard. When she turned, she seemed surprised to see him, as if she'd forgotten anyone else was listening to the music but her. "Wasn't he wonderful? I wish I could play the piano that well."

Luckily, in her enthusiasm over Bach, she seemed to have allowed some of her guard down. She was no longer staring at him as if he were a fox about to pounce on a rabbit.

Simon tamped down the desire to reach out and tuck a stray tendril of that gorgeous red hair of hers behind her ear. "I wish I could plunk out 'Chopsticks.'"

"My parents made me take piano lessons when I was little," Ellen said. "I thought it was torture—I couldn't wait until they would allow me to quit. Now I would give anything if I had just stuck with it." Her lips tilted whimsically. "When I was a kid I always thought boys were the lucky ones. They joined teams. Girls took lessons."

"Don't forget Arthur Murray," Simon said, reminding her of his experience.

"That was self-inflicted."

"True. But like you and the piano, I get wistful whenever I think of Baryshnikov, and what might have been."

Her mouth turned up in a flirtatious grin. "Somehow, I can't imagine you in tights. Besides, I prefer tappers."

"Fred Astaire?" Simon asked.

Suddenly, something in her face changed. A hint of the old sadness returned to her green eyes.

"Is something wrong?" he asked, wondering how Fred Astaire could have broken the light mood between them.

She shook her head. "No, it's just that after Abel . . . I mean, four years ago, I used to have a terrible time falling to sleep. Sometimes I would stay up late watching old Fred and Ginger movies. In one—*Top Hat,* I think—Fred was staying in the room above Ginger's in a hotel and he played sandman by doing a soft shoe to help her get to sleep."

"I saw that one," Simon remembered.

"I would have given a lot to have my own personal sandman back in those days," she mused.

"And now?"

Her lips, upturned in a smile, remained frozen as she stared at him. "Now I'm fine. Perfectly fine."

Simon doubted she was as perfect as she wanted him to believe. He'd seen her yawning at the office a lot lately, and more than once, he'd noticed dark circles under her eyes. Something was causing Ellen to still have sleepless nights.

But apparently she didn't want to discuss them with him. Instead, she was looking anxiously down at her program, with its small portrait of Bach on the front. "I wish I could get my hair to do that," she said nervously, changing the subject by pointing at the composer's neat rows of curls.

"I like yours better," he said, admiring her long, shiny hair that he itched to touch. "How about a glass of wine?"

They got up and went to the lobby, where people milled around, talking and laughing, some just crowd watching. Simon and Ellen stepped into the short line for refreshments.

"Ellen?" a male voice called out. "Ellen Lantry?"

Across the lobby, a tall man sporting a goatee and wearing a black suit with a pencil-thin tie began sidling through the crowds, waving his long arms above his head. Simon felt a pang of jealousy at first, but as the stranger came closer, his smile broad, his gangly arms open, Ellen's face didn't register any recognition at all. In fact, seeing the odd man loping toward her made her turn a pinkish hue and glance around, as though checking to see if there were another Ellen Lantry in the line.

"Ellen! Finally!" The man skidded to a stop only inches away from her, then grabbed her hand and started pumping it as though she were a long-lost friend. "I can't believe it's you!"

Ellen managed a hesitant smile. "I think . . . I don't—"

An expression of mortification crossed his face. "Don't you recognize me?"

Ellen hesitated. "Well, I . . ."

Before she could say anything, he clapped her on the shoulder and let out a burst of laughter. "Of course!" he cried out. "It's the beard! Try this." With one hand, he covered the thick, wiry stubble over his chin. "Guess who?" he challenged her, his brown eyes round, his eyebrows waggling playfully like a villain in a melodrama.

Simon was about convinced the man was a complete lunatic when suddenly Ellen let out a gasp of recognition. Her hand flew to her mouth, and her face drained of color. "Oh! It's *you!*"

"Of course!" the man said, spreading his arms as if beckoning Ellen to step into them and give him a great big old bear hug. Which, judging by the way she stood rooted in place, she wasn't about to do. "It's me!"

The two remained staring at each other, but for Simon, the question still remained. Who was *he?*

THE MUSIC PROFESSOR! Ellen thought, her mind in a panic. She barely recognized him from the picture Abel had shown her. This was terrible! What could she say—what could she do to get rid of the man? And what on earth was his name? She couldn't remember it for the life of her.

Simon *would* have to be here to witness this scene, she thought miserably. The three of them were standing in a tight triangle, each looking from one to the other. The professor seemed especially interested in her new escort. Which made sense, considering that she'd supposedly been writing the man love letters for two months.

"I suppose you two need to be introduced," she said anxiously when the silence had stretched beyond a bearable length. "Uh, professor, this is Simon Miller."

Simon held out his hand. "I didn't catch the name?"

The professor's mouth set in a grim line. "Cliff Webber."

The two said "nice to meet you" at the same time, but neither sounded as though he actually meant it. Then they both turned to Ellen. What now?

She cast around for a subtle way to get rid of the man, then decided to toss subtlety out the window. "It sure was great to see you, Cliff."

"And how!" Cliff got a hold of his enthusiasm, then threw an anxious glance toward Simon. He looked back at her and said in a lower voice, "I thought we'd never get to meet."

"You mean you two have never met each other *at all?*" Simon asked curiously.

Ellen winced. "Well, under the circumstances, you know—it's just one of those things," she explained vaguely. Maybe he would think Cliff had something to do with work or—

"You look older than your picture," Cliff noted.

"What picture?" Simon asked.

"It's a long story," she explained quickly.

"I sure miss your letters," Cliff said in a wounded tone.

Ellen cursed her bad luck as Simon swung toward her with unconcealed amazement in his eyes. "Letters?" he repeated.

Ellen's stomach did a few acrobatic flips.

"You mean you two were correspondents, too?" Simon asked.

"Too?" Cliff pointed from Ellen to Simon, his expression hurt. "Are you two... Did you two also meet in the personals?"

"No," Simon said emphatically.

The professor looked relieved. "I'm afraid I would have felt betrayed if I thought you'd been writing to another man all those months that you were writing to me."

Ellen looked away, but felt Simon's sharp brown eyes boring into her. No telling what *he* thought. She wanted to strangle Abel. How was she going to explain this compulsion for writing strange men to Simon?

"Why would you feel betrayed?" Simon asked Cliff. "Did you two become intimate in your letters?"

She turned on Simon. "That's a private matter," Ellen said.

Cliff smiled and raised a hand in an appeasing gesture. "My epistolary exchanges with Ellen were only on the highest, most intellectual level."

Thank heavens. Ellen rounded smugly on Simon. "There, you see? They weren't even love letters at all. Just epistolary exchanges."

Simon still looked doubtful. "No verbal hanky-panky?"

"No," Ellen said quickly.

"No, no, no." She thought Cliff was backing her up, until she saw him turn a dreamy smile her way. Abel apparently had the man completely besotted. "We were far beyond mere hanky-panky."

Uh-oh. "We were?"

Simon looked perplexed. "I'm not sure I understand exactly what kind of relationship you two had going."

"Nothing—it was nothing," Ellen said quickly. Turning, she noticed a tiny hope of a way out. "Look, Simon," she chirped, "it's our turn in line. I think I'll have something to drink, after all. A club soda with lime, please," she told the man on the other side of the table. She felt as if she were a hop, skip and a jump away from hysteria. "In fact, make it a double."

Simon was now too preoccupied with Cliff to care much about refreshments. Ellen dug through her purse to find money to pay as the two men carried on about the ups and downs of getting to know people by post. Waiting for her drink, she tossed her program down onto the makeshift bar and rubbed her temples, trying to drown out the two men's conversation. When her eyes focused on the program again, she saw her late husband's face framed by Bach's tidy hair.

She nearly yelped in shock at seeing him there.

"Abel!" she cried under her breath. She quickly glanced around, afraid that someone might have heard her.

"What a mess!" he said, the little grin indicating that he was actually enjoying the chaos. "Cliff's showing up here is ruining our evening."

Our? "What am I supposed to do now?" she whispered back frantically.

Bach's shoulders shrugged. "I dunno. Why don't you lie?"

"Lie?" She could have shrieked. "Is that what they're teaching angels up in heaven these days?"

She felt a hand touch her shoulder. "Ellen?" Simon asked. "Are you okay?"

She slapped her hand over the top of her program and whipped around quickly. "Oh, yes," she said brightly. "Perfectly fine."

If Simon's concerned frown were any indication, he didn't believe her. He pointed to the counter helpfully. "There's your club soda. Why don't you take a sip?"

She did better than that. With her free hand she slugged down the entire fizzy glass in one belt. "Yes, I feel much better now," she assured him.

"I wish I could show you some of the things this little lady wrote to me," Cliff continued. "She has the soul of a poet...."

The men returned to their conversation, and Ellen carefully lifted her hand off the program. Abel was still there, superimposed on Bach's face. He twitched his nose uncomfortably.

"Ouch."

"Serves you right," Ellen said, careful to keep her voice a low hiss. "How am I going to extricate myself from this situation? Now I'm supposed to have the soul of a poet!"

Abel smiled again. "Okay, tell them the truth."

In frustration, she took the program and rolled it into a tight scroll. Weren't angels supposed to be helpful? She turned her attention back to Simon and Cliff, but discovered the two hadn't progressed very far in their discussion.

"You see," Cliff was explaining, "we had a perfect exchange of ideas. As Ellen once wrote, 'Letters mingle souls more than kisses.'"

Ellen nearly choked. Desperate to get Simon away before she had to hear any more pearls of wisdom she had supposedly written to a complete stranger, she hooked her hand around his arm and gave him a tug. "I think we should get back to our seats."

But Simon wasn't budging. He was enjoying himself far too much. "I'm intrigued by this philosophical bent of yours."

Ellen lifted her head, trying to project a tiny bit of dignity. "I think what I said about letters and kisses was rather interesting."

"It certainly is. Especially since John Donne said the exact same thing four centuries earlier," Simon joked. "I suppose he is the poet whose soul you borrowed."

Cliff looked crestfallen. "Well," he said, coming to grips with the fact that his stellar correspondent had been less than truthful, "as they say, great minds think alike." The audience had started filing back into the little theater for the second half of the program, and Cliff took her hand in a quick, loose shake. Discovering she was a plagiarist had apparently soured him on her. "I'm glad you've found someone you think will make you happy, Ellen."

She automatically opened her mouth to set everyone straight on that score, but the professor dove back into the crowd, disappearing as quickly and jarringly as he had appeared. She let out a breath of relief. Except now she had to face Simon alone.

His first words were predictably sardonic. "Are you expecting any more men to come out of the woodwork this evening?"

"Don't be ridiculous," she said.

Yet, she was worried about the same thing. She tried to assure herself that the professor's appearance was just a fluke—but she took little comfort in the fact that Austin was a small city, and Abel had picked people out for her who shared similar interests. With Martin, it had been movies. With Cliff, Bach. She considered the remaining correspondents and shuddered. Abel had said one of them was a painter. Would she ever be able to go to a gallery again without the fear of being accosted by a former lover she'd never met?

"I see," Simon said, "you were just writing him as a favor to a friend, too."

Ellen let out a sigh as she plopped back into her theater seat. "Not exactly. If you'll just let me explain . . ."

Luckily, the orchestra started playing before she had a chance to. Which at least gave her a reprieve, some time to think of a convincing lie.

Lies, evasions—what kind of person was she turning into? She was certain Simon was beginning to doubt her credibility—and he didn't even know about the three other men who had been writing to her for two months!

WAS ELLEN LANTRY REALLY a modest, reclusive widow who happened to have a letter fetish, or was she an incorrigible, compulsive liar?

Simon shifted gears as he pulled onto Guadeloupe, the main street that ran past the university. There had to be a rational explanation for her mystery men, but he was still waiting for her to say something. He hadn't heard a peep out of her since the music had stopped, except to say that she was tired and she wanted to go home directly.

After driving another block in silence, Simon cleared his throat and asked tentatively, "Do you answer classified ads often?"

She let out a sigh of resignation. "I can't blame you for being curious," she said. "But honestly, it's just been an odd coincidence that every time I see you..."

"I just happen to meet a man who fell in love with you by correspondence," he finished for her.

She turned in her seat so that she was facing his profile. "A few months ago I began to feel lonely, and... a friend... told me that the personals might be one solution. And to set the record straight, *I* took out the ad."

Well, at least she was being honest. "And you answered some of the letters sent to you."

"A few," she admitted, then added more easily, "I didn't want to take my chances and go out with just anybody. So I wrote to Martin and Cliff, and got to know them a little. Then I went out with Martin, and... Well, you saw the results."

"Not a perfect match."

She let out a short bark of laughter. "Not even close. So that was the end of my letter-writing campaign."

At a red light, Simon considered her words in silence. More important, he tried to put himself in her place. It wasn't so hard. Who didn't feel that kind of crushing loneliness from time to time?

He looked over at her as she combed a hand through her long, gorgeous hair. He would have given anything for that hand to be his. Only the streetlights illuminated the interior of the Jeep, making her pale skin looked especially creamy and delicate. Her green eyes looked different, too. Darker. More watchful. Was she worried that he wouldn't accept her explanation? Or was her impenetrable stare a sign that she felt the same tug of desire in the confines of the Jeep that he did?

She had admitted to being lonely. She probably hadn't had a real relationship with a man for years. For all he knew, he was the only man since her husband who had held her, had kissed those rosy lips of hers.

"Simon?"

He was jarred from his guilty thoughts by her soft voice. "What's the matter?"

"Green light."

As he sped ahead, his mind snagged on those words. Green light? Was that what she was giving him? There were so many contradictions. On one hand, there was the mysterious incident at her house that Friday night. And Martin Mayhew. And her years of relative reclusiveness. And on the other hand, there was what she had told him tonight about being lonely. And the wanting he detected in those jade eyes of hers.

That she would be looking for a steady, exclusive relationship with him seemed to good to be true, yet what other explanation could there be for her sudden decision to cut off two other men she'd been writing to for months?

He pulled up in front of her house and killed the engine and the lights. Suddenly, the dark interior of the vehicle seemed smaller, and rigid with silent tension. He turned and saw Ellen staring at him, her cheeks stained with color, her lips parted slightly.

"Well. This is it," she said quickly. "Thanks so much for the lovely evening!"

Before he could so much as reach over, she had the passenger door open and was halfway out of the Jeep.

"Wait!" Simon said, placing a restraining hand on her arm. "I want to talk to you."

"What about?" she asked, glancing anxiously toward her house. A blue glow emanated from the living room. "Oh, look—I left my TV on. I'd better go right in and turn it off!"

And then she was gone, barreling down the sidewalk full speed. He leapt out of his car and chased after her.

They reached the front door before she turned to him and asked politely, "Did you forget something?"

"No, I think you did," Simon told her.

She twirled her keys impatiently around one finger. "What?"

He cleared his throat, darting an anxious glance around the surrounding houses. "Aren't you going to invite me in?"

She practically hopped in the air at the very idea. "In? In *my house?*"

"Well, yes." What was wrong with that?

Her eyes rounded, and she looked a little panicked at the thought. "That's impossible."

"Why?"

Simon watched as she anxiously licked her lips. He wanted to test those lips himself.

"You wouldn't like it in there," she said. "It's cold, remember?"

He leaned closer. "We could warm it up."

She opened the screen door, but before she could put it between them, Simon stepped in and held it for her. "I assure you, there's nothing to see in there," she told him.

Simon shrugged. "I just thought it was sort of customary to invite your date in ... to talk."

"Oh, I'm afraid I tend to break with custom on a lot of things," Ellen said.

Simon smiled. "Even time-tested dating rituals?"

"Especially those," she said, turning quickly and jabbing her key into the lock. "I think if a woman can afford to pay for her own meal—"

"I wasn't thinking about economics," he said, putting a hand on her shoulder. An answering shudder snaked across her skin, and she swallowed hard.

"Wh-what exactly *were* you thinking about?" she asked him, her voice a whisper as she turned slightly.

"This," he said, leaning in to claim her lips.

They were soft and invitingly warm, and after just a moment he knew that just a quick good-night peck wouldn't do. Definitely not. He wrapped his arm around her waist and pulled her close, nearly groaning when he felt her breasts collide softly against his chest. Deepening the kiss, he tested her reaction. She still had one hand on her key, but as his tongue delved between her lips, he could feel her other hand weave up his back and hook itself around the nape of his neck.

This was surely as close to heaven as a person could get, he thought. For two long, agonizing months, he'd dreamed of taking her in his arms, of kissing her like this. Her birthday kiss hadn't counted. Too fast. Now he felt as if he had the time to truly savor the experience.

There was nothing to compare with these sensations—the smell of her, the warm pressure of her close against him, the movement of her lips. Her tentativeness gave way to a more demanding need for gratification, and together they fell back against her wooden front door, tasting and touching and moving together as if they were kids on a first date. Or maybe he just got that feeling from hearing the sounds of a Three Stooges episode on the other side of the door.

"Ellen . . ."

ELLEN HEARD HER NAME through a blur of sensation. She felt as if she were spinning, though she was positive she was standing completely still, pinned as she was against the door.

It was *who* had pinned her there that made her feel dizzy with desire. Every time she kissed Simon, it seemed as though she'd never kissed another man before, never felt this warm rush of desire coursing through her. He was both physically imposing, hard, and yet achingly gentle at the same time. The combination gave her butterflies, made her legs feel rubbery beneath her.

His tongue didn't force itself against her lips, it insinuated, so that she welcomed the intrusion, reaching up and pressing herself as close against him as she could manage. She could feel the tension coiling him tight, and she smiled inwardly. This was something she'd forgotten about, too— the sweet sensation of having a man willing to lay his desire bare before you. If she wanted, she could open the door and invite...

The television. She heard it and gasped slightly, remembering. She most certainly could *not* invite Simon into her house, which was really no longer just her house at all. With a strength she was surprised she could muster, she pulled herself back, attempting to look anywhere but into Simon's eyes.

"Oh, my goodness! I've got to go," she said. "I mean, *you've* got to go!"

She brought her hand down and pushed against his chest.

He said nothing for a moment, but she could feel his confusion. And no wonder. Not in her wildest dreams had she imagined kissing him like that.

"I think we need to discuss some things," he said.

"Yes, we do," she agreed. Preferably after she'd recovered some restraint! "Maybe Monday, at the office."

"This isn't about work."

"I know," she admitted. "But please, Simon. Let's talk later, okay? I'm exhausted."

She looked up at him then, pleadingly, hoping he would relent. Reflected in his eyes, she could see her own face, flushed and flustered from their kiss.

He looked at her for a moment, then took pity on her. "All right," he conceded, reaching out to brush a single

strand of hair behind her ear in a gesture that was sinfully
tender. He gave her lips a final brush, turned and walked
down the steps. Before he was halfway down the walk, he
turned back. "Monday, then?"

She nodded. Monday was so far away, it seemed very
safe. Especially when she had a long weekend to get through
with her husband.

Her husband, who was just on the other side of that door.

Chapter Five

Ellen slipped inside and collapsed, her back sagging down the door frame. Judging from her physical symptoms, she would have thought she'd just finished running a marathon, or swimming the English Channel. Her heart tripped out of control, she felt short of breath, and how her legs managed to support her she couldn't guess. But she'd only engaged in a simple kiss!

Or was it really so simple?

Aside from the spastic sounds of Moe, Larry and Curly, there was an eerie absence of noise in the room. She looked up and saw Abel sitting on the couch, his hair pulled back in a severe ponytail, his arms knit tightly across his chest. Gone was the puckish, teasing manner he'd displayed during his impromptu visit to the concert hall.

She pushed away from the door, trying to overcome the uncomfortable combination of weak-kneed desire and crushing guilt that suddenly washed over her. "Hi, there," she said, forcing her voice to sound easy and natural.

There was a moment of silence before Abel responded with a clipped "Hi."

"How's everything?" she asked, stepping out of her torturous heels and moving closer to the couch.

He refused to look at her. "Fine."

She took a deep breath. "Aren't you going to ask me what happened after the concert?"

When his head swung to face her, his lips were twisted in a wry sneer. "Oh, I think I can guess. The front door's not that thick, you know."

Ellen felt her face flame just thinking about what had happened. She'd stepped right into Simon's arms with barely a squeak of protest . . . and here sat Abel, listening to the whole thing.

But why should he of all people be acting so high and mighty? "It was just a little kiss," she said, reminding him. "You were the one who got so upset when you thought Martin hadn't given me a peck good-night."

"This was more than a peck," he replied.

"Well what was I supposed to do," Ellen asked, "hit him?"

"You didn't have to get quite so carried away, did you?"

"But when I came back from the date with Martin—"

"This guy isn't Martin."

He had a point there. Ellen felt herself blush again, then steeled herself against that involuntary reaction. She had nothing to be ashamed of. "You didn't behave too well yourself tonight, popping up on my program the way you did," she lectured. "And what was that Cliff person doing showing up during my date in the first place? I suspect you arranged for him to be there to cause trouble."

"I did not."

"Well, at any rate, you're an angel. Can't you control fate a little more efficiently than that?"

"I'm doing my best," Abel defended hotly. "And if we're going to have a discussion about control, how about that kiss that lasted through three commercials!"

So he was back on that again. "I can't believe *you're* criticizing," she said. "What did you think was going to happen? You were the one who wanted me to be alluring and hosed me down with perfume.''

In response to her accusation, he hunched down and returned a glowering gaze to the television. ''Yeah, well, I didn't expect you to get swept off your feet so easily.''

''I wasn't!'' she said. Surely he didn't think she was so fickle that she could fall for Simon this fast!

In fact, she had no intention of falling for Simon at all. If his kiss had taken her by surprise, maybe even made her emotions waver temporarily, seeing poor Abel sitting there unhappy amid his discarded candy wrappers and soda cans reminded her what was at stake. Simon was just a means to an end, a way to keep Abel with her.

Then realization struck her like a bolt of lightning. Abel wasn't just mad about the kiss—he was afraid of losing her. All thought of argument rushed out of her, and she sank onto the couch next to him, inadvertently landing on a chip bag. She turned to him, the plastic crinkling beneath her as she said, ''You said angels didn't get jealous.''

''I'm not jealous!'' he retorted quickly.

She didn't believe him. But how could he think that anyone could ever mean as much to her as he did? ''Don't worry, Abel. Simon's a charmer, but it's going to take a while before I can tell you for sure if he's the one.'' To save his angel pride, she would go along with the ruse of trying to find a mate. But she wanted to reassure him that she wasn't serious about anyone else.

''Humph,'' Abel grunted, folding his arms crossly even as she tried to rest her head on his shoulder. ''I can save you some time. I don't like him.''

Ellen straightened warily. ''Why not?''

''He's so...conventional,'' Abel said, scoffing.

Her mouth dropped open. Simon was hardly a dreary drip. ''What makes you say that?''

"Oh, please," Abel said, rolling his eyes. "He's a *law-yer.* He even dresses like one, in those boring suits. Mr. Rich and Successful. Big deal!"

Ellen smiled, understanding. Abel's antiestablishment streak seemed to have survived just fine. But had he forgotten that *she* had wanted to be a lawyer, too?

"And yet he drives around in that Jeep, like he's cool or something, when it's all just a sham," he finished.

Ellen sighed. A few years ago, she would have agreed wholeheartedly with Abel. Now she saw a bigger sham in Abel, a wealthy doctor's son, running around with holes in his jeans and the same plaid flannel shirt day after day. But she didn't want to point that out now, since he was apparently going to spend eternity as a grunge ghost.

What was she going to do with a petulant angel on her hands? "I think you've been cooped up in this place too long, Abel. Why don't you get out some? Do a few of those good deeds you have hanging over your head," she suggested brightly. "I'm sure it would make you feel better."

"Yeah, right," he said, in full sulk now. "You're already trying to get rid of me."

Ellen clapped her hand over her mouth, immediately wishing she could retract her stupid words. What was she thinking? If Abel fulfilled his deed quota, then he really would have nothing keeping him here. Except her. But he was so jealous, he seemed to fancy her falling in love with any man after one date.

She snuggled more fully against him, dislodging a loyal Hawthorne from his lap. "Oh, Abel, I'm sorry. Don't think I want you to leave—ever. I could date Simon for a million years and it wouldn't change that," she said truthfully.

"Then I don't think you should go out with him anymore at all," Abel said.

She blinked, wondering if she'd heard him right. "Wh-what?"

"I think you should blow him off. Try somebody else, like you said before."

"But Simon *was* that somebody else."

"I thought that Cliff guy looked okay."

"Oh, Abel, please! That guy?"

"He's better than that poser Simon, at least."

"But—" Why was she arguing so vehemently about this? Simon meant nothing to her. Not really.

And yet…not go out with Simon again? That didn't seem fair. What would she say to him, how could she explain? True, she wasn't in love with him, but she liked him. Liked him very much. Who wouldn't?

Who wouldn't want to kiss him again after what she'd just experienced on her front porch?

The thought made her anxious. Maybe she *was* too attracted to Simon for her own good.

"What was the matter with Ed?" Abel asked.

Ellen looked up at him. "Who's Ed?"

"The painter we wrote to."

What was the matter with Simon? a stubborn little voice in Ellen's head insisted. If she couldn't go out on pointless dates with him, she didn't want to go on with pointless dates with anybody. But she couldn't tell Abel that. He had his own heaven-mandated agenda to follow.

At that moment, plan B began forming in her head. What if she *didn't* go out with anybody? She could simply make it seem as if she were. Of course, the only trouble with this idea was Abel himself. But maybe she could remedy that.

"If I do go out with Ed, or whomever, you have to promise not to pop up all the time, Abel," she said. "It makes me nervous."

"You mean like tonight?"

She sent him a sharp glance. "And at the movies—you think I didn't see you in that marquee poster, but I did."

Two sharp stains of color in his cheeks gave him away.

"I have a hard time staying composed when that happens," she told him. "You don't want these guys to think I'm mentally unstable, do you?"

He considered for a moment. "Okay, no more popping," he promised grudgingly.

Ellen smiled and settled down again. This would work out fine, although the first thing she intended to do was write the remaining two of Abel's correspondents and tell them not to expect to hear from her. Maybe that way she wouldn't have strange men running up to her in public anymore.

She grinned, thinking of the look on Simon's face when he'd first seen Cliff—and then realized who he was! She couldn't imagine what he thought of her. Or what he would think when she told him she didn't want to go out anymore.

Her heart felt heavy at the prospect. Simon was a perfect guy. He deserved better than what she was dishing out to him. He deserved . . .

Suddenly, an idea came to her, and she shot upright again. It wasn't an easy thing to do, but perhaps a little personal sacrifice would ease her conscience a little. "Abel, how much *can* you manipulate things?"

He shrugged. "It depends."

"Could you manage to get Simon together with Annie from next door? Wouldn't that be considered a good deed?"

"Hey, that's not a bad idea." Abel rubbed his chin and thought it over. Matchmaking Simon with someone else apparently appealed to him. "Yeah, I think I can do it."

Somehow, Ellen hadn't expected it to be this easy. She suddenly imagined Simon and Annie going out together and frowned.

"Are you sure?" she asked, rethinking the scheme. After all, bringing two people together... Well, she didn't want to be hasty. "I mean, I know you said you can only do so much."

He shook his head. "No, I can manage this, I think."

She forced a smile. "Great."

Sacrifice, she told herself, forcing thoughts of Simon out of her mind. So he was handsome, and charming, and was the best kisser she'd had the pleasure to run into. Other than that, he was still an unknown quantity. There could be any number of terrible things about him that she didn't know about yet. Although she couldn't think of a trait terrible enough that would make her never want to kiss him again.

Stop thinking about it! It would be great if Simon and Annie could get together. And if Abel's matchmaking was successful, it would just be proof—which she really didn't need, anyway—that she and Simon weren't meant to be.

The very phrase "meant to be" just didn't suit her and Simon. She was destined to be with Abel, her husband. It didn't matter that Abel was a ghost and she was a mortal. Or that he was supposed to be beyond earthly desires and her hormones were on overdrive. Or that he was trying to set her up with other men and she seemed to be particularly susceptible to one of them. Every married couple had sticky little problems to work through. Theirs were just a little stickier than most.

Dear Ed...

Ellen had already spent half the morning huddled in an isolated conference room at work thinking about what to write. She tried to conjure up something reasonable to say to Ed, upbeat words that would make him understand her situation more clearly. The truth, naturally, was out of the question. And she just couldn't break it off by giving him no explanation. That would probably cause him to hunt her down to find out where they had gone wrong. Another run-in with these people was the last thing she wanted.

"Ellen?"

She pivoted and saw her neighbor standing uncomfortably in the doorway. "Annie?" she asked. "What are you doing here?"

Even though Annie was dressed for work and looked much like everyone else wandering around Smith, she seemed oddly out of place. She shrugged helplessly. "I don't know." Her eyes were a little dazed, as if she wasn't sure what had hit her.

But Ellen did. Memory assailed her with the force of a blow. This was Abel's doing! He was following through with her request for him to bring Annie and Simon together.

So soon? Ellen chafed at the prospect now that it was upon her.

"It's the strangest thing," Annie told her confidentially. "Would you believe I just woke up this morning and decided I needed to have my will drawn up?" She snapped her fingers. "Just like that. You don't think this means something terrible's about to happen to me, do you?"

"Of course not," Ellen said truthfully. Remembering Simon's kiss of Friday night, she realized that quite the opposite was the case. She had to force herself to continue with the setup. "I'm glad you decided to come here. I could introduce you to one of the attorneys—"

Annie moved into the room, cutting her off. "That's the strangest part of all," she said, taking the next seat at the conference table. "I didn't even know this was the law firm where you worked."

"Then how...?"

"I looked in the phone book under attorneys and found a name." She stared down at a little piece of paper she held. "Simon Miller. Do you know him?"

"Sure," Ellen said, swallowing. She took in Annie's appearance, and noted that her neighbor looked especially cute, dressed in a coral-colored suit, her bob springy and youthful, her makeup just right. In the back of her mind, a devilish little voice said, *Tell her he's no good. Send her to Larry Lambert.*

"What do you think of him?" Annie asked.

Sacrifice, Ellen reminded herself. This was all to appease Abel. No one said holding on to an angel would be a cakewalk. Her voice, when she found it, came out in a startling monotone. "Simon's the best."

Annie pouted. "Oh, great!" she said miserably.

"What's wrong?" Ellen asked.

"I tried to make an appointment with him," Annie explained, "but when I called, they said he was out today."

"Out?" Ellen repeated, worried. What was the matter with him? Was he sick? She considered calling him. What if he had a fever and couldn't make it to a doctor, or—

"So they gave me another man's name," Annie continued, oblivious to the fact that her audience had been sidetracked. She looked down and read again. "Larry Lambert."

Oh, no! Ellen shot up out of her chair and began to pace. This was a cruel trick. Just when she'd screwed up the resolution to set Simon up with someone else . . . How could Abel have fouled this up so completely?

Well, what one hapless angel could mess up, one determined woman could make right again. She simply had to. "Thank goodness you came to me first," she told Annie. "We're going right out front again and change your appointment."

Annie balked. "I'm sure this Lambert guy will be all right," she said. "What difference does it make? It's not like I have any money, or property, or even many valuable possessions. In fact, I just can't figure out why I've got a bee in my bonnet about this will business all of a sudden.''

But Ellen tugged her toward the hallway that led to the reception desk. "Never mind that. If we're going to go through with this, we'd better do it right."

"Look, there's his office." Annie dug her heels in and forced them to stop right outside Larry Lambert's office. "He's expecting me, Ellen."

"The receptionist sent you back?" Ellen asked.

"That's right," Annie said, perplexed yet again. "It's the oddest thing. I was walking down this bright yellow hall looking for Larry Lambert's door, and then I saw that conference room and I felt something tugging me toward its oak door—like the light at the end of the tunnel, only in this case its the dark at the end of the tunnel. Isn't that weird? It was as if some force more powerful than me was dragging me back there."

Ellen shifted impatiently. "That certainly is strange."

"And then I opened the door and there you were. What a weird coincidence!"

"Listen, maybe you'd better come back later in the week when we can get this planned out better," Ellen said.

Annie smiled gratefully. "You keep saying *we,* but please don't bother yourself over this, really. It's just a fluke that I came here at all. And like I said, this whole will business—"

In that instant, the door flung open and on the other side stood Larry Lambert. The ex-football player was tall and brawny, with a boyishly handsome face, so physically he always made quite an impression. And well he knew it. His gaze lit on Annie, and his face broke out in a winning, perfect toothpaste-commercial grin.

"You must be the woman I've been waiting for."

Annie, who had been staring back in rapt wonder at the gorgeous blonde, swallowed hard. Quickly, an answering smile spread across her face. "I sure am!" she said eagerly.

Without another word—or a glance spared for Ellen—Larry pulled Annie into his office and quickly closed the door behind them. Ellen let out a frustrated breath. Nothing seemed to be working out these days. Not even divine intervention!

She had to remind herself that Abel was as yet an unsuccessful angel, which was why he was here with her to begin with. She couldn't bemoan his failed attempts too much. But honestly, couldn't he have figured out that today was the wrong date to play with fate? Simon wasn't even in the office!

Feeling her brow crease with worry, she wondered again whether Simon were sick. He'd seemed fine Friday night. What could be wrong with him? She went out to the front desk to ask Yolanda, who usually knew everything.

"Sick?" Yolanda repeated moments later, her skeptical smirk firmly in place. "If you ask me, he's *love*sick."

Ellen gulped down a breath of surprise. Simon, lovesick? Preposterous!

But what if it were true? "Why do you think that?"

"Because he sounded fine when I talked to him—better than fine. And he is just not the kind of man who's gonna take off work for no reason."

"What reason did he give you?"

"He's a big boy, Ellen," Yolanda quipped, reaching for the buzzing phone. "I don't ask for notes from home."

While Yolanda took her call, Ellen leaned over and grabbed the Rolodex off the reception desk. Even if she didn't phone him today, it would be useful to have Simon's number. She found his card and jotted down his home number.

"Why are you so interested in Simon?" Yolanda asked.

"Just because," Ellen began, reaching frantically for an excuse, "because we're working on a project together and . . . and you know."

Yolanda nodded, rolling her eyes. "Yeah, I know," she said in disgust, grabbing for the handset to the phone again. "Men with great voices call you up and you're not interested. A guy right down the hall is pining away for you and you couldn't care less. Ellen Lantry is all work and no play."

Pining away? Ellen stood stock still, taking in those strange words. Was Yolanda privy to some secret information? She was dying to ask. Unfortunately, Yolanda was engaged with a completely lit-up board right now. Besides, if Ellen started making inquiries about Simon, the receptionist could get the idea she was actually interested in him. Which she wasn't.

She wasn't.

If she were, would she really have tried to play matchmaker between Annie and him? Even though the attempt hadn't worked out very well, she'd given it her best shot. Hadn't she?

Ellen returned to her cubicle, determined to actually get done some of the work she was accused of being so devoted to. She pulled out a brief Harlan Smith had asked her to work on, and proceeded to stare blankly at the file for a good fifteen minutes. Then, almost without thinking, she fished Simon's home phone number out of her pocket, picked up her phone and dialed.

No answer. She tried again, and there was still no answer.

Frowning, she returned the phone to its cradle. Where could he be? At the doctor's? Maybe Yolanda was wrong. Perhaps he really was sick. She flopped restlessly against the cushioned back of her chair, worrying.

The file folder in front of her beckoned, yet Ellen couldn't get fired up about Vern Samuelson's estate just now. Besides, she'd misplaced her legal pad somewhere.

No, she'd left it lying in the conference room.

She stood up and strode with brisk, vigorous steps through the hallways, trying to look like her normal busy self, even if her mind had been helplessly distracted all morning. She gave a brief rap on the door of the little-used conference room but went right in—and nearly fainted when she saw Simon standing there, hale and hearty and suited up for work, her yellow legal pad in his hands.

Her reaction was immediate. Instantly, her stomach did a few flip-flops, and her pulse started beating like a rabbit's. "What are you doing here?" she asked.

His face lit up. "Is this your legal pad?"

Ellen looked at the page, upon which she'd only written *Dear Ed,* and sent up a quick prayer of thanks that she had gotten no further. "Yes, it's mine."

"Then fate must have brought me," he joked lightly.

She grabbed the pad, then felt her face drain of color. "Fate!" Now she understood why Annie had gravitated to the conference room. She looked at her watch, then grabbed Simon's hand. There still might be a chance to get Annie and Simon introduced. "Come on, maybe there's still time."

Simon laughed as she tugged him down the hall. "Say, what's this all about?"

"Never mind," she instructed him. "These things work better if you don't think too hard."

"Sounds interesting," he said. Then he saw her stop in front of Larry Lambert's open door and peer inside.

"Empty!" she cried in despair.

His brow furrowed anxiously. "Are you insinuating that my fate is somehow wrapped up with Larry Lambert?"

She let out a groan of dismay. "That's what I'm afraid of!" She sent Simon a beckoning gesture. "Come on, we might be able to catch them."

Down the corridors they sped, reaching the lobby just in time to witness Larry Lambert putting Annie into an elevator. The two had locked gooey gazes, and didn't notice Ellen barreling down on them until she'd flung herself against the closing elevator doors.

"Hold it!" she cried, stuffing herself in harm's way seconds before the doors could close.

"Are you nuts?" Yolanda cried from behind her fortress.

In confusion the steel portals banged opened and closed against Ellen a few times before she finally calmed them down. She turned to her neighbor, who was looking at her in the same alarmed manner Yolanda, Simon and Larry were. "Annie, there's someone I have to introduce you to," she said.

She held out a hand to beckon Simon to join them and stepped farther inside, but accidentally lost her tentative mastery over the open doors, which now slid shut in her face. The elevator immediately began a smooth descent to the lobby.

"Oh, no," she moaned. "So much for introducing you to Simon!"

"Oh, Ellen!" Annie gushed, oblivious to her misery. "Everything worked out fine. I can't thank you enough!"

Ellen looked into her neighbor's ecstatically happy eyes and finally had to admit defeat. "Thank *me?*" she asked.

"I'm sure I never would have met Larry if it hadn't been through you."

Ellen didn't bother pointing out to the woman that *she* had nothing to do with this terrible turn of events. Annie didn't even seem to remember that Ellen had counseled *against* the meeting with Larry Lambert. The former tight end had completely blitzed Ellen's matchmaking game plan.

She listened patiently as Annie gushed over her new lawyer all the way to the ground floor. All the while, it became acutely clear why she'd wanted Simon connected to someone else to begin with—by himself, he was a loose cannon just waiting to explode her happy little life.

"Will I see you this evening?" Ellen asked Annie.

"Maybe not," Annie said with a wink. "I've got a date."

She departed the elevator, leaving Ellen nine floors to ponder what her next move should be. When she reached her destination, however, she was still working it out. And Simon, all concern, was waiting for her.

"Are you okay?" he asked. Yolanda pretended not to be watching, and Larry had probably long since left the lobby in romantic triumph.

Ellen planted her hands on her hips and looked Simon directly in the eye. "Why were you late?" she asked. After all, his tardiness was what had goofed everything up to begin with!

He looked at her questioningly. "You mean this morning?"

"I mean thirty minutes ago," she told him, tapping her foot impatiently.

"Why?" he asked. "Did I forget something?"

"No, I was just curious. We thought you were sick—and now here you stand, fit as a fiddle!"

With one hand braced against the wall next to her, he leaned closer and asked in a low tone, "Were you worried about me?"

"Absolutely not," she lied. "It's just hard to keep one's nose to the grindstone when everyone else is out to lunch."

"Speaking of out to lunch..."

"No," she said, anticipating his question. "I've wasted too much time on you today already."

She started down the hall, but he was fast behind her. "I was going to ask you about that. Yolanda said you got my phone number."

"Don't you have anything more productive to do than sit around gossiping?"

"Sure," Simon said, "this morning I went shopping."

She shook her head mournfully. "You are completely unrepentant, aren't you."

"It was for a good cause," he assured her. Then a knowing grin crossed his face. "And while we're talking about unrepentant, I might say that you seem to have developed an unhealthy habit of lying."

Uh-oh, Ellen thought. What had he discovered now?

"While I was talking to Yolanda, she said you were telling her about a project we were working on together." His eyebrows rose with interest.

She rolled her eyes in dismay. "I was just trying to figure out where you were," she said in frustration. "Though heaven knows why. Now that you're here I wish you'd go away. Don't you have some more shopping to do?"

He smiled with satisfaction. "Nope. All done."

Persistently good-natured people had their down sides, Ellen discovered. She had the terrible feeling that no matter how many insults and disparaging remarks she hurled his way, Simon would continue to buzz around her like a happy gnat.

"Well *I* have work to do," she said.

"You mean your 'Dear Ed' letter?" he asked.

She clutched her legal pad to her chest protectively. She'd almost forgotten she'd been holding it all this time. "As a matter of fact, yes."

"Who's Ed?"

"A client," she lied.

He made a show of appearing crestfallen. "Shucks. I was hoping it was an old beau, and that your 'Dear Ed' was really a 'Dear John.'"

"Now, why would you think that?"

Simon shrugged genially. "I don't know—maybe because you'd discovered Mr. Right recently?"

She shook her head. "Go back to work, Simon. We'll be lucky to get anything done before the afternoon stretch."

He let out a long-suffering moan. "I nearly forgot."

Ellen felt guilty as she returned to her work area. This was the first time they had spoken since Friday night. Why hadn't she been more honest with him? She owed it to him—not to mention to herself and Abel—to tell him that they shouldn't see each other anymore.

When she rounded the corner to her walled-off cubicle, she stopped in her tracks. On her desk was a little gift bag decorated with flowers. It was filled with tissue paper, and a small bouquet of daisies poked out. Carefully, she moved toward it—slowly, as if all that floral wrapping were just a cover for something explosive.

A tentative peek inside revealed a small box of chocolates, a Bach CD and a small card from a florist shop. Ellen opened the little blue envelope and read its message.

Nothing makes me happier than skipping work on your behalf.

S.

Ellen sank down in her chair with a sigh, her elbows sprawled on her desktop. What a silly, sappy thing to write. What a nice gift. Thoughtful, but nothing too overwhelming. She smiled, reaching into the bag for a chocolate. Simon certainly knew how to play his cards.

He just didn't know how to pick the right partner.

"I DON'T GET IT," Simon said, leaning against the reception desk. "Didn't her behavior seem a little weird to you?"

Yolanda shrugged. "She did seem a little skittish."

"I'll say! And you didn't see the look in her eyes—or the way her face became as white as a sheet when she saw me in that conference room. I wonder if she's sick."

Yolanda's lips pursed skeptically. "Sick?" she repeated in a manner that seemed very self-assured. "If you ask me, I think she's *love*sick."

Simon perked right up. "What makes you say that?"

"The signs are there." Yolanda steepled her fingers in front of her phone board sagely. "She's edgier than usual, and though she'd be the last to admit it, she's slowing down at work. And then there's her appearance. Her eyes are getting droopier and buggier by the day—a fool could see that the woman hasn't slept. She looks like hell," she summed up, "and that usually means one thing."

"Love?" Simon asked hopefully.

"Of the unhappy, unrequited variety," Yolanda said.

But that didn't make sense. Unhappy? Unrequited? Heck, he was ready to requite all over the place for her sake. Unless there was someone else . . .

He wouldn't allow himself to consider that possibility. Martin was out of the picture, and she'd sworn she'd had no interest in that Cliff character. Surely those were all the men she had been hiding away.

And yet, ever since Friday night, he'd had a sinking feeling that Ellen was keeping something from him. Maybe not another man . . . but something. He thought about that freezing house of hers, and her evasiveness.

But what could she possibly have to hide? He seriously doubted Ellen was doing anything criminal in that domestic-looking little duplex.

Perhaps it was just as he thought, and she really was just having a hard time dealing with the fact that she was having feelings for someone after being in mourning for so long. That was a much more workable scenario from his perspective. Because if that were the case, he could treat her hesitation symptomatically.

And if Yolanda's guess was correct, the first thing Ellen needed was what she'd told him she always wanted to begin with: her own private sandman.

Chapter Six

"Pardon me," Ellen said.

Abel, who had been standing in front of the open refrigerator door for what seemed like an hour, scowled as she darted quickly in front of him to grab some carrots from the hydrator. Why all of the sudden did the kitchen seem too small for two people? Everywhere she turned, it seemed, she bumped into Abel, or worse, caught his broody gaze staring at her.

Ellen set about chopping carrots for a salad with more vigor than usual as Abel gave up on the refrigerator and started rooting around cabinets. It would do her good to get off of his high-sugar, high-fat diet. He opened a tin on the counter and discovered the leftover brownies she'd made the previous weekend, when she was still basking in the first blush of Abel's homecoming. Not that she still wasn't happy to have him home...

She frowned as he took not one but two brownies, and he stared back at her, daring her to say something. Ellen knew the tension between them had nothing to do with food. Not really. It was more about what hadn't happened this afternoon. Namely, Simon hadn't been happily set up with Annie. Which meant he was still loose and on the prowl—and she was his prey.

But it wasn't her fault that things worked out the way they did today. All right, so maybe she hadn't ever found the time to tell Simon that she couldn't go out with him again. It had been a busy day.

Right. A busy day spent at her desk, daydreaming about a certain tall, dark-eyed someone . . .

"Angel to Ellen."

She glanced up, startled. "What?"

"I said, be careful with that knife. It looked as if you were going to whack your finger off, you were so lost in thought."

"Oh, I—I . . ." Her words sputtered out, unfinished.

He arched an eyebrow and bit out, "Thinking about a certain work skipper?"

Her mouth fell open. Had he found Simon's card? He must have, or he never would have made that remark. "You've been going through my briefcase!"

"I was just looking for a pen to do the crossword puzzle," he said, taking a bite out of a brownie.

"You were spying," Ellen replied.

"Was not," he said, downing half his brownie in one gulp. "I was just checking up on some things."

"Me."

He leaned against the counter next to her and crossed his arms. His lips turned down in a pout. "You didn't mind when I said that I had been watching you all these years from heaven."

"That's different. Looking down from heaven sounds sweet."

"You only thought so because you weren't interested in some guy back then."

"I'm not interested in Simon," Ellen said, feeling guilty that she could lie so baldly without batting an eyelash. Seeing Abel look so miserable was frightening—she didn't want to lose him—but it was also annoying. Why was he making this so difficult?

"You kept his card," Abel said.

That was a mystery to Ellen. Why had she felt the need to put that blue note in her briefcase? It wasn't as if she had intended to read it over, or store it away in a keepsake box... had she?

She shook her head, dismissing the crazy notion. "You're placing too much importance on that silly note. In fact, I think the problem is that you don't have enough to occupy yourself. Why don't you try writing something?"

"What's the point?" he asked. "Posthumous books are supposed to be written *before* you die."

She couldn't argue with that logic. "Well," she suggested, "Why don't you go watch some of those noisy cartoons you've been into lately?" This was another puzzle. How had the student who once revered Tolstoy and Faulkner turned into a ghost whose heroes were Wiley E. Coyote and Moe? She'd long since stopped trying to keep up with his addiction to loud juvenile television programming. Maybe she could spend a quiet evening in her room reading.

"You want me out of your hair."

"Abel, no." Guilt stabbed at her. "I just thought that maybe you might want some time to yourself."

"I have all day to myself."

"Well it seems as if you're going stir-crazy. Maybe you should get out. Do some of those good deeds you're supposed to be doing."

His pout turned to a full-fledged frown. "There you go again," he said, "trying to get rid of me."

Her hand clapped over her mouth, but it was too late. The damage was done. "Oh, Abel—" She reached out, but he shrugged away.

His expression petulant, he said, "If that's what you want, fine." He stomped out of the kitchen, heading for the door.

Torn between repentance and annoyance, Ellen sped after him. "Where are you going?"

"Out."

She rolled her eyes. "Please, Abel, I'm not your mother—"

"Then don't wait up," he said, storming out.

The front door slammed behind him. Ellen stood staring at it, stunned. Abel was behaving like a bad-tempered teen, but of course in terms of earth years, he hadn't been too far from a teenager when he died. Yet even back then, they had never had a scene like this one. Their marriage had been so brief, they had never even made it to their first fight.

For a moment, she considered going after him. She really hadn't handled the situation well at all. But then again, she suspected they both needed to unwind and blow off some steam.

Ellen padded to the bathroom and drew a hot bubble bath. Determined to get her mind off her problems, she soaked in the water lost in thought until the bubbles had dwindled to a soapy film around the sides of the tub. Realizing with chagrin that she had been thinking of nothing but Simon and was more keyed up than she had been when she started, she pulled her pruny body out of the tepid water and toweled dry.

Nine-fifteen, and still no sign of Abel. Her brow creased into a frown. Was he really going to stay out late? She didn't like the idea of him wandering around alone—yet she had no idea where he would be at this point.

Relax, she told herself. *What can happen to an angel?*

Calmed somewhat by the thought, she slipped on a long cotton nightgown and got into bed. No matter what Abel said, she would wait up for him.

Minutes later, propped against the pillows with a book in her lap and Hawthorne at her feet, Ellen heard a noise. "Abel?" she asked automatically.

Both she and Hawthorne lifted their heads, listening. When she focused on the precise direction the noise had come from, she realized it must have been just a limb brushing against a screen.

For a moment, all was still again. Maybe it had been a squirrel, or the breeze. She was just about to cast her gaze at her book again when she heard a *bump*.

No squirrel could make a noise that loud.

Another *bump* followed, this one definitely coming from the rooftop. And then she heard steps.

Ellen shot out of bed, threw on her robe and slippers, and headed for the phone in the living room, but she stopped just short of picking it up. What if it was Abel on the roof? She didn't know exactly why he would be, but angels were apt to do odd things.

Suddenly, the footsteps on the roof became bolder, louder... more rhythmic. With a frown, her hand clutching the phone tightly, Ellen simply listened. It sounded like an SOS... or as if a crazed folk dancer had taken up residence on her roof!

She padded across the room and slipped out the front door. To see up to the rooftop she would have to leave the porch, but she didn't want to show herself out in the open, in case there really was a lunatic and not her late husband up there. She scoped out the hydrangea bush in Annie's side of the yard and crept toward it. If she could get to the other side, she would have a view of the roof.

She covered the last yard between herself and the bush in a rolling dive, then got to her knees and peeked through the leaves. She had to look away and back again before she could trust that what she was seeing was real, not some crazy figment of her imagination. Not a wild dream.

Up on her roof, silhouetted by a bright quarter moon and a couple of thousand summer stars, a tuxedo-clad Simon, complete with a flower in his lapel, was dancing. Tap dancing!

Slack-jawed with astonishment, she spent several minutes merely staring. In a tuxedo, Simon was even more than dashing—he was heart-stoppingly handsome. Ellen had to remind herself to breathe. He was tripping across her sloped roof with a surprising grace that nearly caused her to burst out laughing—until she remembered the noise he was making. What would her neighbors think?

What if Abel happened to walk up?

Where was Abel?

She had to get this man off her roof!

Making certain she was fully covered by her red chenille robe, Ellen came out from behind the bush and stood below Simon, hands on her hips. "What do you think you're doing!" she called up to him in something between a shout and a whisper.

Simon, spotting her on the ground below, smiled and waved. His feet never stopped moving. "Waltz clog," he answered back.

Ellen rolled her eyes. "I meant, what do you think you're going to accomplish by dancing on my roof?"

"You looked like you needed sleep," Simon told her, "and I remembered what you said about that Fred Astaire movie. So I thought I would do a simulation for you."

She pursed her lips to keep from laughing. Was he insane? "How did you know you weren't waking me up instead of the other way around?"

"Well . . . it *is* only nine-thirty."

Ellen winced at how she must look, all decked out in her robe and slippers when the sun was barely down. "Well your Fred routine didn't work. I'm still wide awake."

Simon abruptly stopped dancing and crept to the edge of the roof. "Okay," he admitted, "maybe I just wanted to see you." He stopped and knelt down, his brown eyes flashing with something more intimate than mere goodwill as he looked down at her.

She felt heat rise in her cheeks, and forced herself to look away. In the moonlight, in a tuxedo, Simon had a more potent effect on her than ever. "Did it ever occur to you that this is a school night?"

He got a devilish glint in his eye. "You're right! Let's stay up all night, watch the sun come up and play hooky tomorrow. What do you say?"

"I say no. I'm tired." And becoming more anxious by the second about Abel showing up.

"Aha! So it *did* work." He sent her a modest bow. "Is there anything else I can do for you?"

"Yes. Go to bed!"

His eyebrows shot up. "Hey, I like that idea."

"Alone!" she clarified, her stomach fluttering in response to his flirtation. She wasn't sure how to react to him—no man had ever danced on her roof before. But she was certain she needed to get a grip on her senses. "Don't you think you'd better come down?"

Simon sighed. "All right. Since you didn't like my sandman act, I'll just have to go back to the drawing board."

"Getting back to earth would be a good start," she suggested.

He smiled. "You sure you're tired? There's a great coffee shop just down—"

"I'm positive," she said.

"You don't have to worry about being underdressed," he said, "I think your bathrobe's very chic."

She immediately slapped a hand up to close the folds of the robe at her neck. Even though she was wearing more clothes than Simon had probably ever seen her in, she felt as if she were practically naked. Maybe it was the hungry way he was looking at her that made her feel undressed. "Simon..."

"Okay, okay," he muttered, "I'm coming down."

In a move that surprised her, he hoisted himself onto the iron trellis on her porch and began climbing down it. Ellen gasped, then stared in awe as he maneuvered down with amazing agility. When he reached the railing around her porch, he stopped, scoping out the best way to jump down without landing in one of the bushes in the beds by the porch steps.

"Wait!" Ellen said in a low whisper. "Let me help you." He paused as she dashed up to the porch and held out a hand to him. "This way," she instructed.

With a smile, he took her hand and let her tug him lightly around so that he would step onto the porch with her instead of dropping to the ground below. But she knew the minute his hand touched her own that he really didn't need her help. He pushed more than she tugged, with the result that they collided chest to chest in the darkness.

"Quick thinking," he told her, keeping his tone down.

Too bad he couldn't tone down his sex appeal. Her response to him was immediate. Everywhere their bodies touched, she felt heat radiating to her core. Her breasts tightened, and she leaned back, seeing the intense desire sparked in his eyes by their collision, and thought quickly that she should flee.

Her feet, however, remained glued to the porch, and before she could give the matter of escaping another thought, his lips met hers with quick and devastating sureness. The swiftness with which he gathered her into his arms took her breath away, and she automatically hooked her hands over his shoulders for support. Then, with a daring that came from days of remembering and imagining, she kissed him back.

And then she was lost. He pulled her closer, and she responded instinctively with a tiny moan of surrender. It felt so good to be held, to feel his hand playing across her back, to feel the tantalizing warmth of his lips against hers, his tongue teasing hers. Wholeheartedly she returned the kiss, reveling in his obvious delight that she did so. His aftershave, his own male scent, even the faint odor of the carnation in his lapel, all mingled together in a heady scent that made her senses reel nearly out of control.

Their bodies meshed together perfectly, pulsing against each other in desire. The world around them felt motionless; only they were caught up in the swirling sensations. One of Simon's hands continued to caress her back, the other moved up to her jaw, a finger tracing its line from her chin to her ear, then down her neck to her collarbone. She sucked in her breath as his hand ventured gently beneath her robe and gown, tracing the swell of her breast, then stopping to tease the hardened, achingly tender bud at its core.

She shuddered in response, breaking the kiss to pull away, a moan in her throat, burying her head against his chest. The sensation was too much, too frighteningly sensual. She heard herself release the moan she'd been holding.

"Simon..." Her voice came out shockingly breathless and raspy, and she felt ashamed for having come so close to losing control. To think she'd been worried about what Abel would say if he saw Simon dancing on her roof—how would he react to seeing them like this!

"You're so beautiful," Simon said, bringing his hand up to trace the sensitive curve of her ear.

Ellen's breath caught. Beautiful? She dared to look into his gaze and was shocked to see her reflection in those dark eyes. Far from beautiful, she looked a mess—a freshly kissed mess. Her hair was mussed, her eyes slightly glazed with passion, her lips a rosy red. It was a startling sight, especially when she considered that anyone could tell what they'd been doing just by looking at her.

"You have to leave," she said quickly, "I need to go to bed. Not that I'll get any rest this night," she said, desperately striving for coherence.

"Too distracted to sleep?"

Too sensually revved up was more like it. She stared at him pleadingly.

His lips turned up in a slow, tender smile. "I'd give a lot to know what keeps you up nights, Ellen Lantry," he said in a low, sexy purr.

You, she thought. *It's all your fault.* But she couldn't speak; she could only stare up into his handsome face.

"I have a feeling you're keeping some interesting secrets."

Was she ever! The conjecture brought her crashing back to reality. The sensory fog around her lifted. Abel had to be prowling around somewhere. If he came upon this little scene—mere days after she'd promised not to see Simon again and especially after their tiff this evening—Abel was likely to abandon her.

She stepped back, covering her reddened cheeks with her hands. "Simon, you *have* to go now."

His smile disappeared, and he stepped forward. "I don't want to, you know that," he said. "Leaving you now is the hardest thing I've done in a long, long time."

Her mouth felt as dry as dust, and she swallowed. Lord help her, she wanted him, too. But the wanting had to stop—now.

"Simon, please," she begged. "I think we should consider that our farewell kiss."

At first he seemed not to register her words. Then his handsome face twisted in puzzlement. "Farewell?"

"I meant to tell you earlier. This afternoon. I don't think we should see each other anymore." If only that were possible! "Except at work, of course."

"You mean—"

"I mean *never*."

His gaze was disbelieving, and not a little angry. "Never, Ellen? That's not what your lips were saying just a few seconds ago."

"I know, I'm sorry."

"I'm not," he said. "You'd have to be the best liar in the world to convince me that what you were feeling during that kiss wasn't real, Ellen."

He apparently wasn't going to let her weasel out of the situation easily. "Please, Simon. I can't explain now, but this is an unworkable relationship for me," she told him, hoping he didn't hear the shaky catch in her voice.

Apparently, he did. Suddenly, his expression was all concern. "Ellen, is there something wrong? Some trouble you're in?"

"No!" she said. "I just think you're too—" *Too what?* Good-looking, insistent, intelligent, charming? What characteristic could she come up with that wouldn't contradict her argument?

He stood before her, as speechless as she was. "Aren't you being premature, especially considering that all indications so far point to the fact that we'd be dynamite together?"

"That's just it—I don't want dynamite, or anything explosive. I'm a quiet person. Reserved. You're too...too much."

"I don't think you mean what you're saying."

She folded her arms across her chest, tugging the robe closed where he'd pulled it open. "I believe I'm a better judge of that than you are."

His lips twisted sensually. "If how you respond to our being together is any indication, maybe not."

"I'm not going to change my mind," she warned him. "What will it take to make you accept that?"

He considered, rubbing his jaw thoughtfully. She felt awkward staring at him, yet she couldn't force herself to look away, either. At that moment he seemed just what he was—a hunk in a tux. A man who knew how to kiss her senseless, and knew he knew it. How long could she resist him if he came knocking at her door?

"Resistance," he said.

Ellen blinked. Was he a mind reader? "Pardon me?"

He smiled. "You asked what would make me believe that you're not going to change your mind, so I told you. Resistance. In two weeks we've had one date and three kisses. That doesn't show a very good track record for resistance on your part, Ellen."

She felt her cheeks warm and shrugged helplessly. "Yes, but...well, I'm *telling* you how I feel."

"But it contradicts what you're showing," he said. "Which leads me to believe that one part of you is lying. What I'm trying to figure out is, which part. And I'm going to keep at you until I figure it out. Deal?" Surprisingly, he stuck out his hand for her to shake.

"All right," she agreed, screwing up her lips in a wry smile. "I'll show you resistance."

He grinned as he took her hand and squeezed it. "And I'll show you persistence."

She pulled her hand free before he could tug her into his very inviting arms again. "I'm sure you will."

"Well, good night," he said, then added with a sly grin, "Sleep tight. That's what this was all about, after all."

She watched him stroll to where his Jeep was parked several houses down. He'd obviously wanted to hide it so his appearance would be a surprise. As if there were any doubt of that!

Something inside her, a heavy pressure in her chest, made her want to run after him, to take back her words, to tell him he was right. That resistance wasn't nearly as satisfying as a kiss, as feeling his arms around her cocooning her in a pleasure she had never experienced with such force before.

She turned back to her door, trying to train her thoughts on more pressing matters. Like finding Abel. Thank heavens he hadn't been a witness to her torrid kiss with Simon!

Unfortunately, someone else had. Suddenly, Annie popped out of her doorway. "Oh, Ellen!" she exclaimed, grabbing on to Ellen's robe to stop her. "How exciting! Wasn't that the man from your office today? He's so good-looking!" Her expression turned to one of stern rebuke. "But you are forever tossing good ones away! What's the matter with him?"

"Oh . . . it's a long story," Ellen said.

"You must be even more particular than me," Annie said, then shook her head. "I just don't think it would ever work out for Larry and me."

Ellen frowned. This didn't surprise her, but still . . . "Already? How do you know?"

Annie's voice was heavy with disappointment. "He took me to this sports bar after work. The whole time he couldn't keep his eyes off the baseball game. I figure if even on the first date he's more interested in a large-screen TV than me, then we're in trouble."

"You're wise to duck out early," Ellen told her.

"Yes, but that's Larry—how about this guy you nabbed! I wouldn't duck out on him for all the tea in China!"

"Oh..." Ellen said, reaching for an excuse. "There are complications."

"Well, hey. If he gets too complicated, send him on over. I'd love to have a crack at figuring him out."

Great. Annie was just about twelve hours too late!

Ellen smiled halfheartedly as Annie zipped back into her apartment. Somehow, the idea of Simon and Annie going out seemed even more unappealing to her than ever.

Before she had any time to analyze this thought, however, she saw car lights coming down the street. Was it Simon, coming back? Ellen hopped off the porch and ran into her yard to check. But instead of a sporty Jeep, a white midsize sedan with Austin Police Department written across it pulled up in front of her house. And Abel was slumped in the back seat!

The cop driving rolled down his window. "Is this her?" he asked Abel, who nodded curtly without even looking up. Double checking, the policeman asked, "Are you Ellen Lantry?"

"Yes," she answered anxiously.

"Have you got any ID on you?"

"ID?" Ellen asked, alarmed. What did he think, that she carried her driver's license in her bathrobe? "What happened? Is Abel okay?"

"We picked him up. He'd gotten into a fight with a lady on the road."

A fight? Ellen swung a curious gaze back to Abel, who merely scowled in return.

"She started it," he insisted.

"Anyway, we broke it up and brought your friend home."

"Thanks," Ellen said as Abel got out of the car. "Thanks a lot." She still couldn't believe her angel was out beating up on women.

Abel glanced up at her absently as he made his way up the sidewalk to the house. "I didn't know if you'd still be up."

"Of course," she said, as if running around in the dark in her nightclothes were nothing out of the ordinary. Then she noticed something odd about Abel's face. "Your lip!" she cried. "You've been hurt!"

He touched his swollen bottom lip. "Yeah, right. So much for good deeds," he said sheepishly.

"You mean the woman the officer was talking about?" Ellen asked. "You were trying to help her?"

"Can you believe it?" Abel asked, shambling back to the house. "I saw this lady fixing a flat tire and decided this was my big opportunity. But when I went up to her she said, 'Buddy, unless you're from the AAA, you'd better move on.' And when I took another step she stood up and whacked me with a lug wrench."

"That's terrible!"

Abel grimaced. "You're telling me. I'll never make it in heaven at this rate."

Ellen stopped in her tracks. Was he so eager to get back already? She couldn't help feeling a little wounded at the idea. But then, why wouldn't he want to return? She wasn't doing much to make this a heaven on earth below for him. Just the opposite. Ever since he'd arrived, she'd been in turmoil over Simon, which hardly made her stellar company. Then she'd practically chased him out of the house this evening with her carping. And the minute his back was turned, she'd hopped right into Simon's arms.

Some grief-struck widow she'd turned out to be!

"Come inside," she said, determined to be more agreeable, "I'll make you some hot chocolate."

"Nah, you'd better get to sleep," he said.

"Not a chance," she said. As if she could!

Memories of Simon flashed through her mind. His smile. Then the dark intensity of his gaze as he'd bent to kiss her. The firestorm of desire he'd stirred up inside her... Oh, this was terrible.

Resistance, she told herself. Whatever Simon was stirring up inside her was merely lust. It wasn't love. Not like what she felt for Abel, the man she'd vowed all those years ago to share her life with.

From now on she was determined to be a better companion, like old times. She put an arm around him and squeezed, and was pleased when he hugged her back. Usually he seemed to stay distant from her.

"I'm sorry about this evening," she told him when they were back in the house. "I don't know why I was so shrewish. I didn't want to chase you away."

"Nah," he said, shaking his head. "It was me. It's like you said. Maybe I'm going stir-crazy. It's different when you're down here and you're not... well, like everybody else."

She nodded. It wasn't so hard to put herself in his shoes. How often after Abel died had she felt like she was completely out of sync with the rest of the world?

He smiled that cute, boyish smile of his that made her heart skip. "I know this has been stressful, with me throwing all these men at you. But believe me, I appreciate it, babe. I know you're just doing it for me, right?"

She gulped guiltily and returned his smile. "Right."

"I love you, Ellen," he said, pulling her to him. To her shock, he pressed a light kiss against her forehead. "Now, what do you say we do next?"

She waited for a moment. Waited for the kiss to set off sparks, if not a firestorm. But nothing happened, other than that warm feeling of being thoroughly, completely loved. And that sensation was worth all the sparks in the world.

Wasn't it?

"We're going to tend to your lip and then we'll see what's on Nickelodeon," she said, taking his hand and tugging him toward the bathroom. Which would just be the first step in proving to herself—and to Simon—that she was absolutely, one hundred percent positive about her own heart.

"SIX, SEVEN, EIGHT. Come on now, feel the stretch!"

Eight lawyers—two of them partners—five administrative aides and three paralegals stood in their stocking feet in the main conference room for the afternoon stretch. Today's session was being led by Harlan Smith himself, who, being the most zealous about this ritual, was also the toughest.

"Come on, folks!" The room let out a collective groan and their leader admonished, "We don't want workaholics working here at Smith—we want *healthy* workaholics!"

He roared at his own joke and bobbed back up for the final phase. "Everybody shake!"

This was always Simon's favorite moment—the shakedown. Seeing all his co-workers flapping their arms and jittering around the room was worth fifteen minutes of his day. It at least made him take work more lightly.

And God knows his mood had been in need of lightening lately. All week long, he'd been expecting to speak to Ellen again in private, but she'd never given him the opportunity. Every time he saw her, she was speeding toward somewhere else, dashing down hallways, into conference rooms, onto elevators. Not the type of behavior that promoted intimate conversation.

He hardly knew what step to take next. In the past weeks he'd bought so many flowers that his Jeep had practically blazed a new trail between his home and the florist. His gestures were always met with polite thank-you notes on office stationery, and his invitations to lunch were turned down cold.

Her resistance was pretty good.

So far. Something about Ellen gave him hope. Maybe it was still that initial tug he'd felt when he'd first looked into her eyes. Or maybe—more likely—it was the way she responded when they kissed. Like they were simply meant to be together.

As if beckoned by his thoughts, in that second Ellen sped into the room, red-faced, flapping her wrists as she kicked off her shoes. She tried to be inconspicuous as she took a place in the back row, then nearly groaned out loud when she turned and saw Simon next to her.

"Everybody rest!" Harlan bellowed from the front of the room. The office let out a collective sigh as he marched over to his exercise bicycle, hopped on and began to peddle. "I thank everyone for their patience during office remodeling. As you know, further work will be underway in the weeks ahead. After much discussion among the partners and myself, I have agreed—reluctantly, mind you—to change the wall color from yellow to—" his lips turned down in a disgusted pout "—dove blue."

Celebratory glances were exchanged, but not a peep was heard. "Just remember," Harlan continued in a paternal bellow, "beautiful surroundings make a better workplace. Now, everybody, go back to work," he instructed. The old man's sharp brown eyes zeroed in on Simon and Ellen in the back row. "Everybody except Mr. Miller and Ms. Lantry."

The two of them exchanged puzzled glances. "Were you stealing company pencils again?" Simon accused jokingly.

They came forward, Ellen marching ahead determinedly to meet whatever instructions the boss had to give her. "Is anything wrong?" she asked Harlan. "If it's about Mr. Samuelson, I've been on the phone with him three times today and—"

"As a matter of fact, this *is* about Vern Samuelson," Harlan said. "I've gotten a call from a lawyer representing a nephew in California. It seems this nephew is rather concerned that uncle dearest is going to sink the family fortune into this monument business."

"Isn't that Mr. Samuelson's right?" Ellen asked.

"Yes, of course, of course," Harlan said, "but we want to give our client sound advice, you know. Help him avoid further legal entanglements."

"I understand," Ellen said. "Naturally that makes sense."

"Glad you see it that way. Because I'm sending you two down to see Mr. Samuelson and check the whole business out in person."

Ellen's jaw dropped, and she turned to look at Simon. The moment Harlan had mentioned his going to see Mr. Samuelson, Simon had felt a shooting pain in his stomach. Mr. Samuelson was one of Smith's most notoriously difficult clients—one Simon would have been just as happy never to work with. But then it registered that the man lived in San Antonio. Which meant a day trip to San Antonio. A whole day. With Ellen along.

"Brilliant idea," Simon said, suddenly liking this idea very much. "Where are the Samuelson files? I'd love to take a look at them."

Ellen shot him a withering glance, then turned back to Harlan. "Wouldn't *you* like the opportunity to go see Mr. Samuelson in person, Mr. Smith? He thinks so highly of you."

"No, no," Harlan said. "I think it's best to send Simon. That way Samuelson won't feel as though we're trying to talk him out of anything—it won't be as intimidating as if it were me down there."

Simon looked at Harlan, his skinny legs poking out of green shorts and encased in sports socks pulled up to his knees. Intimidating? He was the head of a venerable old law firm, but still . . . he looked more like a Jack Lalane castoff.

"And since you're my assistant, Ellen, and have talked to the man, he should feel very comfortable with you there," Harlan said. "You two just sit tight and I'll arrange a meeting for sometime next week."

With those words, they were dismissed. Ellen, her face showing a strained resignation, turned and walked toward the door. Simon followed her.

"Looks like we're taking a road trip," he said once they were out in the hallway.

She grunted and marched straight to his office, barging inside and barely waiting for him to close the door before she turned on him. "You planned this!" she accused.

Simon was flummoxed. "Planned what?" he asked, trying to ignore the way her flushed cheeks looked. Even when she was angry, she had him completely smitten.

"You planned for Harlan to send us down to San Antonio together. That's more than persistence—that's sneakiness!"

He came forward, but her cool glance stopped him. "I did nothing of the kind," he assured her. "But I can't deny that, had I had the foresight, I would have."

Her lips pursed skeptically. "I don't believe you."

He shrugged helplessly. "It's the truth. I can't help it— I'm old-fashioned. I still haven't progressed beyond the flowers-and-candy approach, even though it seems to be getting me nowhere."

She ducked her head a little. "Oh, that reminds me. Thanks for the flowers."

"Don't mention it."

At his words, she stepped forward, tossing her arms in frustration. "That's just it!" she cried, distressed. "I *have* to mention it. You send them every day."

"I warned you."

"Don't you ever run out of money?"

"No, I budget it specially. I call it the Surrender, Ellen fund."

She couldn't help laughing. "Well your war chest is bound to deplete someday. And as for going to San Antonio—"

He held up a finger. "That wasn't my doing," he reminded her.

"Count it as an incidental victory for your side."

He came closer, careful to keep his arms folded in front of him. "Do you think it could ever happen that we would both be on the same side?"

She looked away, and he swore he could see a shadow of regret crossing her face. "I'm afraid not."

He sighed. "Look, Ellen. I know you've got some kind of secret—"

"No, I don't," she interrupted quickly. "Please, Simon, can't we just be friends?"

He leaned against his desk and regarded her for a moment. "We don't kiss like friends."

"I know," she said. "We have to put a stop to that."

"Kissing?"

"Yes, definitely."

He considered the offer. Not that he believed for a moment that it would work. But it did allow him an opening. What did he have to lose? The charm-and-flowers approach wasn't working.

"Okay," he said, taking a gamble.

Her eyes widened in surprise, then narrowed suspiciously. "You're agreeing?"

"Sure." He smiled. "I'm new to town. I need friends."

She paused for a moment before asking hesitantly, "It wouldn't *bother* you just to go out—I mean, without any romantic... stuff?"

"Not at all," he assured her with growing enthusiasm. "In fact, I think I'd like it better."

She drew back as if he'd dealt her a blow. "Oh." Now that victory was in her grasp, she didn't seem to know what to do with herself.

Simon grinned. "Do you play Scrabble?"

She looked at him as though he'd lost his mind. "What?"

"You know, the game?"

A look of utter confusion crossed her face. "Well, yeah, but—" She stopped, then tilted her head doubtfully. "*Scrabble?* Is this some kind of a trick?"

He laughed. "Not at all," he lied. "I can't deny I've enjoyed sending you things, but if you're not interested, you're not interested." He finished with a shrug. "So we'll be friends."

She watched him skeptically. "Simon, are you *sure* this is what you want?"

"Why?" he asked. "Would you rather I stick with the romantic approach?"

"No!" She waved her hands adamantly. "Friends is fine."

"Great, why don't we get together this weekend? Maybe for a movie, or just sit around and talk. Play games. Get to know each other. We could meet at your house—"

"That's not possible," she said, interrupting him. "I'm busy this weekend. Very busy. In fact, I rarely have time to spare. Unless you'd like to go to lunch or something."

Simon snapped up the offer. "Love to."

"Oh. Good." She looked befuddled, and began backing toward the door. Most likely, she was a little confused at how, after rejecting two weeks of lunch invitations, she'd managed to wind up issuing one herself. "Well fine then," she said, continuing her backward crawl to the door. "How about this afternoon?"

How about every day? "Great," he said.

She smiled limply. "I'll see you."

He waved her out the door, sweating it lest she detect his reverse psychology tactic and cry foul play.

It seemed too easy—until he realized the hard part had just begun. His heart sank with dread, and his lips turned down unhappily. He'd promised to treat her like a *friend*— as in gin rummy and platonic lunch dates.

How long could that last?

Chapter Seven

Ellen pushed her grocery cart down the aisle, numbly piling her basket with junk food. Not that she could eat any of it. After living with Abel for just a few short weeks, she'd gained five pounds. And that was the least of her problems. Abel was still pushing her to go out with his correspondents, so tonight she was out on the first of her fake dates. She'd told Abel she was meeting Ed the painter at a bar to avoid the awkwardness of not inviting him in the house.

It was all so turned around. She should have been happy to have Abel back, should have been trying to spend every minute with him. But his being an angel really threw a wrench into the situation. She would have given anything at that moment for someone to talk to. A friend.

Of course, she did have a friend. That was why she was so strung out in the first place! Being *friends* with Simon was just as stressful as enduring his flirtation. She still didn't know how he'd managed to twist the situation around like he'd done, but she'd never expected him to stick to his platonic pledge. Not in a million years.

But he had. Nary a flower had arrived through the rest of the week. No more notes, either, or senseless little gifts. Just long talks over lunch about their families and growing up.

Simon was a terrific listener, and he had a bottomless capacity for humor. He was a great friend.

Friend. He frustrated the hell out of her.

How had his attitude changed so quickly? It was as though he had an electric switch in his brain. Granted, she was glad that he no longer pressed for a relationship she couldn't pursue, but that didn't erase the physical attraction between them.

Or was she the only one who noticed it? Once when they had accidently touched fingers reaching for a little paper package of sweetener, she had blushed to her hair roots while Simon had remained unfazed. Whenever she got into a car or elevator with him or sat down across from him at a restaurant, she tended to stammer for a minute, as though it took her mind a moment to adjust to the quickening of her heartbeat and the slight light-headedness she always felt in his presence. But Simon never stammered, or giggled nervously, or knocked things over.

It seemed almost inhuman! Or maybe he hadn't been as crazy about her as she'd thought.

"Ellen! Hi!"

Annie tugged on her arm to get her attention, and Ellen looked up in surprise to see her neighbor right next to her, accompanied by a tall man. She had no idea how long she'd been standing in front of the corn chips, lost in thought.

"Don't you look terrific!" Annie said, giving Ellen's outfit a thorough once-over—as well as her heaping grocery basket. "Are you going to a party?"

"Sort of." Ellen had dressed for her "date" in a slinky green dress, but she felt rather foolish now when confronted with someone who had a real escort. She looked up to see who Annie had managed to find so quickly to replace Larry Lambert. The man was tall and rather good-looking . . . and very familiar.

Recognition made her gasp. "Cliff!"

He smiled. "Hi, Ellen."

Ellen blinked in confusion. "But how . . . ?"

Annie beamed. "Ted set us up."

"Ted?"

Annie laughed. "Your brother. Wasn't that nice of him?"

Ellen didn't know what to say. "Very nice," she agreed finally. *Brother?* Last she'd heard, she was still an only child.

"He came next door one evening to borrow some cocoa, and then he saw some doughnuts on my table and I offered them to him, and before I knew what was what, I was giving your brother my life story!"

The doughnuts cinched it. Annie had to be talking about Abel. But Abel had introduced himself as her *brother?* The idea didn't sit well. Couldn't he at least have said "old flame"?

"You know, I'd seen that guy around once or twice, Ellen. Can you believe it? I thought you had a secret lover!"

Ellen let out a weak chuckle. "No secrets here."

"I was so glad Ted told me about Cliff."

"And I never even knew you had a brother," Cliff said.

"Of course I told him about you," Ellen assured him.

Annie giggled. "Well it all turned out lucky for me!"

She and the professor exploded in mirth as Ellen looked on, still in shock. How had Abel—*Ted!*—managed to engineer this? What seemed even stranger was the fact that the two looked like a good match. In spite of her happiness for her friend, it made her feel even more blue than she was before.

She dumped a box of crackers into her cart. "I hope you two have a good time," she told them. As if that were in any doubt. They couldn't stop smiling.

"Bye, Ellen," Annie said. The professor waved, picked up a liter of soda, and then the two were off.

Off to what? she wondered briefly. Probably something unbelievably fun, while she...she still had three hours to kill. She couldn't spend all that time wandering aimlessly through the frozen food aisle in her green dress and high heels.

She thought of alternatives. A movie? Or perhaps she'd buy a book and go somewhere and read for a few hours, but that didn't sound very entertaining, either. She wanted to be part of a giggling couple, with a whole evening stretching before them.

Ellen sighed and pushed forward, on to cookies. No sense in dreaming about things out of her reach. She nosed out into the main aisle and collided with another cart. "I'm sorry—"

"Excuse me—" a male voice said simultaneously.

Ellen looked into the face of the shopper she'd just rammed into. Her mouth fell open in shock. "Simon?"

He looked just as surprised as she was. "Ellen!" he exclaimed, then he gestured behind him, pointing in amazement to the checkout aisle where Annie and the professor stood, still chuckling. "Wasn't that...?"

She nodded. "He's going out with my neighbor now." That light-headed feeling she got around Simon returned full force. He looked especially good tonight in a red short-sleeved knit shirt that casually draped over his broad shoulders. And he was wearing those jeans that fit him like a glove and did strange things to her heartbeat.

"That's terrific!" A broad smile beamed at her before he thought to sober his expression. "I mean, you aren't upset by this, are you?"

"I think it's nice that they got together," she answered truthfully. It was *how* they got together—through brother

Ted—that she was having a little trouble accepting. Now that he'd promised not to pop in on her life, Abel was obviously finding other adventurous uses for his time.

"You're dolled up," he noted. She felt a little shiver run through her as he took in her outfit with obvious appreciation. Then his gaze returned to her face, darkening curiously. "Do you always dress like this to go to the grocery store?"

"I was just..." She thought about lying again, and telling him that she was on her way to a party. Annie had swallowed that explanation easily enough. Or she could tell him she had a date—one who was inordinately fond of junk food.

But she didn't. When she looked into those eyes, she found herself incapable of saying that she had other plans, especially involving another man. The one in front of her, with his flashing brown eyes and killer smile, stole all her attention.

"I had something to do earlier," she lied, "and I was just picking some things up."

His eyes bugged when he glanced into her cart. "You must have a great metabolism!"

She looked down at the piles of high-fat, high-sugar food she'd thrown in there, feeling queasily self-conscious. "I have a bit of a sweet tooth."

"Yeah, but you still manage to keep that great figure!"

It was the first real compliment he'd paid her in days—ever since their "just friends" agreement—and she felt herself blush like a foolish schoolgirl. Even though his admiration for her shape was couched in his wonder that she could eat like a garbage disposal, his words gave her a giddy lift.

"Thanks...I guess," she said.

He paused for a moment, until she was forced to look at him, to stare into those eyes of his and feel her knees go weak. "Are you busy this evening?"

Her breath caught. *Say yes. Say yes. Say yes!* But she couldn't say anything.

He took in her hesitation and continued, "I could follow you back to your house and—"

"No!" Ellen said, panic spurring her. She couldn't let him anywhere near her house, especially not when she wasn't supposed to go back there herself. At least not until eleven.

"Just for a friendly evening," Simon said persuasively. "You know, I've never even been inside your place."

Friendly. She was beginning to hate that word.

"It's nothing special, really," she told him. She had to distract him from even the idea of visiting her house. "I'd much rather..." What would she like to do? Her feet were killing her, so she couldn't bear the prospect of a walk.

"I know," he suggested, "there's a great little pub downtown not far from my house. How about it?"

It was certainly a better idea than her house, yet when she looked out the window she saw Annie and the professor driving away. To a destination unknown. Given her track record with Simon, being out in public was risky. No telling who they were likely to run into.

"Actually, why don't we just go to your place?" she said.

His face registered pure shock. "Really?"

She couldn't believe the words had popped out of her mouth. *Are you insane?* Whenever they were together they were like kids unable to keep their hands off each other. She thought about the last time she'd been alone with Simon outside the office, when he'd kissed her senseless on her porch. She didn't want a repeat of that...did she?

"I'm sorry," she said hastily, wheeling quickly for the checkout lane, "I didn't mean to invite myself over. If you have other plans—"

"I couldn't think of anything I'd enjoy more." He paused for a moment, then his lips quirked up into a smile. A devious, sensual smile, she thought with a flutter, until his next words set her straight again. "Just a friendly Saturday night together. Doesn't that sound great?"

"Great," she agreed listlessly. How could someone be so amorous one week and so buddylike the next?

She sighed. This weakness for Simon was terrible, and given her tenuous relationship with Abel, dangerous. She should be treading lightly and trying to avoid Simon at all costs, buddy or no. Instead, she had invited herself to spend an evening in the lion's den.

LOOKING AT ELLEN'S LONG, slim legs as she kicked off her high heels and wiggled her stockinged toes in the thick pile of his living room carpet, Simon wondered how much his willpower could withstand.

For days he'd been squiring Ellen around on prim lunch dates and joking with her good-naturedly at the office. And she was great company. Open—as long as they weren't talking about her present private life—funny, and *friendly.*

It was driving him nuts.

He loved talking to her, but every so often, as he sat across a table from her, his gaze would alight on her lips. And he would remember what she felt like, tasted like. Or maybe they would accidently brush arms as they walked, and for a moment he would feel absolutely incapable of thinking of anything else but how it felt to pull her into his arms. Sometimes he would catch a whiff of her perfume while holding a door open for her, and the sensation would nearly drive him over the edge. The longer he restrained himself from intimate contact, the more his desire increased. He felt like a teenager again, or worse—like a primitive in a business suit.

But Ellen remained as cool and distant as ever. She showed none of the tortured signs that he felt.

After steeling himself to the sight of her padding around his apartment barefoot—her toenails, he discovered, painted a tantalizing shade of red—he handed her a soft drink. "Would you like to watch a movie?" he suggested. "I could pop in a tape."

She wrinkled her nose. "Please, no television."

His mind clasped on to that statement with an unshakable curiosity. "Really? I got the feeling you watched a lot of television."

Her eyes widened in dismay, as if she'd just been caught in a fib. "I sometimes keep it on, you know... for background. Hawthorne likes to watch the images flicker. She took a deep gulp of her drink and looked around quickly. "Do you have a pet?"

"No," he said. "I wanted to get a kitty once, but the woman I was going out with was allergic to animals."

Her lips formed a surprised circle at the mention of Jennifer. "What happened to this woman?"

Simon fought against the frown he felt tugging at his lips. "She went back to her husband. Her ex-husband."

"Without any warning?" Ellen asked, offended for him.

He smiled. "Not really. That's what it seemed like at the time, but all along I guess I must have known. You see, I knew her ex, too. Sometimes Jennifer—that was her name—would fly into bouts of resentment toward him, and I would remind her that he wasn't so bad, that it took two to make a marriage. In hindsight, I realize that she never took much convincing."

"It just shows how persuasive you are," Ellen said. "Maybe you should have gone into family law. Your mediation skills could be the country's solution to the high divorce rate."

Simon laughed, then shook his head. "I wouldn't want to go through all that turmoil again. Relationships are difficult enough without having to deal with ghosts of past affairs."

Ellen's expression became a sorrowful blank. "That's the truth."

"I didn't mean—"

"I know." She looked around, obviously searching for something to change the subject. "Where's that Scrabble board of yours?" she asked.

He stared at her skeptically. "Are you serious?"

"Sure," she said. "I can't think of anything I'd rather do. Can you?"

He had to pinch himself on this one. Actually, he could think of about three million things he'd rather do with Ellen, none of which she'd probably appreciate his bringing up.

"Not a thing," he lied, getting up and roaming to the entry hall closet for the game. He tried not to envision the hours ahead, sitting across from her, drinking in her appearance. Dreaming of what he would actually rather be doing. He had no doubt who would win the game.

When he came back into his living room with the board, she was standing next to the sliding glass door that led out onto a small patio.

"How cute," she said, looking out at the small iron table and chairs outside. They looked out onto a postage-stamp yard filled with shrubbery and a large shade tree. "Could we play outside?"

"Sure," he said, flipping the latch on the door, "grab the glasses." He stepped out and enjoyed the feel of the warm night air. It was dark, but there was enough light shining from the inside to illuminate the little table where they would play.

"It's so beautiful tonight," Ellen said in a breathy voice as she stepped out beside him.

He looked down into her face and was nearly bowled over by the magical things the colors of night did to her pale skin. Her eyes sparked like cool emeralds as she gazed up to the heavens. He would have given all he possessed to be able to kiss her.

But he couldn't. Not until he was positively, one hundred percent sure, that was what Ellen wanted.

"Shall we begin?" she asked, glancing over with a gleam of challenge in those eyes.

Simon took a step back. "Sure."

Friends, he reminded himself. If she could stand it, he could.

Maybe.

OF COURSE SIMON WON. There was never any doubt that he would in Ellen's mind. How could she concentrate on whether *zip code* was acceptable as one word? All she could think about was how damn sexy he was in that short-sleeved shirt, how muscled his arms were, how broad his shoulders. Given her shaky feeling as she looked at him it was a miracle she kept from knocking her tiles off their little plastic holder. No wonder he'd managed to commandeer every triple-word score on the board.

Pull yourself together.

She glanced at Simon, who was having no trouble deciding where his final tile should go. He plopped it down smack in the middle of a tight cluster of little words, creating several new words and an impressive number of points. While he was busy pegging up his score, Ellen dropped an *S* onto the beginning of *tank* and considered herself lucky to have managed that much.

"You win," she conceded, flopping back in her chair. It was a relief to have the game over with. They could wind down, polish off their now fizzless drinks, and she could get out of there before she did something completely silly, like leaping over the table and into Simon's lap.

"I wish I knew what you were thinking," Simon said in a low, quiet voice.

She caught her breath, glad her face was tilted up and he couldn't see the flush that was surely washing over her cheeks. "I was just thinking about . . . what a coincidence it was that you found me this evening."

"It was no coincidence," he said.

She stared at him squarely. "Then you sought me out?"

He shrugged. "Not exactly. I think I'd put another label on what brought me there."

She tilted her head and shot him a wry glance. "Such as?"

"Fate."

Ellen nearly shrieked. She just couldn't believe in fate. Otherwise, she might believe that she and Simon *did* belong together. . . . They certainly stumbled over each other enough. "Coincidence," she insisted.

"All right," he agreed, "call it anything, call it divine interference, if you want to."

Which she didn't.

"Something happened to me the very first time I laid eyes on you, Ellen," he concluded, his deep brown eyes melting her heart right along with her words.

Her hands gripped the arms of her chair, holding her in place for dear life. This was not the time to lose her head, not when she was supposed to be out on an imaginary date. Not when Simon had just told her about Jennifer, the woman who had betrayed him by returning to her former husband. Not when she was so unsure of her own feelings that to weaken would be to betray two good men. Or, more specifically, one good man and a heavenly body.

Unfortunately, Simon's heavenly body had recently captured her fancy, overcoming her scruples about poor Abel. What kind of person was she? *A person who craved this kind of attention,* a little voice in her head chimed. She had opened up to Simon in the past few days in a way that she hadn't been able to do with anyone in years. Talking to him made her realize just how lonely she had been. It was so wonderful to have someone who actually cared what she thought about. It had been so long.

She looked straight into Simon's deep brown eyes and felt her resistance slipping away.

He leaned forward and she shot to her feet, almost tripping when her hands refused to let go of the chair. It fell to the ground behind her, and she scurried around to pick it up. Simon did the same—more gracefully, she noted with shame—and their hands met grappling for control of the chair.

The warm pressure of his hand was like a jolt of electricity through her system. "Simon..." she warned, but clearly it was *she* who needed a warning.

He came closer and clasped both his hands on her arms until they were inches away from each other. Her heart pounded like a jackhammer against her ribs. Those eyes. There was no escaping them, not when they looked at her so intently. When she closed her own, she could imagine him bending down to kiss her....

But instead of him bending down, she leaned upward. Likewise, her hands, almost of their own accord, looped around Simon's neck, pulling him down to meet her halfway. When his arms finally enfolded around her, his lips tasting hers greedily—or was it the other way around?—she felt herself sigh with relief. Whoever the fault lay with, she felt she would have died without kissing him.

The warm summer air, the light breeze, the nocturnal music of chirping bugs and distant traffic all seemed to serenade them as they tasted and touched. Ellen felt the now-familiar sensation of turning to putty in someone's arms. Simon's lips were warm and insistent, his hands playing across her arms, over her back, down to her buttocks and back up again, and she felt herself moving against him impatiently.

With one smooth motion, he pulled her into the chair they had just upended, bringing her down on his lap and tugging her close to him. She gasped at the intimacy of this new position, then found herself moving with pleasure against him. Briefly, they stopped kissing long enough for her to see the fierce wanting in his eyes, and as she moved, she could feel a pressure against her thigh, evidence of his desire. Her body stiffened involuntarily in response, but he held her firm, close.

When his lips met hers this time, they tested and coaxed, cajoling her, relaxing her against him. She moved against him tentatively and heard him emit a raspy groan.

"I knew we were more than just friends," he said. "That we were destined . . ."

"Mmm," she moaned, sucking in a gasp of pleasure as he nibbled at her ear. But in the back of her mind, the words niggled at her. *If they weren't friends, what were they?* Simon wasn't referring to their being co-workers . . . he meant they were destined to be *lovers*.

The word sent up a bright red flare in her mind, and she put her palms against his chest. "Oh!" she said, her breath coming in rapid pants. She didn't look into his eyes, she didn't dare. There might be persuasion in them, and she wasn't sure she had the willpower to resist.

"I want to make love to you, Ellen."

She was certain her face was a flaming, embarrassed red. When she reluctantly looked up, her reflection in his dark eyes confirmed it. "Oh, Simon! What about our pact?"

"Pact?" he asked.

"You know," she reminded him, " 'just friends?' "

To her utter amazement, he threw his head back and laughed, his white teeth gleaming in the moonlight. "Are you kidding?"

She squirmed uncomfortably in his lap, then feeling his hardness, realized this was the wrong thing to do. "But I thought..."

"I don't know about you, but friends rarely have this effect on me."

She ducked her head, ceding the point, then felt her chest swell with indignation as realization hit her. "You planned this."

All innocence, he asked, "What?"

"This! You just wanted to catch me with my guard down so I would, would..." *Jump into his arms* was the correct phrase, but she wasn't going to give him the satisfaction of hearing her say it.

"Guilty as charged," he agreed. Sputtering with outrage, she attempted to push herself out of the chair, but his arms held firm. "Don't you see, Ellen? I had to find some way to make you understand that we were meant to be together like this."

"Oh, please don't blather more about fate," she begged, still struggling to get up.

"If our bumping into each other doesn't convince you that we were meant to be, maybe our inability to be alone without kissing should."

"That's your persistence."

A dark eyebrow arched smartly on his forehead. "If I recall, *you* were the one who instigated this tonight."

Her mouth dropped open—and remained wordless—at the truth in his statement. Smiling, he released his grip on her arms and she sprang to her feet.

"Thank goodness we stopped ourselves in time!"

He caught her arm before she could dash inside, pivoting her back to him. Her insides turned to liquid as she was caught in his intent gaze.

"Was it in time?" he asked. "I think it's too late to go back to the way you were."

Feeling her stomach flip uneasily, she crossed her arms. "And just how was I?"

"You were living in the past, Ellen," he said, "surviving on memories."

Some of the old anger returned, the resentment toward those who lectured her when they themselves had never suffered loss. "You make me sound like some kind of nut!"

"Living in the past is no way for you to spend your life," Simon told her gently. "Not forever. Not when there's someone in the present who wants you."

The words pierced her heart, making her quiver anxiously. He wanted her, he didn't love her. He'd just said as much. Why *would* he love her, when he obviously considered her a fanatical widow? The trouble was, she was waiting for a sure thing, the kind of relationship she'd had with Abel.

There might be a man in the present who wanted her, but there was also a man from the past in her present who loved her. To forfeit the latter for the former would be a bad trade-off.

But to put her feelings into words seemed impossible. "I've got to go!" she cried, turning and fleeing into the house.

"Ellen, wait," he pleaded, following her.

"It's late." Nearly eleven o'clock—a safe hour to go back home. Grabbing her purse off the couch, she turned back to him, a smile frozen on her face. "I enjoyed our game."

He didn't smile in return. "You realize you're running from something inevitable."

Her body tensed, and she started back toward the door. "Not inevitable," she mumbled.

He caught her wrist and forced her to look into his eyes. "Promise me you'll at least think about us, won't you?"

She wanted to laugh at the outrageousness of his question. As if she would be able to think about anything else! But she had to try—had to. "I'll probably see you Monday."

He looked at her oddly and released her hand. "Of course you will. We're going to San Antonio, remember?"

Ellen suppressed a sigh of despair. How could she have forgotten their visit to Mr. Samuelson? Harlan had sprung it on them Friday. "That's right," she said gloomily.

A day alone with Simon. How would she ever survive?

Chapter Eight

"Cliff is a dream boat," Annie said.

Abel, Annie and Ellen were having Sunday morning coffee on the back porch deck Ellen and Annie shared. Before Ellen even had a chance to read the comics, Annie had spilled all the details of her date with the music professor, and also filled them in on their upcoming date set for the next day.

Abel, wearing his "Ted" hat, took a long sip from his coffee cup and seemed inordinately pleased with his matchmaking skills. "That's love for you," he mused. "It'll sneak up on you when you least expect it."

Annie sighed.

Ellen rolled her eyes at the mention of love.

"What's the matter with you, grumpy?" Abel asked.

"I'm not grumpy," Ellen said, her very tone belying her words. The truth was, she hadn't been in a good mood since leaving Simon's house the night before. How could she be? She had a deceased husband who wanted to set her up but was jealous of other men, and a persistent suitor whom she had to resist but who managed to undo her every time with his toe-curling kisses. And Simon could be so irritating! Why was he interested in her anyway, if he thought she was so dedicated to the past? Why couldn't he just leave her alone with her ghost!

Maybe for the same reason you keep jumping into his arms when you should be avoiding him like the plague...

"Maybe she didn't have a good time last night," Annie suggested to Abel. "Although I can't imagine not having a good time with that man of hers!"

Abel's ears perked right up. "What man?"

Ellen felt a stab of panic. "You know," she told him, "Ed."

"Ed?" Annie frowned. "I thought his name was—"

"Ed," Ellen insisted.

"I couldn't believe it when we ran into him at the market right after seeing you," Annie said. "I bet he was there looking for you, Ellen."

"You two met at the grocery store?" Abel asked suspiciously. "I thought you were going to a bar."

Before Ellen could think of a lie, Annie laughed. "Oh, I think the grocery store is much more romantic in its own way, don't you, Ted? Just think of it as love where you least expect it—in the frozen foods. But I could have sworn the guy's name was..."

Ellen wished she could sink through the floorboards of the deck. "I—I think I'll get some more coffee."

"Now I remember!" Annie exclaimed. "That guy you work with is named *Simon.*"

Ellen, standing, laughed nervously. "Oh, *him.* But my date wasn't with Simon. It was with Ed. Ed's a painter."

Annie frowned in confusion. "But when I saw him last night, I naturally assumed—"

Abel frowned at Ellen. "You didn't tell me you ran into Simon last night."

Ellen shrugged helplessly. "He just appeared."

"He has a habit of that," Annie said. "Every time he shows up here I keep wishing he were chasing me instead of Ellen."

"He's not chasing me," Ellen corrected her. "We work together, that's all." Trying to inject some truth into her conversation, she added, "Just like tomorrow. Simon and I have go to San Antonio for the day." She said it as though she dreaded it, which she did, but not for the reasons she would have them believe.

"What for?" Abel asked, his dismay plain.

"To talk to Vern Samuelson." For Annie's benefit, she explained, "The dear old man is rich as a king and completely dedicated to his late wife, but his long-lost relatives don't want him to spend the family fortune on a monument to the woman."

"How selfish!" Annie exclaimed. Then she frowned in consideration. "How much money are we talking here?"

"Why should that matter?" Ellen asked. "He loved her— she meant more than money to him."

"Well, sure... but you can get a little nutty about these things," Annie said. "A person has to live. They just can't survive on memories, like those crazy old ladies in books who live alone and keep cats. That would be too weird."

Ellen thought of her years alone with Hawthorne and felt stung. This was the second person in twenty-four hours who had spouted off about living with ghosts. Was she the only one in the world who thought such dedication was touching? She turned to Abel. He should have a whole different take on the subject. "What do you think, *Ted?*"

His brow crinkled, and he looked away uncomfortably. "I don't know...."

"I guess some people think that you can find only one love in a lifetime, but not me," Annie said. "Otherwise, I'd be sunk. I've been falling in love with a different guy every six months since I was fourteen.''

''Mr. and Mrs. Samuelson were married for fifty-one years,'' Ellen said.

''I guess that could make a difference,'' Annie allowed.

Ellen and Abel's gazes locked. The Samuelsons had had fifty years, but he and Ellen had barely had five weeks. Was their love any less strong, their tie less binding? Ellen felt torn. She still wanted all the things she'd dreamed she and Abel would have—a home, a family, years and years together. But if Abel didn't think he could give her that, that he couldn't stay...

''Maybe it's not wrong for some people to live with ghosts,'' he said, looking up at her.

Ellen sucked in a breath. Was he conceding that all his matchmaking schemes were hopeless where she was concerned? She stared deep into his amber brown eyes for an answer and waited.

''Maybe some couples were just meant to be,'' he said in a soft voice.

Ellen felt a smile break out across her lips. If Annie weren't there she would have thrown her arms around him. There! Finally, she had convinced him. If Abel would just say he would stay with her always, and stop pushing her toward other men, she could relax. Then she would definitely be less susceptible to Simon. Wouldn't she?

Well, Simon simply wouldn't even be an issue anymore. It would just be her and Abel, together again. Of course, it would be tough going through life with such a secret, but what was life without a few challenges?

''Okay,'' Annie admitted. ''Some couples. But those are one in a million, I'll bet.''

Ellen's smile faded as she looked at Abel, who appeared to be lost in thought again. He had said *some* couples, too.

Was he thinking that they were one of those one in a million?

ELLEN LOOKED DOWN at the map of San Antonio in her lap and pointed to the left. "There should be a gate on this block."

Simon turned the Jeep onto the tree-lined road and drove slowly. They had spent an hour and a half together in complete silence except for the radio blaring oldies tunes at them—Buddy Holly and Chuck Berry and the Supremes. Tunes that Ellen could silently bop along to without having to think about their Saturday night kiss, or how good Simon looked first thing in the morning, with his hair still slightly damp and his after-shave wafting over to her side of the Jeep. No doubt about it, the man did things to her.

She forced herself to think about Abel, and his statement about couples being made for each other. That was what she wanted. Only she had been made to be part of a couple with Abel, not Simon.

Abel, she repeated silently.

Seeing Mr. Samuelson would be good for her. Seeing his selfless devotion toward his late wife would remind her of how she herself used to feel before Simon had knocked her for a loop.

After a little ways they found it—a dark, ivy-covered iron entrance that opened onto a gravel drive of huge live oaks with branches curving over the path and overgrown shrubs. In the distance lurked a rambling old two-story brick house. The ramshackle mansion was reminiscent of one that might appear in a gothic novel. *Where an old lady who kept cats might live...*

Stop it!

"It's a little eerie," she said, then added, "but charming, don't you think?"

Simon shot her a dubious glance. "In its own decrepit way, I guess."

"Actually, I think it's exactly right."

After years of speaking to Mr. Samuelson on the phone, Ellen expected him to live in just such a gloomy place. She imagined at one time the estate had been carefully tended and manicured, the flower beds bursting with summer flowers, but now the old house and grounds looked as though the life had been sucked out of them. Vern Samuelson was too heartbroken to care about his surroundings.

Ellen sighed wistfully. Poor, poor man.

"Exactly right if you're into cobwebs and wheezing pipe organs," Simon muttered as he parked in the little-used drive.

Ellen shot him a warning look, and they made their way up the cracking front porch steps and knocked with the old, weathered brass lion's head. Then they waited.

After what seemed an eternity, an elderly woman opened the door suddenly, and Ellen and Simon were nearly knocked off their feet by a blast of cold air and the blaring of a swinging Frank Sinatra tune. The frigid temperature was a shock after the warm air outside—and the dance music seemed to come from another world entirely from the glum, dark garden they had come through.

Ellen glanced anxiously at Simon as Frank beckoned them to come fly away—and was glad to see that his confusion was just as profound as her own. The housekeeper beamed a sunny smile at them that also clashed with the gloomy surroundings. And there was something else in the woman's appearance that made Ellen do a double take; something about her eyes . . .

Before she could figure out what exactly she found disturbing about the maid, from behind the door a hand suddenly reached out and yanked Ellen across the threshold. All at once she found herself being whirled and twirled across the glossy white marble of the entrance hall, her feet stepping automatically in time to the peppy beat. Then, in a dizzying move, her partner, who so far was only a short, balding blur to her, stopped short and dipped her low to the ground.

"At long last, we meet!"

Ellen heard her backbone pop in a few places and looked up into the man's eyes. She could hardly believe it. Vern Samuelson! *This* was the sad, reclusive widower she'd spent so much time on the phone with? His few black and gray hairs were slicked across his balding head in a debonair manner, and he wore a navy suit with a brightly printed yellow-and-red tie. But aside from his grooming, his whole manner was the exact opposite of what she would have expected. His cheeks were bright, his blue eyes happy and clear, and despite his short, elderly frame, the arms that held her were definitely robust.

"Mr. Samuelson?" she asked with a gasp.

He let out a sharp, boisterous laugh and brought her upright again. "Of course!" he bellowed, stepping back and clicking his heels to attention. "And you're Ellen. Pretty as a picture!"

Ellen cleared her throat and glanced uncomfortably at Simon, who was still standing in the doorway, his arms hugging his briefcase to his chest to warm himself, his lips twitching up in amusement. She shot him a withering glance and gestured toward him for Mr. Samuelson's benefit. "This is Simon Miller, the attorney Mr. Smith told you about."

Vern Samuelson looked at his housekeeper. "Show him in, Louise. The man doesn't seem to know whether I've stolen his girlfriend or not."

"Oh, no—you've got the wrong idea completely," Ellen sputtered helplessly.

The old man winked joyfully at her. "Ha! Have I?" He laughed again, a jarring sound Ellen had never heard over the phone in all their conversations together. "Don't worry, Ellen. Some men are just blind when it comes to love."

Love? "No, you see . . . I mean . . ." Her attempt to right this wrong impression trailed off when she caught sight of the housekeeper again. Had he called her Louise?

Noticing her confusion, Mr. Samuelson cocked his head impishly. "Odd coincidence, isn't it?" he asked.

His wife's name had been Louise. And his wife, in the one picture they had on file of her, bore a striking resemblance to the short, pink-cheeked lady in front of her now. "Yes . . ." Ellen said, swallowing, "it *is* a coincidence."

In fact, it was downright spooky.

"Louise came to me yesterday, in answer to an ad."

Something clicked in Ellen's brain. "An ad?"

"Yes, for a housekeeper. Oddest thing," Samuelson mused, "I'd forgotten all about it until she showed up at my door." He chuckled lightly. "But you see, I've always liked the name Louise. So maybe it isn't such a coincidence at all that I hired a housekeeper with the same name as my late wife." Mr. Samuelson asked Louise to bring tea, then escorted his two disoriented, shivering guests into a mahogany-paneled study.

They sat down around a large oak desk to get down to business. Old Blue Eyes was still crooning away. Loudly.

Simon tugged on his coat, trying to get warm. "I know I talked to you last Friday over the phone, sir, but I thought it would be convenient if we went over some of the details."

"Oh, you mean the monument?" Samuelson asked, as if it were something he rarely thought about instead of his

long-standing obsession. "We can forget all about that," he
assured Simon, dismissing the subject with a wave of his
hand. He looked eagerly from one to the other. "Do either
of you play croquet?"

Simon tilted his head, caught off balance by the sudden
change in subject. "Do you mean you're changing your
will?"

"Yes, I've become convinced that Louise might not have
thought that the monument was the best way to spend our
money . . . so I've decided to leave half to a nephew of mine
and half to charity. What do you think?"

At first, Simon seemed as startled as Ellen felt. But he
couldn't have been. Because Ellen, sensing the invasive hand
of Abel Lantry in this setup, knew exactly how Mr.
Samuelson suddenly understood what his late wife's wishes
would have been. Louise the housekeeper not only shared
the same name and looks as the late Mrs. Samuelson, she
was the late Mrs. Samuelson!

Ellen, who should have been used to these things, felt
momentarily faint, and weaved a bit in her leather chair.

"Are you okay?" Simon whispered to her.

Ellen nodded weakly. "I'm fine."

Mr. Samuelson smiled paternally at her. "You'll perk
right up with some hot tea, won't you?" He laughed. "I've
spent hours with this little lady on the phone, so I know she
likes her caffeine!"

Ellen barely heard Mr. Samuelson and Simon discussing
the drafting of his new will and what it would entail. She felt
sick. Was that *really* Mrs. Samuelson? The eyes and hair
and clear, creamy skin were the same as the pictures of
Louise Samuelson. But how could that be? Had she lived
with a ghost for so long that she was actually beginning to
see them in other people's houses, too?

Moments later she heard the soft footfall of a woman's tread, and the study door opened.

"Splendid!" Mr. Samuelson said, rising to his feet to do the honors of pouring for his guests. Ellen noticed him clap his hands together lightly, as if trying to warm them. As if he weren't quite acclimated to the temperature yet, either. She knew the feeling well.

She took her steaming cup and shivered, especially when she glanced into Louise's face. She looked exactly like the woman in the picture, except that her hairstyle was softer, more silvery. She couldn't disguise the open kindness of her face, however, or the sparkle in her blue eyes.

"Whattaya know!" Samuelson cried, hopping to his feet when a new song came on. "It's our favorite!"

He did a little jig around his desk, relieved Louise of the heavy silver tray with the tea things, and pulled her to the center of a large Oriental rug to the tune of "Fly Me to the Moon." Bashful at first, yet game, Louise moved easily to the upbeat tempo, and when her eyes met Samuelson's, Ellen had no doubt where the old man's sudden euphoria had come from. From the angel in his arms.

Ellen cast a glance aside to Simon to see whether he had noticed anything odd happening. But as he took his first sips of tea, he appeared oblivious to the presence of a heavenly creature in their midst.

Ellen didn't know why, but the sight of the older, obviously deliriously happy, couple made her feel a wave of self-pity.

Except… This *had* to have been engineered by Abel. She had told Abel about the Samuelsons the night before last. Then, the very next day, "Louise" arrived on Mr. Samuelson's doorway as a housekeeper. Very clever—as long as no visitors came by who had known his wife, or seen pictures of her. But Mr. Samuelson had been a recluse for years now.

Even Simon, who most assuredly had glanced at the photo of Mrs. Samuelson in the file he was holding, hadn't detected the truth.

Or perhaps Ellen was simply more adept than most at spotting angels. She also knew genuine happiness when she saw it—and she saw it in Samuelson's eyes right now as he looked lovingly at his long-lost Louise. She felt tears starting to gather and pinched herself to keep them back.

His euphoria struck a chord in her...a sad, wistful one. She remembered that happiness so well, could recall the exact emotion she'd felt when she'd discovered Abel on her couch on her birthday. But she hadn't felt that happy since. Almost immediately, conflict had entered her life once more. Mr. Samuelson looked perfectly content to spend the rest of his days with an angel—but she was still, in her own uneven way, trying to move on with her life. Trying to live.

And not doing a very good job of it.

Maybe the Samuelsons were one of those one in a million couples Annie and Abel were referring to. They were gloriously, infectiously happy—unlike her and Abel. Was that what her late husband was trying to tell her with this little show of his?

Ellen looked again at Simon's handsome face, smiling broadly as he watched the husband and wife, and felt more conflicted yet. Would he have been smiling if he'd known he was staring at a ghost? Like Annie would have said—and Simon, too—there was something weird about the whole setup. Maybe it was hypocritical, but seeing someone living with a ghost seemed strange to Ellen. Yet Vern was so happy....

Perhaps what she was experiencing was ghost envy, unbelievable as it seemed. Especially when the dance ended and Mr. Samuelson brought Louise's hand up to his lips for a kiss. She heard herself sigh with longing at the tender gesture. Simon had done that once....

She felt keyed up. Conflicted. And more than she had in years, she felt an almost painful yearning to grab on to life, to happiness. To Simon.

"I don't suppose there's much for us to do today," Simon told their client when the romantic tableau had broken up. "If you'd rather tend to this some other time..."

"Oh, let's forget business," Mr. Samuelson said, waving away the very idea. "You must stay for lunch. I told Louise to prepare an extra-special meal in honor of your coming, and she's a fantastic cook."

Ellen, feeling hopelessly mixed-up inside, tugged on Simon's sleeve. If only she could get back to Austin, to Abel, to her version of normalcy. "Shouldn't we—"

"We'd love to stay," Simon told him before she could grit out an objection. He looked over at Ellen. "Wouldn't we?"

She nodded unhappily at the thought of enduring hours more in the midst of such strange yet perfect bliss. How much more could she take before she snapped? "Sure. Love to."

"TURN THAT WAY," Ellen instructed, pointing left.

Simon hesitated at the gate leading out of the Samuelson estate. "But I thought the interstate was the other way."

"It is. But a great Mexican restaurant on the river walk downtown is that way," she answered. "Turn left."

He smiled and bowed toward the steering wheel. "Your wish is my command. But didn't we just eat?"

"We didn't eat any margaritas," she told him. "And I could use one. Or twelve."

Simon glanced at her curiously. "I guess this does call for a celebration," he admitted, looking down at his watch. Five after five. The workday was over. And if Ellen wanted to spend an hour or so more in his company, who was he to complain?

Fifteen minutes later they were ensconced at a table at one of the cafés bordering the San Antonio River where it wound through downtown. The day was warm, but they were shaded by a tree and soon Ellen had her icy margarita to cool her. A salsa band played a seductive song with a cha-cha-cha beat in the background, and Ellen swung her leg in time to it. The unconscious movement sparked something inside Simon—namely, the urge to pull her into his arms.

Yet there was an odd look in those green eyes of hers that kept him at bay. She'd been behaving rather strangely all afternoon. They had spent longer with Mr. Samuelson than he had expected, so maybe she was just worn out.

As designated driver, Simon had ordered an iced tea. "Cheers," he said, lifting his glass. "Here's to deliriously happy clients."

Ellen shuddered as she took a swallow. Clearly, she didn't drink much.

"Strong?" he asked.

She shook her head. "It's perfect." That wild look was still in her eyes as she took another gulp. "Simon, do you believe in the supernatural?"

He would have laughed if she hadn't seemed so dead serious. "You mean witches and the Loch Ness Monster? No."

She tilted her head in challenge. "What would you say if I told you Louise the housekeeper was an angel?"

"I'd agree with you all the way," he said, smiling. "And if you want my opinion, I'd say Mr. Samuelson is well on his way to falling in love with her."

She downed about half of her drink. "I think you're right."

"Is that what's bothering you?" he asked, leaning forward.

"What?"

"The idea that some people are given love twice in a lifetime."

She appeared to shrink back from him, but her gaze remained locked with his. She took a sip of her drink and swallowed. "It's not the quantity, it's *who* the person they fall in love with is that bothers me."

He felt a sudden dryness in his throat. The way she was looking at him ... it was almost as if she were referring to *him*. But Ellen wasn't in love with him, much as he would have liked to think she was. The only thing certain about their relationship was the red-hot desire he felt whenever he was around her.

"Don't you think Louise is good enough for Vern?"

An odd little smile touched her lips. "On the contrary. I'm sure she is."

"There, then. What's to say someone can't be just as happy the second time around?"

"Oh, Simon," Ellen said with a moan. "You don't know how I would like to believe that."

"So why don't you?" Even though he didn't understand what had her so balled up over this afternoon, he felt a gut-tightening response to her obvious confusion. Instinct told him that she was more concerned about their relationship than Mr. Samuelson and his housekeeper's, and he wanted to take her into his arms, kiss all her doubts away....

"Isn't Mr. Samuelson evidence?" he asked her, his voice coming out more gravelly than he'd anticipated.

Her eyes sparked in response. "Evidence of what?"

"That happiness can return to a person's life—totally unexpectedly."

"I'm not sure of anything anymore...."

A roguish grin tugged at his lips. "Also, I think I witnessed another miracle today."

Her head snapped up from her drink. "What was that?"

"I saw you dance."

Ellen laughed, remembering. "I was so surprised!"

He loved to see her smile. "Me, too. Only I was afraid he was going to drop you."

"Thank goodness he didn't. I would have spilled all over that slippery marble floor!" She chuckled at the memory of being spun around, then, just as suddenly, the smile left her lips and she stared at him in curiosity. "You weren't really worried, were you?"

Simon felt something pierce his heart, remembering how it felt to see Ellen being twirled around in the arms of another, even for a few seconds. "No," he answered.

Her shoulders sagged a little.

"To tell you the truth, I was jealous."

Her eyes widened in surprise. "Jealous? You?"

He smiled. "Surprised?"

"But I thought..." She lifted her shoulders helplessly. "After all, it was just Mr. Samuelson...."

"I'm beginning to wonder if I could stand to see you in anyone else's arms."

Her eyes rounded, and she swallowed in an almost-audible gulp. "Simon, please. We're barely even friends. We argue all the time."

He reached out and took her hand. "But I even love to argue with you, Ellen. Especially when it's over subjects like whether we should go out on a date, or whether I should kiss you like I want to right now."

She sucked in a quick breath. "Simon!"

A young man came to their table, bearing a camera. "Would you like your picture taken?" he asked.

Simon jumped at the opportunity. "Sure," he said, already scooting his chair closer to a surprised Ellen. He turned to her with a smile, taking in her delectable red lips, her flushed cheeks, her surprised green eyes. Clearly, he'd caught her off guard with his kissing comment.

They were so close he could have leaned down and kissed her right then. He felt incredible heat just thinking about it. The camera flashed, but Simon didn't pull away; his gaze remained pinned on her. "If we can't be friends, what would you like to be?" he asked, his voice coming out deeper than normal.

Lovers, he thought, trying to telegraph the answer to her with his eyes.

Slowly, a wicked smile tilted her mouth as she looked at him, green eyes sparkling so that he thought for a hopeful moment that she had received his message. Her head did a little shake to the sexy, *obstinato* beat of the music. "You really want to know?"

"Only if it's something more intimate than a pal."

She licked her moist lips teasingly. "Oh, it is."

His heart skipped a beat and seemed to squeeze uncomfortably against his chest. "Okay, surprise me."

"Your dance partner."

She surprised him, all right. And it took him no time at all to take her up on that offer. Simon stood, stepped around the table and offered her his arm.

When he was standing over her, Ellen hesitated just a moment, her green eyes wavering between Simon's face and his outstretched hand. Finally, she took it, and with a gentle pull he brought her to her feet, close to him. He was always amazed by how delicate her tall, willowy frame felt so near to his.

Within seconds, they were on a little patio dance floor, moving in rhythm to the sensual music. Their loose embrace seemed just as agonizing as holding her full against him would have been. From the way Ellen talked, he'd always assumed she wasn't much for dancing. But now she twirled and shimmied with an assuredness that would have put Isadora Duncan to shame. Just being near her was driving him insane. Yet when the song ended and a slower song started, he pulled her into his arms without missing a beat.

He'd been wrong. Holding her closely *was* more agonizing.

He looked down into her half-closed eyes and remembered kissing her, how she had responded to his every touch and caress as if they had been made for each other. He wanted to kiss her now, but kissing her was never enough. Each time, she had pulled away, leaving him unsatisfied.

He felt her sigh restlessly in his arms, felt her breasts rub gently against him as she did so. Her cheek nuzzled his chin sensuously, and her gentle breath whispered against his neck. His dry throat tightened.

He didn't want to kiss her. He wanted to make love to her. And he got the strange feeling that she wanted him to.

She sighed again and languorously draped her wonderful hands around his neck, where one manicured finger teased and twirled the short hair at his nape. A hot shiver worked its way down his spine, causing him to tense. Ellen felt it and smiled.

Maybe it was that margarita she'd gulped down, or perhaps it was just the sight of the deliriously happy Mr. Samuelson that had done it, but something had definitely gotten into her. She seemed wild. Reckless. He'd never imagined her to be so sensually frank, so boldly desirous, before.

His hands moved down her back, pulling her hips closer against his. The contact stoked up a whole new fever inside him, but he was past caring. He wanted her to know exactly how he felt, even if he couldn't say it in words. He bent slightly and nuzzled the top of her head, loving the softness of her red hair, the light, sweet perfume that he knew was so much her. To tell her he wanted her, wanted to spend the night making love to her, would put this delicate moment at risk. He didn't want Ellen to bolt away from him tonight.

And so he would dance with her. Dance until one of them broke down and admitted to wanting the other.

He wasn't certain he wouldn't be the one to cry uncle. Holding her slim body, which fit and moved so perfectly against his, was sheer torture, especially when it seemed that she knew exactly what she was doing to him. Yet he couldn't have let her go if his life depended on it.

And why should he? A little torture of this particular type was exactly what he'd been craving. . . .

Chapter Nine

She wanted him to make love to her. Knew it with terrifying certainty. And now the evening was almost over.

Simon's Jeep swung into the empty parking lot just after sunset, its radial tires spitting gravel. The top was down, and Ellen's hair flew out in disarray behind her. Her whole body tensed as she caught sight of her little Toyota in the parking lot, waiting to take her back to her house. She didn't want to leave him.

She couldn't remember the last time she'd felt this way. She tried not to look at Simon, even though it felt as if there were an electric current snapping and popping between them. Each time she did peek to the side, she was met with those brown eyes of his boring into her—only now, instead of upsetting her, their intensity completely matched how she felt inside.

She wanted to make love with him. The words repeated insistently in her brain, as they had ever since they'd started dancing together. She'd almost told him so then, but she had been too afraid. Afraid of what would happen if he took her up on her offer. Or even worse, if he didn't.

"Here we are." Simon's voice definitely lacked enthusiasm as they came to a stop.

Both of them looked in silence up at the tall building looming before them.

"Home," Ellen joked.

If only she *were* home already. She didn't feel like getting out and situating herself in her own car, then making the drive to her own house. Or perhaps she just didn't want to leave Simon yet.

Couldn't he sense how she felt?

If only she could tell him the truth, she thought despairingly. Their day was over, and soon this tentative, delicate moment would be, too. But what could she say? *I'm living with an angel but I think I'm falling for you....*

Somehow she doubted those were words every man was dying to hear. The silence stretched.

Couldn't he see that she was just waiting for him to reach across and kiss her? She looked searchingly into his eyes.

He looked away. "Maybe I should follow you home."

Her heartbeat picked up. Did he not want to leave her?

Unfortunately, her house was someplace Simon could not go. She shook her head sadly. "I only had two margaritas—and that was a few hours, eighty miles and about twenty dances ago."

His brow crinkled in worry. "Yeah, but two margaritas is pretty heavy for you, isn't it? The strongest thing I've ever seen you drink is club soda."

"Now you know why," she said, laughing tightly. "I turn into a dancing fool."

"Was that the drinks?" he asked. "I was hoping it was because you'd finally found the right partner."

There was a dark glint in those brown eyes of his, and enough truth in his words to wipe the smile from her face. *The right partner.* Was he?

She cleared her throat. "I'll be fine," she assured him. "Thanks for driving."

The second she pulled on her door handle, he immediately leapt to action. "Let me escort you to your car, at least," he said. Her Toyota was a scant five steps away.

The last thing Ellen wanted was to draw out this frustrating goodbye scene in the middle of the parking lot. Hurriedly, she grabbed her briefcase from the tiny back seat and scampered to her car, which was locked. By the time she'd put her briefcase on the top of the car, fished her key out of her purse and opened her door, Simon was at her side.

She looked up into those eyes of his and couldn't help remembering another time—her birthday. Had it only been a few weeks ago? He'd followed her out to her car, talking her ear off with all his big plans for the evening. And then, out of the blue, he'd kissed her.

Would he try to kiss her now? Couldn't he see that she wanted him to? Was dying for him to? Practically would have *paid* him to?

The few feet between them pulsed with desire. Both of them remained motionless—it took every bit of exertion Ellen had not to hurl herself toward those arms that had held her so tenderly in a slow dance only two hours earlier. She could feel a similar tension in Simon, too. As if all his efforts were being concentrated in reining himself in.

Stop reining! she wanted to tell him.

"So...I guess I'll see you tomorrow," she said awkwardly. A vision of Simon's lips capturing hers as she was trapped in the front seat of her car flashed through her mind.

Simon hesitated. "Sure, tomorrow," he agreed, not moving. "Listen, are you certain you don't want me to follow you home?"

She imagined him following her to her house, following her into the living room, through her bedroom door.... Her head shook adamantly, as much to drive away the tantalizing image as to indicate the negative. "That won't be necessary. But thanks."

His lips lifted in a polite, tense smile. For the first time, she noticed tiny little lines at the edges of his eyes. Laugh lines, of course. How could a man like Simon have escaped having them? She longed to reach out, to trace each little line with her fingertip. Instead, she buried her fists in her jacket pockets.

"Well...I guess this is it, then," he said. If he sounded as reluctant to leave as she felt, did that mean he was also as conflicted about where they stood as she was?

"Where they stood" at the moment was rooted to the pavement, unable to break away. Ellen felt as if the soles of her shoes had become one with the tar. She was relieved when finally Simon seemed to gather the necessary energy to move.

He audibly bit back a sigh, then, in a surprise gesture, reached out to take her hand, which was still buried in her pocket. She nearly jumped in shock at the feel of his warm, roughened skin on her wrist, which was the closest thing to her hand that he could grab.

"Good night, Ellen," he said.

She felt a slight tug and knew that was her cue. She could have stepped forward at that moment, into his arms, into his embrace. She could have just admitted that she wanted to jump back into his Jeep, drive to his house and spend the entire night in his bed. God knows, she did want to. But everything seemed so uncertain. They were in a parking lot, for heaven's sake.

She stood her ground until finally that faint smile returned to his lips. A smile of resignation?

"Good night," she told him. Firmly. There was no tremor in her voice. No mixed messages.

He got the one message clear enough. Nodding, he pivoted and returned to the Jeep, jumping in and reaching for the ignition in one fluid movement. Before she could gather her composure enough to finally open her own car door, he was already pulling out of the parking lot.

She sighed. That was it, then. A weird, lovely day, an evening of carefree abandon... all had ended in a wristshake in the law firm's parking lot. Which was good, she told herself. They had cleared a major hurdle. She hadn't weakened just out of mere physical desire. And after this trip, there would be no more reasons for her and Simon to be thrown together after hours. Everything would remain strictly business.

This was good, she repeated to herself as she shakily got into the car, turned the key in her ignition and pulled into reverse. This was just the way she wanted things. No matter that her insides pulsed erratically in a hollow, disappointed throb.

She pulled back jerkily and heard a loud *thwack!* of something hitting the gravel outside the car. She braked, rolled down her window and poked her head out to look. The briefcase! She'd been in such a disappointed erotic funk that she had forgotten to take it off of the roof of her car.

She killed the engine and stepped out to retrieve the case. It was then that she noticed she had the wrong one. If it hadn't been dark, and her nerves so frazzled, she never would have mistaken Simon's for her own.

She sighed. She could switch with him tomorrow morning. Or she could run it inside the building now. Or maybe...

She peered down the road, where Simon's Jeep had just disappeared. He probably didn't have that much of a head start on her. And he might need to do some work at home....

Strictly business, she said to herself as she jumped back into her car. Her pulse had picked up again, and it was with quite a bit more gusto that she backed up and pulled out of the empty lot. She drove the fifteen minutes to Simon's house without thinking, moving on instinct alone. She cranked up her radio, and the speakers blared Mary Chapin Carpenter crooning "Shut Up and Kiss Me" to a seductive country beat. Ellen sang along mindlessly until she pulled up in front of Simon's house.

His Jeep was in the driveway. He'd probably just gone inside.

Ellen picked up the briefcase and marched up to the front door. *Just hand it to him,* she coached herself. No explanations were necessary. She was just doing a good deed, as co-worker to co-worker.

The door opened and Simon stood before her, his eyes lighting up with surprise. As before, both of them stood speechless, yet the mood was different now. It was even more electric with anticipation.

Ellen's mouth was as dry as dust as she looked into those knowing brown eyes. "I just ..." Who was she fooling? Maybe she *should* have thought of what she was going to say, scolding herself for being virtually incoherent now. To compensate, she simply held out the case to him with a heavy, shaky arm.

He gave it the briefest of glances, then planted his hand solidly over hers. "Why don't you ..." When words failed, his eyes beckoned.

Inside.

Mesmerized by those velvety brown depths, and electrified as always by his mere touch, she moved past him across the threshold. As her shoulders brushed lightly against his chest, she felt herself go boneless again. Felt her heart start beating erratically, so that it was hard for her to catch a full breath of air.

They turned in a circle near the doorway, still joined at the briefcase handle and their gazes locked. The door was kicked shut lightly, leaving them alone in the silent house. She had been here just two nights ago, but it seemed different now—more silent, more shadowy. More intimate. Suddenly she felt the need to say something, to fill the charged air between them. Her lips parted, but no words came. His eyes locked on her lips as she brushed her tongue against them.

His eyes darkened, and something inside him, some tiny thread of control, snapped. Before she could blink, the briefcase was unceremoniously dumped, and in the next moment, Ellen found herself in his arms, seeking relief to the tension that had been building and building between them since he'd first offered her his hand to dance back in San Antonio.

His mouth claimed hers in a swift, deep kiss, and she grabbed his shoulders for fear of being knocked off her feet with the power of it. Her hands snaked up across the soft cotton of his shirt, taking heed of the muscular shoulders just beneath the surface. She finally looped them around his neck, anchoring herself as she pushed closer against him.

This wasn't like before. There was more hunger than playfulness in the way his tongue probed hers, in the desperate way they clung to each other, his hands roving across her back, down her hip, her thigh, and back up again. And all the while, they were moving, turning, twirling, in another slow, erotic dance toward the interior of the house.

It would have been much quicker to simply walk to the bedroom, but Ellen couldn't bear the idea of separating even for a moment. She felt a rush of warmth inside her as he probed ever deeper, stopping only for brief moments, to kiss her lips again, her chin, her neck, and then his lips would move up again, feverishly seeking her mouth. One of his hands moved around to tease the tip of her breast, and she released a moan of pleasure so deep she wondered whether it really could have been her own voice. Her hands moved, too, playing with the short, soft down at his nape, then plunging up to bury themselves in the thick locks of his dark hair.

In wordless agreement, they parted only long enough to discard her silk shirt, and she stood before him, her back leaning against the door frame to his bedroom, in only a thin ivory camisole. He bent to kiss her again, impatience and desire lighting his eyes as she reached forward to undo the tiny buttons of his blue business shirt with trembling fingers. As each little button was freed, she bent and kissed the skin beneath, reveling in the slightly salty taste of him, and teasing the hard, flat nipples she found there with her tongue. She worked her way down, discovering a light matt of brown hair on his chest, and she couldn't help running her hands through it, her cheek across it, noting the labored movements of his chest as he struggled to breathe evenly.

Finally, when she pulled his shirt free and began to loosen his belt, it became too much for him. With a primitive, un-lawyerlike grunt, he lifted her easily into his arms and carried her to the bed. She half expected to be tossed unceremoniously onto the mattress, and probably wouldn't even have minded, but instead, he eased them both down so that she faced forward, straddling precariously on his lap. Her skirt was pushed out of the way, so there was one less barrier between herself and the evidence of his desire rubbing gently but firmly against her stocking-clad leg.

She tossed back her head and allowed herself to be stroked and petted. With both his hands and his lips, he began to touch every part of her. Starting with her earlobe, he worked his way down her neck, delivering kisses and gentle nips as he went. Then he pushed aside the strap of her camisole and gingerly touched the sensitive skin there, moving cautiously but surely down to her breast, which already ached for his touch.

She moaned again, and writhed gently against him as his lips gently fondled the tight rosy bud. With growing urgency, she moved against him, responding to his ministrations and needing more, much more.

She had forgotten about this. The consuming heat, the willing relinquishment of reason to sensuality... Simon followed her unspoken wishes and finally lifted off her camisole, tossing aside his own shirt as well, and for a moment sat watching her, the heated desire in his eyes unmistakable.

"Ellen," he breathed, his voice low and hoarse, "you're so beautiful." He swallowed, then looked her in the eyes directly. "Are you sure...?"

Her throat felt dry, cottony. *Sure?* She longed to tell him how much she wanted him, how impatient she was, how eager, but her voice wouldn't come. Instead, she attempted to tell him in movement, nodding mutely, then caressing her hands up his muscled arms, across his shoulders, down his back.

She was surprised to find him as responsive as she had been to his touch. As each moment of exploration passed, she felt even more sure. Sure that she wanted him more desperately than she'd ever wanted anything in her life.

He stopped her, cupping her face with his hands. "Has it been a long time for you, Ellen?"

"Mmm." The sensual moan was the most she could manage. A long time? She could never remember feeling such feverish need.

"We'll go slow," he promised her.

She groaned. *Slow.* She was practically in agony....

But as he proceeded to shed the rest of their clothes, one piece at a time with the promised leisure, she began to see the wisdom in his way. Every moment he prolonged their wait, caressing her newly bared skin to results she had never imagined, she came closer to understanding the power they held over each other, and was able to respond in kind.

Simon gave in a way that made her feel wild, but he also received her ministrations with an appreciation that made her understand the word *sharing* for the first time. The elemental man-woman tug between them, which had seemed so strangely disturbing all the weeks she had been trying to resist him, seemed completely natural now, with all their barriers down.

As they moved, ever more entwined, skin against skin, Ellen realized again that she had forgotten completely this combination of bliss and longing, the fierce desire tearing at her, if ever she had known it. She'd certainly never experienced anything like the spiraling sensations as Simon began stroking the center of her womanhood, slowly, building her desire to a fever pitch until finally she was ready to welcome him to her, moist and hot and aching.

He made love to her with a restless patience, and Ellen saw in his face all the wonder that she herself felt at the feeling of utter closeness. His eyes brimmed with emotion and a caring for her that made her cry out for more than the sensations building inside her. Every second he drew out their lovemaking was both agonizing and wonderful. And when finally she lay beneath him, spent and senseless from her release and cradling him against her, she knew neither of them would have rushed one single moment for all the world.

SOMETHING WAS ANCHORING her to the bed. Putting off that inevitable moment when she would wake, Ellen kept her eyes closed and smiled in her half sleep. She felt deliciously rested, but she could still stand to sleep for another ten hours or so. And maybe she would have to, if she couldn't figure out how to rid herself of whatever it was that had her pinned to the bed.

Sometimes during the night Hawthorne would crawl up on her shoulder for a nap, but this didn't feel anything like her cat. In fact, this didn't feel anything like her bed, either. The sheets beneath her naked—naked?—body were stiffer than hers, newer, and the pillow her head rested on was fluffier than the old ones on her bed. Ellen's nose wrinkled in an investigative sniff. An odd smell. Musk.

Man.

Her eyes snapped open and she half turned to find Simon, fully, spectacularly, undressed, lying against her, one arm draping possessively over her shoulder. She gasped, remembering suddenly what had led her to be in Simon's bed, and felt a hot flush creep over her entire body.

Her first instinct was to get up and run, but she ignored it and instead went with her second, far more intriguing, impulse, which was to stare curiously at the man who had just made love to her so expertly. His dark hair was an adorable jumble on his head—mussed, no doubt, by her own hand. His eyes were closed, but his lips were turned up in a secretive smile that reminded her of her own a few moments before.

Taking in his broad shoulders, his chest with its light dusting of coarse dark hair that narrowed to a single trailing line at his stomach, she would like to have thought that even in his unconscious he was as moved by their lovemaking as she had been. Certainly his manhood, swelled with desire, still pressed insistently against her thigh.

And yet, these things were different with men. Digging deep into her memory, she recalled that males could look on moments like this more casually than she ever could. Her heart had been broken once by reading too much into what one college boy had callously told her was simply "a roll in the hay." Was that what Simon would call this?

He didn't seem the callous type, especially not now, when his face was boyishly appealing in sleep. She had to fight the urge to reach up and comb a hank of hair off of his closed eyelids. But in answer to her doubts, memories assailed her—of the tenderness in his eyes as he had entered her. And his words, asking her if she'd been certain of what she'd wanted. And his patience. His infinite, nearly maddening patience. These weren't the trademarks of a callous womanizer.

And yet...it had been so long for her. Aside from her one bad experience, there had been only Abel.

Abel. She tried to put him out of her mind, but he returned to niggle insistently at her conscience.

He was the one who had started all this, she thought heatedly. Seeing Mr. and Mrs. Samuelson together had made her so confused, so envious. Oh, she wanted that kind of love again. She'd thought she'd found it again with Abel. By bringing the lovebirds back together, was Abel trying to send her a not-so-subtle message? After all, he'd gone to great pains to tell her that *she* couldn't have a ghost live with her forever. Why could Mr. Samuelson?

But the strangest thing was, seeing the Samuelsons had made her rethink the idea of holding on to Abel forever. So she'd turned to someone vital, alive. To Simon. And in return, Simon had taken her into his arms and shown her precisely how much she had been missing of life, how pleasurable being a woman could be.

Ellen let out a long, uneasy breath. And yet Simon had said nothing of love, even in his most heartbreakingly tender moments. He hadn't whispered words of deep emotion, promises of forever—or even of a few days. For all she knew, to Simon their physical uniting had been completely in the moment, their carnal release the result of an overlong day.

But to her it meant so much more. While she herself was torn between earthiness and the ethereal, she had no idea what he felt. This evening she had bared herself to him like a raw nerve, yet he hadn't made any assurances. All she knew for certain was that he wanted her, and that he was a relentless pursuer when he knew what he wanted.

She lightly traced the corded outline of muscle on his upper arm. Did she want him? Oh, yes. She felt completely vulnerable to his six-feet-two-inch combination of determination and tenderness. It seemed to be a mixture she had little will to resist. If she let herself, she would fall head-over-heels in love with Simon in a heartbeat. But could she afford to let herself? Maybe she needed to back away, to give herself time to adjust to the idea of loving someone new....

She thought about Abel. His love had seemed a sure thing. But what about now? She wasn't so certain that he wouldn't pull out on her and hotfoot it back to heaven, especially if he found out about her and Simon. The very idea pierced her to her core, causing her to sit up.

Simon's arm fell away, over to the pillow her head had just vacated, and his mouth pursed for a moment. Ellen didn't want to wake him. Not until she had things sorted out a little better. Her heart hammered against her rib cage as she stared at the shambles of a room. Clothes were everywhere, evidence of their frenzied trip to the bed. And then her gaze caught sight of the clock. Half past eleven!

Before she could say Cinderella, Ellen jumped out of the bed and started throwing on clothes. She couldn't believe it was almost midnight. Abel knew she'd had a trip to San Antonio today—would he be waiting up for her?

Guilt washed over her. Guilt and remonstrance. She *never* should have drunk those margaritas.

Yet even as the excuse came to her, she realized that it was flimsy. Drink hadn't seduced her, Simon had. She'd gone into his arms, to his bed, because she had wanted to, had found it impossible *not* to.

Could she really be falling in love? she wondered as she hurriedly hunted for her shoe. For four years she'd been in mourning—so deep her husband had come back to her. Could it be a coincidence that Simon just happened to appear in her life at the same time Abel took out that classified ad? He'd even known her birthday, something she'd never even told Yolanda. And what about all those times they'd "bumped into" each other? Abel had to be behind this . . . although he'd denied it.

Maybe he'd taken out an advertisement for the attorney position for Smith in the want ad pages, just like the one he'd put in the personals, or the one he must have taken out for a housekeeper that Louise Samuelson had returned from heaven to fill. Which meant that what she was falling into wasn't really love . . . it was just a divinely inspired, elaborately devised trap. Only Abel was being cagey, and trying to make it look like the whole romance came about naturally and that he didn't like Simon. Her late husband was very clever.

But he couldn't fool her. She wasn't about to be drawn into a relationship borne out of some angelic voodoo. After all, what would happen when Abel decided to pack up his fairy dust and return to heaven? Would the celestial aura of desire around her and Simon lift, leaving them wondering what on earth had ever brought them together?

Who could tell what would happen? That's what made her leery of the whole business. Men were untrustworthy to begin with; men under the influence of heavenly spirits were bound to be even more unstable. That's why she wanted to keep Abel with her. The angel she knew was better than the mortal she didn't.

She found her shoe, shoved it on and finally followed up on that first instinct of hers. She ran.

SIMON SMILED, NOT QUITE sure whether he was dreaming, or if his fantasy had finally come true. He opened one sleepy eye and looked at the red digits of his alarm clock. It was just before midnight. What could be better? He had the whole night in front of him, and Ellen sprawled out beside him.

Still half asleep, he stretched, grabbed a corner of his comforter, and turned over, intending to cover himself and Ellen at the same time. But instead of capturing his lover in a snug embrace, all his arm met with was bare sheet.

She was gone.

Simon sat up, confused. He *hadn't* been dreaming, had he?

Not possible. He could see the indentation her body had made on the sheets and pillow beside him. Her perfume still hung in the air. Even more conclusive was the empty foil packet next to the clock and the underwear hanging on his bedpost.

He reached forward and retrieved the camisole, moving the whispery fabric across the back of his hand. It was so light, so delicate, like Ellen herself. In fact, she was so light and delicate that she appeared to have vanished into thin air.

He looked around curiously. Where were the rest of her clothes?

Becoming more concerned, he got out of bed, tugged on a pair of Levi's and went to the living room. The light was still on, and Ellen was no longer in his house. When he looked out his window, her car was gone.

She'd sneaked out on him. But why?

Damnation! Simon muttered under his breath as he walked more purposefully back to his bedroom, gathering up his clothes as he went and randomly putting them back on. So much for a leisurely night of lovemaking. So much for dreams coming true.

He'd been all kinds of a fool for not putting on the brakes—but in all fairness, *he* wasn't the only one who'd done the accelerating to begin with. When Ellen had arrived at his door under the lame guise of returning his briefcase, she'd seemed so willing. So eager. It had seemed so natural to take her into his arms, to kiss her. After that, he'd lost control. He admitted it. Week after week of pent-up desire had caused him to snap. He'd only composed himself long enough to ask once whether she was certain she wanted to take this next step. Of course, given the fact that at the time they'd been half naked and all over each other, it could be that she wasn't thinking clearly.

Judging from his empty house, the lady was having more doubts than she admitted to.

Well, if she was, then she would just have to tell him about them now. He wasn't going to wait and give her time to think up excuses and rationalizations for running out on him.

ELLEN FELT LIKE a teenager sneaking guiltily up the back stairs of her parents' house. Only this was about a thousand times worse!

She pulled her car into the driveway, got out and ran up the walkway. In her hurry to confront Abel, she almost tripped over Annie, who was sitting on the top porch step, one hand cradling a diet soda, the other propped morosely against her chin.

At the last minute, Ellen gingerly sidestepped her neighbor. "Annie! What are you doing out here?" She glanced down at her watch. It was almost midnight.

Annie sighed. "Moping."

The answer made Ellen stop and take notice. It wasn't like Annie to mope. "What's the matter?"

Annie clucked her tongue in disgust. "What else?" she asked. "Men!"

Ellen could certainly sympathize with that sentiment. Suddenly, she remembered the music professor. "I guess Cliff didn't turn out to be a prince, huh?"

"Ellen, believe me, the closest that man comes to earning a royal title would be King of the Skinflints." She rolled her eyes just thinking about it. "You know, I didn't want to complain in front of Ted. He was so nice to set us up. And I really didn't mind starting our dinner date at the grocery store, or going out early to catch the movie matinee bargain rate. And I agree that sitting at home listening to the Brandenburg concertos over and over on old LPs is also good, thrifty entertainment. But I don't buy the old 'tipping is un-American' argument."

"You had a fight about how much to tip a waiter?"

"I couldn't help it," Annie admitted. "I used to be a waitress, and believe me, five percent is not acceptable."

Ellen shook her head sadly. "You couldn't find a way to work this out?"

Annie pouted unhappily. "You think I'm too picky, don't you. One little thing bothers me and it's all over. Well, two things. I never liked goatees—do you?"

Ellen lifted her shoulders. ''I'm hardly an authority in these matters,'' she admitted honestly.

''Oh, come on,'' Annie chided. ''You were married to that great guy Ted always talks about, you're out with a different guy every weekend, and now Mr. Suave is chasing you.'' Her bright eyes gave Ellen an assessing once-over. ''Haven't you just come back from a date with him?''

Ellen blushed, and stammered, ''N-no, just a business trip.'' Naturally, she'd been in such a hurry that she'd left her briefcase in Simon's car. Again.

This time it could just stay there till morning.

''Oh, that's right.'' Annie tilted her head skeptically. ''Funny. I never come back from business trips with love bites on my neck.''

Instinctively, Ellen's hand reached up to cover whatever evidence there was of her appalling lack of control.

''Don't worry, it's tiny,'' Annie assured her. ''Your brother probably won't even notice.''

Abel. Ellen threw a careful glance at her door, dreading facing him. ''Have you seen, uh, Ted tonight?''

''What a doll!'' Annie exclaimed. ''You know he promised to set me up with a new guy?''

''He did?''

''Yeah, he says he's a real nice man. Smart, and artistic, too.'' She sighed again. ''Maybe he'll renew my faith in the opposite sex.''

From what she'd seen of Abel's dream boats, Ellen was more apt to fear they would renew one's faith in cloistered celibacy.

''And the best part of all,'' Annie said enthusiastically, ''is that I won't have to worry about him being a cheapskate, because he's a very successful dentist.''

Ellen bit back a groan. ''Martin Mayhew?''

"D.D.S.," Annie confirmed, smugly enunciating each initial. "Do you know him?"

At that moment, she sensed it would have been wrong to rain on Annie's parade. Dreams of Martin Mayhew seemed to be all that was keeping her neighbor together. "No goatee," Ellen said. Unfortunately, he was otherwise about as far as you could get from the perfect hunk Annie had been dreaming of. "Well, I guess I'd better go in and see what Ab—Ted's up to."

Annie frowned, temporarily distracted from her lonely-heart concerns. "Oh, he's been gone for a couple of hours now."

When it was almost midnight? Abel had never stayed out this late before! "Did he say where he was going?"

"Not to me." Annie got up from the stair and went to her own door. "I wouldn't worry about that cool little brother of yours. He can take care of himself."

Ellen frowned as she went into her apartment. Where had he gone?

When she flipped on the light, she got a huge shock. The apartment was clean! Spotless! The weeks of soda cans had been bulldozed away, the house had been vacuumed free of crumbs and orange Cheez Doodles dust, and every surface appeared shiny and clean. Hawthorne came running up to her, clearly disoriented. The place hadn't been this spic-and-span since Abel's return.

Something was terribly, terribly wrong.

Then she caught sight of the little dining table all decked out for a candlelit dinner for two. Her best white linen tablecloth was draped over the table. The places were set with her good china—the china Abel's parents had given them for their wedding—and crystal wineglasses. He had even taken the time to fold the napkins into little shapes and placed them, restaurant-style, in the center of both plates.

That last touch affected her most. How romantic—and so like Abel. She could just picture him sitting on the couch all day, attempting to perfect his folding technique to impress her. But of course, he couldn't have had too much time to practice, given that he had cleaned up so much. He must have really wanted to give her the quiet, romantic evening together that she had craved since his homecoming....

And she had given up on him. Disappointed him. Betrayed him.

Numbing guilt struck her like a punch to the stomach. For a few moments, Ellen couldn't move, couldn't take her eyes off that table. She could just imagine Abel sitting there behind one of those plates, waiting for her to get home. Hour after hour after hour. Had he known where she was?

Ellen was overcome with remorse. How did she know Abel hadn't been watching her all day on the sly? He'd promised not to pop up in her life, but that doesn't mean he hadn't been secretly watching. In which case... She shuddered to think of what he could have seen.

Curious, she strode to the kitchen and opened the refrigerator door. On the top shelf were five cartons of Chinese carry-out, unopened, from their favorite restaurant years back. Ellen kicked the door closed and put a hand to her temple, trying to think, trying to get past the guilt.

Had he decided to move out? He said he couldn't return to heaven unless he did some good deeds, and he hadn't been very successful in that area so far. Which meant that he was probably out trying to make up for lost time. But at midnight? Austin wasn't exactly a den of vice, but neither was it Mr. Rogers' neighborhood. Crazy ghosts with ponytails were apt to meet some bizarre characters.

Her heart started racing at the thought of Abel out there alone, especially if he thought she had deceived him. What if he did something desperate?

Oh, why hadn't she controlled herself better? Why hadn't she come straight home?

She dashed into her bedroom, stripping off her clothes as she went, then changed quickly into a pair of jeans and a red T-shirt and sneakers. She would simply have to comb the city until she found him. It was her fault he was out there, anyway, maybe risking his life so he could get back to heaven.

Leaving one light on, she snatched up her purse and ran to the door. When she threw it open to run outside, a man stood on the other side of the screen. Ellen nearly shrieked with fright.

"Simon!" she cried, her chest deflating once she realized he wasn't an ax murderer. But he was also the last person she expected to have to deal with tonight. She gave him a slow glance, from his boot-clad feet, up the pair of blue jeans that hugged his legs and hips, to the familiar shirt that she herself had stripped off of him mere hours before. Her cheeks heated at the memory.

Then she saw the hard, suspicious glint in his eye. Maybe he wasn't a criminal, but he was looking at her as if *she* were one. And it didn't appear he was going to let her get away.

He raised his fisted hand, at which she involuntarily flinched, only to open it and leave her ivory-colored camisole dangling from his finger by a whispery strap.

"Going somewhere, Ellen?"

Chapter Ten

"You *really* don't have to do this."

"I can't think of any better way to spend a warm summer night," Simon said, but of course that was a lie. In spite of the fact that it was a gorgeous night and the top was down, with Ellen next to him and the stars above them, he couldn't say that cruising hospitals was exactly what he wanted to be doing.

And he was worried. Not only had Ellen divulged the news that she lived with her brother Ted, whom Simon assumed was somewhat eccentric, she appeared hellbent on believing that something disastrous had happened to the guy when there was absolutely no evidence to back up her fears. And she was just as bent on trying to convince Simon that she didn't want him along.

But there was no chance he was letting her out of his sight again, especially not while she intended to be out in the middle of the night going to places like police stations and emergency rooms and the Salvation Army men's shelter.

This Ted must be a little off center, a real black sheep. No wonder she'd been hiding him. Simon assumed that her brother was the shadow he'd seen in Ellen's house the night of her birthday, which made him inordinately happy. But why was she so frantic to find him right this minute? From the sounds of it, Ted, though strange, was a full-grown man.

"Don't take this the wrong way, but are you sure this is about your brother, and not about us?" he asked gingerly as they waited at a red light. After all, in the past half hour, she hadn't mentioned their lovemaking of mere hours before, while he could hardly think of anything else.

She squirmed in the seat next to him. "This has absolutely nothing to do with you, except that you insist on driving. I would get rid of you if I could."

"You can't," Simon replied. "You know, your brother's probably just out having a good time. Kids do that when they're . . . how old, did you say?"

She crossed her arms. "Twenty-three. He's *not* a kid."

He wouldn't have pegged Ellen for being an overprotective big sister. "What does Ted do for a living?" he asked, trying to figure out where her brother might hang out.

Ellen hesitated slightly. "I guess you could say he works for a messenger company." She swallowed. "Most of the time."

"You mean your brother's unemployed?"

"Temporarily," she admitted. "But now I'm afraid he's gone out to find work. . . ."

In the middle of the night? Poor Ellen. She didn't seem to know young men very well at all. "Maybe we should try Sixth Street," Simon suggested, naming the downtown strip known as the hub of the nightclub scene. He didn't want to insinuate that Ted was a ne'er-do-well, but . . .

She sent him a withering look. "We'll try the emergency rooms," she corrected him sternly, her jaw set stiffly. She turned, looked out the window, and sighed. "*Then* we can go down to Sixth Street."

"THIS IS THE LAST ONE," Simon noted as they approached a red-painted door.

At one in the morning, Sixth Street was still alive, but barely. The blare of live music emanated from select clubs; most of them were a bit more subdued, since this was only a Monday night. Or, more precisely, a Tuesday morning.

Ellen tried to edge away from Simon, just in case they did find Abel in the last bar. She had repeatedly tried to convince Simon that this wasn't his business, but he'd insisted on coming. Now, as she stepped across the threshold into a dank, dark pub that smelled of old beer and stale cigarettes, she felt his hand at her waist.

Trying to avoid his touch, she took a half leaping step into the wood-paneled room, nearly tripping over a chair in the process. Simon, of course, reached out to steady her, nearly folding her into an embrace. It was hard to resist the warmth of his arms, even when she was on pins and needles. Smelling his masculine, musky scent, which made her dizzy with memory, didn't help matters any.

Still slightly off balance, but determined to keep her head, Ellen pushed herself away again and immediately spotted Abel at a corner table with two other guys who were practically lookalikes, listening to Elvis on the jukebox and drinking beer. Of course, he'd been watching the whole little scene. His eyes were practically shooting daggers at Simon.

Ellen was seized with conflicting emotions. Relief that Abel was here, safe and sound. Regret that she hadn't been able to ditch Simon. And finally, confusion. Abel hadn't been out risking his life doing good deeds at all. Instead, he'd been out whooping it up with some newfound buddies.

Ellen took a closer look at the flannel-clad fellows he was with. Their skin was pale, as if it hadn't been exposed to anything brighter than the glow of the jukebox, except maybe a halo or two. The one on the left was older, with brown hair that fell across his forehead. He looked strangely familiar—probably because he and Abel and their other buddy were birds of a feather. More slackers from beyond.

Ellen couldn't help feeling a little indignant. She'd been so worried!

Abel glanced up, noting her expression of dismay. "Oh, look, guys," he drawled, "it's Mama Lantry, and does she look ma-a-a-ad!"

That wasn't root beer he was drinking—a fact that caused her a moment of shock. No wonder Abel was being stopped at the pearly gates, if this was the way he behaved!

Now, however, she had to worry about getting him home, not to heaven. "I'm not your mother," she said, adding pointedly, "I'm your *sister*, Ted."

Alerted by her cue, Abel weaved up a little straighter and shot another glare at Simon, who was standing slightly behind her.

The older of his friends looked at him in fuzzy confusion. "Ted? I thought your name was—"

"I lied," Abel said.

The two angels at his side snorted with laughter. "Uh-oh!" one of them cried. "There will be heck to pay for that!"

"You'll be doing cloud duty in Siberia if you don't watch it, bud!" joked the other loose-lipped celestial.

Ellen tapped her toe impatiently and answered Simon's questioning glance with a look that said, *See what I have to contend with?* She was beginning to feel a little maternal at that. If only you could ground angels! "Ted, you haven't met Simon."

Simon held out his hand, and Abel shook it curtly. "Have a sh-seat," he beckoned. "Meet my friends, Jack and Doug."

"Ted," Ellen begged, "it's the middle of the night, and I've been searching all over town for you. Simon will give us a ride home."

"Oh, all right," Abel bit out, throwing Ellen a resentful glance that let her know he thought she was the biggest kill-joy who ever walked. At this point she barely cared.

Out drinking! Before he'd earned his wings, even, Abel was turning into a fallen angel. Of course, *her* behavior to-night hadn't been exemplary, either. She remembered her blissful abandon at Simon's house and felt a blush heat her cheeks.

"It was nice meeting you," Simon said politely to Jack and Doug as he snaked an arm about Ellen's waist.

They smiled, then waved to Abel. "Nice seeing ya, bud. Have to do it again sometime."

Abel shuffled out behind her and Simon. Feeling self-conscious about him staring at Simon's arm looped around her, Ellen attempted to step out of his embrace, but only managed to do an awkward side hop, and tripped on an uneven floorboard.

"You're having more trouble staying on your feet than I am tonight," Abel noted bitingly.

Ellen frowned at him as Simon reached out and caught her arm. "Are you okay?" he asked. His voice dripped concern.

"I just tripped."

"Maybe Simon can *carry* you out to the car," Abel sniped.

She glared at him and walked on ahead. This was the first time the two men had—knowingly—been in each other's presence, and it was turning out to be every bit as awkward as she had feared. When they reached the Jeep, she pulled the seat back for Abel and got into the front herself, leaving him to stew behind her. She looked in the rearview mirror and saw him slumped back there, with his arms crossed and a pout on his lips as he looked from her to Simon.

She felt guilt wash over her anew. Whatever it was Abel suspected had happened between her and Simon couldn't be too far from the truth.

Simon glanced at Abel in the rearview mirror. "You know, that friend of yours named Jack…he looked sort of like Jack Kerouac. You know, the writer from the Fifties?"

A chill shot through Ellen. *That's* who that had been! All this time, she'd thought Abel had been joking about being able to make introductions to famous ghosts.

"Yeah, some coincidence, huh?" Abel said, smiling enigmatically. "You two have a nice trip to San Antonio?" he called up to the front.

Simon, oblivious to the tension between the two of them—or perhaps just unaware of his own role in it—answered, "Sure did." He turned a million-dollar smile on Ellen. "Didn't we?"

Ellen winced.

"You were gone long enough," she heard Abel mutter. "I waited dinner."

She felt herself seeping down farther in her seat. "Oh, Abel, I saw. I'm so sorry."

"We went out to unwind a little afterward," Simon explained before she could stop him. "Had a little fun."

She hazarded a glance back. Abel was not amused.

But what right did he have to be angry? For weeks he'd been ignoring her, pushing her out the door, throwing men in her path. Now she even suspected Simon was one of those men. This wasn't exactly a situation of her own making.

Or maybe it was. She'd had a choice. She could have just picked up the briefcase and driven home. Abel had probably been there at the time, waiting for her.

She felt as low as a worm.

"Here we are," Simon announced as they pulled up in front of her house minutes later.

Before Ellen could step out of the car, Abel vaulted out of the back seat, mumbled a quick "thanks for the ride" to Simon, and headed inside.

Simon looked over at her and smiled. "Guess he sensed we wanted to be alone?"

Ellen was horrified by the idea. "Look, Simon, we can't—"

"I know," he admitted, "it's late. I can see now why you're so tired all the time. You've obviously got your hands full at home. Why didn't you tell me about your brother?"

She shrugged mutely.

He laughed. "And to think, I was so jealous. I couldn't imagine what you were hiding in that apartment."

She chuckled along, then frowned. "Why didn't you ask?"

He looked at her as though the answer were obvious. "I respect your privacy, Ellen. And it wasn't as though I thought you were hiding a secret lover behind those closed blinds." He laughed again. "Not for long, at any rate."

She stared at him in amazement, feeling more duplicitous by the moment. "Look, Simon—"

"I know. We need to talk."

"No—"

"Tomorrow," he said. "You must be tired right now."

She sighed. "Yes, I guess I am." And anyway, she wasn't sure *what* to say at this point. Abel was angry, Simon was amorous, and she was torn between the two of them.

Quickly, Simon leaned over and planted a tender kiss on her cheek. At the light brush, every atom in Ellen's body screamed for her to turn and meet his lips with her own, to throw her arms around him. Before she could even react, however, he reached across her and popped open her car door. "Good night," he said.

Ellen sucked in a steadying breath and stumbled out of the Jeep, not sure if she was ready to face Abel just yet, but not really having any alternative. Life had been much, much easier back when she was a *lonely* widow.

"And Ellen..."

She turned, and he sent her a last, brief grin. "Don't be too hard on the kid," he told her. "Remember how rough it was when you were his age."

Not nearly so rough as it is now, she wanted to tell him. She sent him a nod and a limp wave as he drove off down the street.

When she entered the living room, Abel was on the couch, waiting for her, the scowl on his face utterly predictable. He hadn't even turned the television on.

Ellen swallowed anxiously. That was a very bad sign.

"Hungry?" he asked peevishly. "There's Chinese in the fridge. But of course, you and *Simon* probably ate already."

She moaned. "Oh, Abel—I'm so sorry. If I had only known..."

"Would it have made any difference?"

"Of course! You can't imagine how worried I was when I came home. I went to the hospitals, police stations—"

He looked up. "You did all that?"

She nodded. "I thought maybe you were so anxious to leave that you were out doing good deeds and had run into trouble again. I was nearly out of my mind with worry." *And guilt,* a voice in the back of her head reminded her.

"Your disappearance just came at the wrong time. I think I've had one of the strangest days of my life—well, since the day you showed up, at any rate." She arched an eyebrow. "By the way, I met Mrs. Samuelson."

For the first time tonight, a genuine smile lit up his face. "That was the first part of my surprise for you today."

"For me?" Ellen asked.

"Of course. What did you think? I knew how much you sympathized with Mr. Samuelson."

"I thought maybe you meant the opposite . . . that maybe *we* weren't meant to be together."

"No way!" Abel said, shooting up from the couch. "Weren't they happy together?"

Ellen felt tears burn in her eyes. How sweet of Abel to engineer the reunion just for her. Why hadn't she understood that was what he was doing? "They nearly broke my heart. They were so happy, so romantic."

"I knew they would be. Unfortunately, I only seem to have succeeded in getting you in a romantic mood for someone else's benefit. Or maybe you just don't like me anymore."

"Oh, Abel!" Ellen cried, sure her face was flaming. "That's not true. I only. . ." How could she explain? She walked over to the couch, taking Abel's hand as she passed. "I just got so confused. I couldn't understand, if you could bring Vern and Louise together, why we couldn't be that happy, too. I thought you were telling me that we weren't one of those one in a million couples."

He sank down on the couch next to her. "How could you think that, babe? I did it for you, to show you that we were. I guess maybe you don't have much faith in me."

Hearing the words put her to shame. For four years, she'd pined away for this man—or ghost, or fledgling angel, or whatever he was. Her faithfulness to him had known no bounds, not even those of heaven and earth. Now, within the space of a few weeks after he'd returned to her, she had already taken him for granted.

How had that happened?

She kept trying to think of ways to believe that it wasn't her fault. But it wasn't Simon's. And it wasn't as if she and Simon were in love, either. They'd just lost their heads. But even losing her head wasn't like her. She was sure she never would have slept with Simon under normal circumstances. Abel had to be meddling....

How, then, could she explain the Chinese dinner he'd arranged while she and Simon were together?

She took a deep breath, screwing up courage to ask the question that had been plaguing her all evening. "Abel, did you get Simon his job at Smith?"

Again he denied it. "Of course not. I never saw the guy until that day in his office."

Ellen wasn't sure she believed him. "But you know, he showed up around the time you took out that personal ad."

"Give me a break."

She sat up a little straighter. "What?"

"I can't believe you'd think I'd actually send you one of *those*."

"One of what?" Ellen persisted.

He rolled his eyes. "One of those smooth operators women really fall for. I told you how I felt about the guy."

At the time, Ellen had thought he was merely jealous. Now she worried that Abel truly did have a better perspective on Simon than she did. God knows, it was hard for her to keep her head on straight when she was around him. Maybe she wasn't the best judge of his character.

"Some men are just untrustworthy," Abel lectured her, "and that Simon's one of them."

Untrustworthy? Simon? Something inside her balked at the idea—or was this simply more of her naiveté showing. "What makes you think so?"

He let out a disbelieving sputter. "Please! Say, you aren't hopelessly smitten with this guy or anything, are you?"

She was more than smitten; she was completely embroiled. But she couldn't tell Abel that. "No, no," she said, getting up and pacing anxiously. "I just thought that maybe you'd had something to do with him. He keeps talking about fate."

Abel looked at her as if she were completely naive. "Get a grip! That's just what a guy like that would talk about. Don't you remember what your mother told you? Men like him are just after one thing. After that, they cool down fast enough."

The thought made her suck in a shocked breath. Simon wasn't like that! she wanted to scream.

But what if he was?

Yet his smiles, his teasing, his openness—it all seemed so sincere. "Simon is Mr. Honesty," she defended.

"Yeah, right," Abel muttered. "Believe you me, I bet it won't be long before you see his true colors. Scratch Mr. Honesty and I bet you'll find Mr. Heel." He turned on the television with the remote and leaned back. Ellen followed suit. He seemed surprised. "Aren't you going to bed?"

"No, I'd rather stay here with you for a while."

He smiled, a warm, beckoning smile, and she put her head on his shoulder and sighed. "This is nice."

"Just like old times," Abel said. He switched to a movie channel that was playing a black-and-white Cary Grant film, something she actually liked to watch.

"Don't ever think I lack faith in you, Abel," she said, "or that I don't like you anymore. It isn't even a matter of 'like.' I love you."

"I know," he said, resting his chin against the crown of her head.

The words should have struck her as arrogant, cocky, lacking in maturity, but they didn't. It seemed so natural to be sitting here with him, such a relief after the tense day.

And yet, when she tried to focus on Cary Grant, another dark-haired, dark-eyed man came to mind. When she thought of Simon, the man she knew, Abel's warnings about him sounded so ridiculous. Yet she couldn't completely discount his admonitions. After all, he was, in a sense, a higher authority.

At the same time, images of the day kept swirling through her mind—the Samuelsons, dancing with Simon, making love with Simon....

Abel *couldn't* be right. The very idea of Simon being the manipulative type was laughable.

So why wasn't she laughing?

HE WAS LOSING HER. What a bummer!

Abel hadn't missed the look in Simon's eyes when he stared at Ellen. The man was completely besotted. Genuinely.

And then there was Ellen herself. She'd been flustered, and had blushed every time Simon had opened his mouth or even looked at her. And the times he had actually touched her, she'd practically tripped all over herself. Who was she kidding?

Even now as she stared with glazed eyes at the TV screen, he knew she was thinking of Simon.

He knew he should be happy for her. Hadn't he thrown himself into the task of making men fall in love with his wife? Now she was turning to someone else, just as he'd asked her to. But it wasn't at all how he'd expected it to be.

Not for him, at least.

The real trouble was this Simon guy. He was so obviously all wrong for Ellen. Who was he, anyway? Some lawyer. A big noise. He'd thought Ellen would have more imagination in her choice of mates than that.

Simon. He clucked his tongue in disgust. But what could he do? Ellen seemed to like him.

Maybe he'd been harsh, telling her the guy was a phony. He didn't know whether he was or not. But it was good to keep Ellen's guard up, just in case. When it came to men, she was just a babe in the woods.

But was Simon the wolf he'd painted him as being?

Suddenly, a devilish little smile tugged at his lips. Maybe he was or maybe he wasn't, but Abel was certain he wasn't the man for Ellen. So what would it hurt if he just stepped in and hurried things along their natural course? It wasn't as if he was killing Ellen's odds of ever finding someone. He would just be helping her be more *selective.* He had all the time eternity had to offer; he could just stick around until he found someone appropriate for her.

And in the meantime, he would be there to lend Ellen a shoulder to cry on when she discovered that Simon Miller wasn't the pillar of virtue she thought he was.

"YOU KNOW WHAT Simon said to me the other day?" Yolanda asked, hovering around the water cooler as Ellen stooped to get a drink. This was the second time today that Yolanda had sneaked away to whisper something about Simon in Ellen's ear. Not that Ellen could think of anything else!

As Ellen drank down a cup of water, Yolanda continued, "He asked, 'Any messages?' and I said, 'No,' and he said, 'Okay, thanks.' "

Ellen waited for a punchline that never came. "That's it?"

Yolanda giggled. "That's it. Just 'Okay, thanks,' in that sexy voice of his." She giggled again. "Isn't that cute?"

Giggling? It wasn't exactly normal Yolanda behavior. Of course, years on the phone had made her hypersensitive to people's voices, and Simon did have an exceptionally sexy one. Maybe she'd just now taken notice, unbelievable as that seemed.

Still, thinking about Abel's words of the night before, about Simon being untrustworthy, Ellen decided that Yolanda might be just the right person to provide her with some useful information. "Does Simon get many calls from women?" she asked, keeping her tone as nonchalant as she could.

"Not usually," Yolanda answered. "Just clients, mostly. Sometimes an older woman calls—his mother, I think."

Ellen nodded, feeling vindicated in her trust of the man.

"But that was before today."

Her stomach flopped over anxiously. "What happened today?"

"What *hasn't* happened, you mean," Yolanda corrected her. "That phone hasn't stopped ringing all day. I've been flooded with calls for Simon—and the man's not even here yet!"

Ellen's lips turned down in a frown. She hadn't noticed that he wasn't around the office yet. Where was he? "These calls he's getting . . . are they work-related?"

Yolanda snorted in derision. "All I've heard this morning are young, sexy female voices purring on the other line."

Her mouth felt thoroughly dry. "Really?" She could hardly believe it. But why would Yolanda lie?

When she looked up, she saw the man himself coming down the hall toward his office, looking like a wreck. His dark hair was so mussed it was practically standing up on end, his tie was loosened with one end flapping over his shoulder, and his white shirt had grass stains all over it.

"What happened!" Ellen exclaimed. Even so disheveled, the sensuality in his eyes and movement struck her like a blow.

"You look like you were run over by a truck!" Yolanda said.

"Actually," he correctly her wryly, "it was a police car."

SIMON SHOOK HIS HEAD as he watched Ellen bite into her burger. "I don't get it. Why on today of all days would every woman in Austin wanting a divorce try to call me?"

But Ellen was still preoccupied with the policewoman who had stopped him this morning. "You say you got those grass stains trying to get her car unstuck?" she asked skeptically, looking at him as though she thought he'd taken a roll in the hay with the lady cop.

"Yes!" he cried in frustration. "I don't even know why she stopped me in the first place. I could have sworn my license tags were up to date."

She stared at him as if he were a criminal. And why not? He'd spent a better part of the morning in the back of a police car. The aura of crime had probably rubbed off on him.

"Now, what about these women?" she asked, bringing him back to problem number two.

It was the damnedest thing. Eleven women he'd never heard of all decided to call him in the space of two hours. It was the sort of freak occurrence Larry Lambert probably dreamed of—but to Simon it seemed more like a headache. "I guess I'll try to field some of them out to other attorneys," he said. "I'm pretty full right now."

Ellen, across the table from him, remained silent.

He reached across and grabbed her hand. "This is so frustrating. I bounced out of bed this morning, eager to see you, to talk to you, and now all I've done is complain the whole time we've been out."

"Don't worry," Ellen told him, pulling on her hand to retrieve it. She picked a french fry off her plate and nibbled at it. "It's been very...educational."

Uh-oh. He didn't like the sound of that. He opened his mouth to speak, but the waitress came by to refill his iced tea. It was her fourth trip over to the table in under a half hour, and he was beginning to feel waterlogged.

"Can I tempt you with dessert?" the waitress asked, slipping an extra lemon into his tea with a wink. She barely splashed Ellen's empty glass. "Flan, mousse...me?" She let out a flirtatious laugh.

Simon smiled halfheartedly. "No, thanks," he told her. "Ellen?"

Ellen's eyes had widened incredulously, and she barely bit back a laugh as she told the waitress, "None for me, either." When the waitress was out of earshot, she said to Simon, "I doubt she was offering me the same selection."

Simon lifted his shoulders, completely confused. "I don't get it. Why me?"

She looked at him sharply. "Maybe women just gravitate toward you naturally."

"Are you saying I'm some kind of playboy?" he asked.

Her expression turned serious, as if she were about to turn the subject to what had happened last night, when suddenly she glanced up. "Don't look now, but it appears your troubles aren't over yet."

Simon swung around in his seat and nearly groaned. Two well-dressed women were bearing down on their table—and it was too late to duck away.

"Simon Miller!" one of them squealed. She was a well-dressed woman, about his age, with long blond hair. "Don't you remember? We all went to law school together!"

She and her companion, a petite brunette, stared at him with unblinking expectation. "I'm Trisha," the brunette said, trying to jog his memory.

Simon smiled blankly, his mind a panic. "Well, what a surprise!" He couldn't remember these two for the life of him.

The brunette, Trisha, sent a knowing smirk to her companion. "We went out for two months, and he doesn't even recognize me!"

Two months?

Across the table, Ellen stared at the women, stunned, then looked at her watch and tossed down some money. "I told Harlan I'd be back by one," she said, nearly breaking his heart when she pushed her chair back and got up. There was still so much he wanted to tell her, so much they hadn't discussed . . .

Wouldn't he have remembered someone named Trisha?

"Oh, did we interrupt something?" the other woman asked, plopping herself heedlessly in Ellen's vacated seat.

With a heavy heart, Simon watched Ellen retreat into the busy restaurant. Would he ever get to sit down and talk to her, heart to heart?

Would he ever be free of all these women?

Chapter Eleven

Ellen hesitated to go in, yet she felt drawn to Simon's house like a magnet. It was no use sitting around her place, trying not to think of him, pretending to be interested in television shows she hadn't enjoyed since she was ten. The more she moped around the house, the more she felt Abel's eyes watching her, waiting for her to tell him he was right.

And the more compelled she felt to pay Simon a visit, to prove that Abel was wrong.

Or was he? Simon hadn't seemed to do anything to encourage women to swarm around him today. He just had a charming personality. Naturally women would flock to him. She just hadn't noticed this before now because she'd been one of the flock herself.

She'd been so certain he would call this evening. Or maybe even come over. After last night, after the emotion he'd moved inside her when they made love, she was so certain Abel had been wrong. Of course, that certainty had been sorely shaken when she'd witnessed him being unable even to recognize someone he'd gone out with for two months!

But the phone had remained silent, and no one had come to the door except her paperboy for a renewal. And here she was. But what should she do now? There was no briefcase to ease her way this time. She was sure she was showing a pitiable lack of restraint in even coming this close to knocking on his door.

Gathering her courage, she finally stepped out of the car. Now that she was on her feet she felt much better, especially when she remembered the forlorn look on Simon's face when she'd abandoned him to Trisha. He would probably be *glad* to see her.

After taking what she considered an eternity to answer his buzzer, Simon finally opened the door. It looked as if he'd just got back from the office, which made Ellen feel somewhat relieved. If he'd been working late, that would explain a lot. He was still wearing his suit pants and shirt, although his tie was gone and his dark hair was mussed.

"Ellen!" He stepped forward slightly, his expression agitated. "What are you doing here?"

She crossed her arms anxiously. *What are you doing here* was never a good sign. Neither was the fact that he was practically throwing himself in front of her line of vision into the house. "Have I come at a bad time?" she asked. As though the answer weren't obvious!

"Well . . . yes," he said frankly. "Actually, I was just on my way to see you, but I've had a surprise visitor and—"

Trisha, no doubt, Ellen thought, biting her lip.

"Why don't you ask her in, Simon?" a voice called from behind him. A *feminine* voice.

Simon, with tiny beads of nervous sweat practically popping out on his brow, groaned quietly. "Ellen, this is awful," he said in a low voice. "You won't believe what's happened. . . ."

"Let me guess," she said. "At lunch you and Trisha got caught in a time warp."

"Trisha?" He spoke the name as if he'd already forgotten her again. "No, I left her back at the restaurant. But you see, I was just on my way to your house when I found Jennifer on my doorstep."

"Jennifer?" The name came as a sharp shock. This was the woman he'd gone out with before, his old co-worker.

His mussed hair and loose, rumpled appearance suddenly took on a whole new meaning... all of it pointing to the fact that Ellen was creating a very awkward situation. Hadn't she noted his adorably rumpled hair after they had made love? She felt her face flush red with mortification.

"Why don't you come inside?" Simon asked her.

Her mouth dropped open in astonishment. Did he think she had no pride at all? "No, thank you," she said, trying to gather her wits. "I just thought I would drop by."

She knew the excuse sounded lame, but his wasn't much better. "This isn't the way it looks," he defended.

"Well, whatever it is, three's usually a crowd, anyway. I'm sure we'll have plenty of chances to speak to each other at work."

She pivoted to leave, but he reached out a hand to stop her.

"Do you mean that?" he asked, looking into her eyes pleadingly.

A part of her wanted him to at least *try* to explain right now. To tell her that Jennifer was only passing through, or, better yet, that Jennifer was here to ask him to be best man at her remarriage to her ex-husband. Anything.

But another, stronger part of her just wanted to bolt away from the door as fast as she could. Because deep down she feared the real explanation would be that Jennifer had left her husband again.... And remembering how torn up Simon had said he was after he lost Jennifer, she would have to be happy for him getting a second chance. Just as she was happy for the Samuelsons. And herself, when Abel had come back.

She tugged her arm free. "Of course I mean it," she said, not sure whether she was lying or not.

"Ellen, wait—"

But she didn't wait. She didn't stop moving until she was in her car at a red light two blocks away, and then she collapsed in a nervous, confused heap against her steering wheel. Abel, it seemed, was right.

How could she have misjudged someone so completely?

"PICK CHERRIES!" Harlan Smith bellowed over the heads of his staff. "Ready? One, two, three..."

Ellen picked listlessly. A day had passed, but the few times Simon had attempted to call her, someone—someone *female*—had beeped in on his call waiting. Last night after she returned home she'd given up even answering the phone and had spent the evening over at Annie's. Her neighbor was excited about her upcoming date with Martin Mayhew, but Ellen was skeptical. Annie was trying to keep an open mind about this one, but anyone as picky as she was might be apt to be turned off by a man hypersensitive about tooth decay.

Ellen sighed and lifted her hands high above her head, following Harlan Smith's lead. Down the hall on her desk were two bouquets of flowers and several Post-It notes' worth of apologies from Simon, all of them saying that he could "explain" Jennifer. Meanwhile, every woman in the office had made a circle around him during the afternoon stretch. Suddenly, he'd become inapproachable—by her, at least.

Of course this, as Abel had said, was the way men like Simon preferred to operate. Even though Simon had Jennifer hanging around him, he probably wanted to keep Ellen in the palm of his hand—just in case—which would explain the few charmingly worded yellow stick 'ums. She felt like a fool.

But she wasn't going to be blinded by the flower treatment again. Not this time.

As for Monday night, she tried not to think about that. Maybe four years of chaste living had simply made her hormones go temporarily haywire. But she couldn't so much as look at Simon without remembering the feel of his hands roaming her body, or wanting to relive those endless moments of passion she'd experienced with him. Being in his arms hadn't felt like meaningless desire.

As she did a twist from the waist, she saw Simon, twisting the wrong way, gesticulating at her and mouthing something she tried her best not to understand. She practically popped her hip out of joint in her attempt to turn away, to pretend she hadn't noticed him. That became harder as he began to edge his way toward her. They performed a subtle pas de deux, snaking through their sweaty colleagues. The minute the afternoon stretch was over, she darted for the door.

"Whoa, Ellen," Harlan called after her. The big boss caught the back of her shirt, forcing her to stop. "I'm glad to see these stretches give you so much vim and pep!"

She smiled limply—until she saw Simon coming up behind Harlan.

"I just wanted to tell you what a great job you did with Mr. Samuelson. Everybody's happy."

"Oh, don't thank me," Ellen said. *Thank my late husband.*

"I know, it was teamwork." Harlan beamed, his silver hair like a halo around his head. "That's the spirit I like to see! And to that end, I've decided I've been hogging your services. Maybe I should pair you up with some of the other associates more often. You and Simon work well with each other."

Ellen nearly choked, especially when she saw Simon's smile as he bore down on them. "Pairing up" with Simon again was just what she was trying to avoid!

"What a wonderful idea," Simon said enthusiastically.

Harlan turned. "Then you agree I've been hogging Ellen?"

Simon glanced over at her. "Naturally, I can understand that impulse."

Oh, brother. Ellen had the impulse to flee, and she went with it, glancing quickly at her watch. "I—I think I hear my phone," she blurted out.

"From here?" Harlan seemed shocked by the announcement. And why not? Her cubicle was half a building away from where they were standing.

Fortunately, before Simon could catch up with her, Yolanda snagged him in the hallway. "Eight more messages for you, Simon," she heard the receptionist admonish him.

Ellen barely left her desk for the rest of the day, dreading the prospect of running into Simon. To be truthful, she half expected him to pay her a visit, or at least ring her at her desk. Instead, he avoided her, which left her feeling like a rabbit being chased by an invisible wolf.

At the stroke of five, she grabbed her purse, crept away from her cubicle and made a dash for the elevators. When the doors closed, she sank back against the wall in relief. She'd made it through one day—surely it would become easier with time. All she wanted now was to go home, change into jeans and spend the rest of the night with Abel, relaxing. Maybe she could go a whole evening without once thinking of the name Jennifer.

Besides, now it would be her and Abel again, just as she always wanted it to be. All these weeks, she'd thought he'd been neglecting her, when maybe it was the other way around. She tried to imagine cozying up together on the couch—although it was hard to be cozy in a room that was sixty degrees. Perhaps she'd invest in an electric blanket on her way home.

She went out into the bright early evening and strode briskly down the sidewalk—but not fast enough. From behind her came the sounds of someone running, sprinting right up to her. And before she could even turn to see who it was, she felt herself being lifted—no, hoisted!—over that someone's shoulders. Ellen yelped in dismay.

"Put me down!" she hollered. "Help!"

Stray office workers stopped and glanced around, their eyes bugging as they saw her being abducted by a tall man in a gray suit and dark sunglasses. Ellen managed to look down and get a glimpse of his face. Just as she suspected!

"Simon! What are you doing?"

"Kidnapping you," he replied evenly, loping toward his Jeep. He slowed only enough to dump her into the back seat and then hopped in front and peeled out of the parking lot. Before she knew what was what, they were headed north on the expressway that skirted the town.

"This is insanity!" she cried, poking her head between the front seats.

"It's also the only way I can get you to talk to me."

"I *would* talk to you," she said, "but we always seemed to be interrupted."

"If you'll just give me a chance to explain . . ."

Not that she had any choice in the matter now, she thought crossly. By ducking out of work right on time, they had managed to beat the worst rush hour traffic, and within minutes Simon darted off an exit and took the Jeep up several winding backroads.

"Where are we going?" Ellen asked.

"Mount Bonnell."

"That's where teenagers go to make out!" Ellen protested.

He waggled his eyebrows in the rearview mirror. "It's early yet. Maybe we'll beat the crowds there, too."

They did. Simon pulled up to the curb and offered her his arm as she stepped out of the car. To their right was a steep stairway cut into a rocky hill. Ellen balked, but he gave her a gentle shove forward, reminding her that she was, technically, a prisoner.

After climbing more than was probably wise in her work shoes, she came to a huffing, puffing halt at the edge of a steep hill overlooking Lake Austin. She'd never even been here before, but she could instantly see why the place was a favorite with kids. The view, as the Clearasil crowd would say, was awesome.

Simon took her hand and led her over to a bench, onto which she gratefully collapsed. "This place must have more steps leading up to it than Mount Olympus!"

He sent her a mirthful glance. "Good, maybe now that you're all tuckered out, you'll listen to what I have to say."

"I told you, I *would* have listened to you back down at sea level. *I'm* not the problem."

"But that's just it!" he said in exasperation. "I'm not, either. Do you know what torture it's been to spend the past days thinking about you—about us—and Monday night, and not be able to see you alone?"

His words were like a balm, but Ellen tried to remain objective. "Then what about Trisha?"

He shook his head. "I don't know her! Then, yesterday night I was on my way to see you, to explain all about her, but when I opened my door Jennifer was standing there. I had no idea where she came from. We haven't seen each other for almost a half a year."

"She just drove down all that way, without calling first?"

He nodded. "She said she and her husband were having problems, so she decided to come see me. Can you beat that?"

"It certainly seems odd."

"The frustrating part was that she couldn't tell me exactly what was wrong with her marriage—just that she woke up that morning feeling unhappy. And that she had to see me." He shook his head. "That's what she kept saying—that she just *had* to come see me. Like some sort of weird compulsion."

A terrible niggling suspicion was developing in the back of Ellen's mind. But it just couldn't be... "What exactly spurred her to come see *you?*"

"Now, this is really strange," Simon ruminated. "She said she opened up the paper, and there was an ad for Smith in the paper, and my name was listed. Why would Smith be advertising in a Dallas paper?"

"I don't know," Ellen lied. She knew exactly why.

"That's why I was such a mess when you came by," he went on to explain. "I'd been listening to her story for nearly an hour, pressing her for details that she couldn't provide. Poor woman. I felt sorry for her, but in the end I sent her back to Eddie. I think she just got nostalgic or something."

"Or something," Ellen agreed. And she knew exactly what that something was—more of Abel's meddling handiwork, in a slightly more twisted design.

An angel? He was behaving more like a devil now!

She began to seethe, thinking about the torturous day she'd spent, doubting poor Simon. And herself. She'd been convinced that she had behaved recklessly, foolishly. And perhaps she had, but she hadn't been completely wrong about Simon. Abel no doubt was also behind all of the women who'd been plaguing him in the past few days, too.

Her late husband had ensured that Simon had no free moment to speak to her, and he'd done it in such a way that would raise doubts about him.

Simon took her hand and asked tenderly, "You didn't really think I didn't care for you, did you?"

"I guess I've been sort of mixed-up lately."

"You've just been under stress, because of your brother."

"You've got that right."

He nodded. "You shouldn't let him run your life. I can understand your worrying about him, but he needs to learn to take responsibility for himself."

Ellen's jaw worked furiously as she thought about it. Abel *was* trying to run her life! What's more, he was being scheming and deceptive about it.

"You know," Simon told her in a low voice, "someday you're going to have to let him go."

"Oh, he'll be around forever," Ellen said, still steaming.

Simon laughed. "But someday you won't be."

His statement brought her up short. "Where will I be?"

He dropped a kiss on her lips, then looked at her with that aching tenderness she was beginning to know well. "Have you ever thought about getting married again, Ellen?"

Married?

She jumped so high she nearly fell off the cliff. Shooting to her feet, she leapt at least three flagstones away from Simon before turning. Seeing her shock, he stood abruptly. "Did I say something wrong?"

"I've *never* thought about getting married again," she said adamantly.

He held up his hands in a calming gesture. "Look, I'm sorry. I didn't mean to upset you."

"I'm not upset!" she cried. "I just think that's a little premature, to say the least."

Simon looked bewildered. "But after Monday, and then Monday night, I just assumed that things had...progressed...a little."

Ellen felt heat wash over her just at the memory. "Of course they have," she admitted, forcing herself to calm down. What he said was only logical, from his perspective. But *marriage?* That would never work—it couldn't! She was married already. He couldn't get the idea that their relationship was anything more than a...

Well, what *would* you call it? Given her odd position, she lacked the correct vocabulary for what Simon was to her.

"Listen, forget what I just said," Simon said, hazarding a few steps forward and taking her hands again. He pulled her gently to him and looped his arms around her waist. "We'll take things one step at a time."

It was like when they'd danced together. Fitting herself against Simon this way felt so right. Her hands naturally seemed to snake their way up his chest, around his neck. He kissed her again, more passionately this time, and she let all the tensions and doubts she'd built up over the past days melt away as he held her closely in the evening light. All except one.

One step at a time...it sounded good in theory. But how could she tell Simon that the top step was already occupied by an angel?

Or, more correctly, a devil?

"WHAT KIND OF ANGEL are you!"

Abel looked up in surprise and pressed the mute button on "Gilligan's Island." "What do you mean?"

Ellen dropped her purse in the chair by the door and looked at her late husband through narrowed eyes. "Don't try to play innocent with me, Abel. You've been plaguing Simon all week."

"Have not," he said petulantly.

Ellen rolled her eyes. "Thirty divorce clients just happen to drop in on him in a two-day period?" she asked, ticking off his laundry list of offenses. "A cop stops him and he spends half a morning in a police car? *Two* old girlfriends show up out of the blue?"

His lips twisted in a lopsided pout. "I only did it to show you what kind of person he really was."

"But that was you, not him! The Simon I know doesn't have the faults you accuse him of." She paced furiously across the little rug by the couch. "And to think you sat there just two nights ago, lecturing me about having faith in you!"

He pulled his long hair out of its ponytail and shook it out for a moment, thinking. When he looked back up, his brown eyes were mournful. "I guess I'll have to go, then."

"Oh, not tonight, Abel," she said, growing exasperated. "I always get so nervous when you go out on your good deed runs. And they never work."

"I mean forever, Ellen."

Her heart stopped beating. "What?"

"If you're going to be like this," he told her challengingly, "then I'll just have to go back to heaven."

She couldn't be sure if he was serious or not. Most likely this was just a heated threat. "But why?"

"I would think that's obvious. You're in love."

Ellen felt herself drop into the chair, and she sat before him, stunned. "That's not true!"

He rolled his eyes. "Yeah, right."

"But it's not," she insisted. Why was everyone being so difficult today?

"Listen to the way you talk about the guy," he said, a hint of disgust in his tone.

"But that was only because I felt sorry for him," she defended. "Simon's a nice person, a good friend...."

Abel looked her straight in the eye. "I think your good friend smudged your lipstick," he drawled.

Automatically, Ellen's hand lifted to her lips, so recently kissed. A wave of guilt crashed over her. "Oh, Abel," she begged, "don't get the wrong idea." But that wasn't the problem, she realized. Abel had the right idea...*she* was the one in the wrong.

He shook his head sadly, looking away. "I don't want to make you miserable, Ellen."

"You don't!" she protested, moving to the couch.

He shrugged, then confessed, "I never guessed how hard it would be to watch you fall for another guy. That's why I did what I did. I was jealous, like you said. All those years in heaven, I was rooting for you, babe. I wanted to see you happy, I really did. But when push came to shove...I couldn't stand the thought of you with someone else."

His words touched her like none he'd spoken since his return. They brought back the memory of how she'd felt for so long. Completely bereft. All those years, it had seemed like she was just sleepwalking through life. If she felt different now, it was only because she had Abel back. Without him, her life had been heartbreakingly lonely.

And how would he be if he left here? She tried to imagine him up in heaven again, without her, away from the life he loved so much.

Tears filled her eyes. "I was so alone without you, Abel," she said. "Sometimes I used to wonder how I would keep going."

He nodded. "I hear you. The other night, when I saw how Simon looked at you, I thought I was losing you forever."

Ellen's heart hurt. She felt so torn. A tear splashed down her cheek and onto the hand that Abel was holding. She looked at their hands, joined together, and remembered their hasty, giddy wedding, right after her twenty-third birthday. Their days together had been so few. Maybe that's why it was so hard to think about letting go.

Maybe that's why she simply *couldn't* let go.

Whatever pain it cost her, she knew she had to make a decision, now. For nearly a month, Abel had been trying to make it easier for her, but she'd been living in halves, which wasn't fair to herself or anybody else. Especially not Simon.

She blinked, then looked up at him. "Abel," she confessed, "Simon did mention something about marriage tonight."

He held his breath.

"I told him it wasn't a possibility. And I meant it."

Abel looked relieved, but said, "That still doesn't mean I'm not in the way here...."

"You're not," she assured him. It was now or never. For days she'd been emotionally limping along, half attached to two men, somehow entertaining the harebrained notion that they could all work something out. But that wasn't going to happen. She knew that now. The decision was up to her.

She took a heavy, painful breath and announced, "I'm not going out with Simon anymore. It's over."

For the first time in what seemed like ages, a genuine smile touched Abel's crooked mouth. "I know it's been bumpy these past few weeks, but from now on, we're going to be together and happy, forever, like the Samuelsons."

"Forever." She smiled sadly.

"This calls for a celebration. A big one!" Abel tapped his chin thoughtfully. "Now... what excuse do we have coming up for having the mother of all parties?"

Ellen shook her head. He was shameless. "Could you be thinking of your birthday?" It was a week and a half away.

Abel snapped his fingers. "I knew there was something I was forgetting!"

"I bet you would have remembered," Ellen said wryly.

"I'll have to get to work on the plans, and the guest list. Anyone from work you want to come?"

Ellen frowned, remembering at least one person she would have loved to invite. But that couldn't happen now. She was resolved.

Abel reached out with his hand and tilted her chin up so that she couldn't help but look at him. "Hey...are you sure this is what you want?"

"I'm sure," Ellen said. But when she hugged her arms around Abel's chest, the only thing she was sure of was that this was the hardest choice she'd ever had to make in her life.

NORMALLY, ELLEN WAS a Christmas and Easter churchgoer. But ever since Abel came back, she'd been a regular.

At the end of the Sunday service, she got up and made her way out with the rest of the congregation. For the past week she'd trudged along, getting back to a routine, straightening out her life. Abel was in a good mood, planning for his party. Ellen had called up the university and found out when law school classes began in the fall. No more deferments. Finally she was fulfilling the dreams she'd always had for herself. And once classes began, she wouldn't have to deal with Simon at work every day.

She frowned, thinking about the many ways she'd avoided him. There were only so many times she could duck away from him, ignore his notes and screen her calls, but she just couldn't bring herself to face him yet. It would be too painful to look into those brown eyes of his and not be able to tell him the truth. She was so tired of lying.

But as she walked out of the church into the drizzly late morning and saw Simon waiting for her at the bottom of the steps, she realized that she would have to face him, sooner than she had planned. She took a deep breath and descended the few steps, trying desperately to think of excuses for her recent behavior. *Stop being a coward,* she told herself.

"Hi," he greeted her, stepping forward and reaching out to help her down the last step. Gracious, old-fashioned gestures of courtesy like that were so natural with Simon, she thought wistfully. He looked more devastatingly handsome than usual in his freshly pressed Sunday clothes—dark gray trousers and a striped shirt with suspenders and a paisley tie. Even though it felt as if it might start pouring at any moment, he must have given into the heat and left his suit jacket in his Jeep.

"Were you just out here waiting?" she asked.

"No, I was inside, in the back." He smiled. "I noticed you were up where the action is, front pew and center."

She returned the grin. "Best to make your presence known where it counts."

"True," he said, walking her down the tree-lined walkway to the parking lot. "Unfortunately, I had to sneak in late. It took me a while to get Ted to tell me where you were."

"Ted?" She'd been wondering how he'd found her. She swallowed, always a little anxious when it came to Abel's dealings with others. "He didn't want to tell you where I was?"

"I had to wake him up." Simon sent her a lopsided smile. "I don't think your brother likes me very much."

"I'm sure it's nothing personal," she lied.

He looked her straight in the eye. "Maybe it's just because he knows you didn't want to be found."

Ellen stopped walking, her heart pounding nervously. Leave it to Simon to cut to the chase when you least expected it. "What makes you think that?"

He shook his head sadly. "You haven't exactly been seeking me out the past week."

"I know, but I've been so busy and..." She shrugged. "Well, I've been busy." She started walking again.

He took hold of her arm, gently but firmly, and turned her toward him. "A week and a half ago we had the most wonderful day. We talked and danced and then made mad, passionate love together. Are you so busy that you've forgotten that?"

She felt something like a knife twist inside her at the memories his words evoked. Forgotten? She'd been trying to fill up every single second of each day in order not to give herself time to remember...and still she hadn't been able to get the man off her mind. "I haven't forgotten," she admitted.

"Then what's wrong?" he asked. When she didn't answer, he added, "Look, if this is a bad time for you, maybe with your trouble with your brother and all of that, I understand. All you have to do is say so."

"This has nothing to do with Ted," she said defensively. "I just decided that things were moving too fast. I thought maybe we should give each other some breathing room for a while."

He looked at her doubtfully. "I know we said we'd take it step by step, but—"

"I think we should sort of put the brakes on what's happening between us," she said quickly, before she could talk herself out of it.

He breathed out a frustrated breath and combed a hand through his damp, slick hair. "'Slowing down' and 'putting on the brakes'—that doesn't even make sense! We've been sputtering along in fits and starts since the beginning. And as for giving each other space, I've only been in your house once," he reminded her.

His words made her feel lower than the low. Everything he said was true, and she couldn't bring herself to summon up more lies and evasions. What Simon deserved from her was the truth. The whole truth. God knows it had been welling up in her long enough, until she thought she might explode with it if she didn't tell someone. If Simon cared for her, he would understand.

She took a deep breath and squinted up at him through the light mist. He was waiting for her response. "I have something to tell you," she said.

"I'm listening."

Several people in their Sunday best walked past them, glancing curiously. This was not a conversation Ellen wanted overheard. "Come here," she said, gesturing. She ducked beneath the branches of a huge old live oak tree, away from the sidewalk.

Simon followed, an eyebrow arched in curious expectation. "This must be interesting," he said, crossing his arms when she came to a stop on the other side of the tree's massive trunk.

Ellen swallowed, struggling to summon the right words. Finally, looking down at her palms and rubbing them together nervously, she blurted out, "I'm sorry. I never should have gotten involved with you, Simon. I had no right."

For a moment, aside from the twittering of birds and the sounds of cars driving out of the church parking lot, there was silence. "Why not?" he asked finally.

She screwed up her courage to look at him. Here went nothing. Or everything.

"Because I'm living with an angel," she explained.

Chapter Twelve

The silence returned, and stretched, as Simon's face registered her words. Ellen could hear the blood rushing in her ears, and suddenly felt awkward at having blurted out the truth like that. But how else could she say it?

"An angel?" he asked finally, his voice beyond skeptical.

She squared her shoulders. "Well, he's not a full angel, exactly. More like a ghost," she corrected herself. A fat drop of moisture from one of the branches above plunked her on the head.

"A ghost," he repeated slowly.

Ellen swallowed. "It's Abel. My husband."

Simon stared at her, dumbfounded.

"He came back to me a month ago, on my birthday," she continued, anxious to fill in the awkward void. "You...well, you remember that day."

He squinted, then held up a hand in a halting gesture. "Wait. You're telling me that you're living with your husband? Your *late* husband?"

She nodded, relieved to have finally confessed, and to be understood. "Yes, exactly! It's been so terrible not to be able to tell anyone. Especially you—well, and my parents, of course. And his parents, too. Those poor people have been—"

"Ellen," he said, cutting her off. "Are you feeling all right?"

Her jaw snapped closed. "I feel fine."

He couldn't keep his shocked gaze off of her. "Then you must be crazy—or think I am!"

She took a step backward. "But surely this makes sense to you now. I couldn't invite you into my house because of Abel, don't you see?"

"Abel!" he repeated. When he spoke, it was in a loud, slow voice someone might use with a toddler. Or someone who was exceptionally loony. "Ellen, that's your *brother* you're living with. Ted, remember?"

She shook her head. He didn't believe her! "No, I lied," she explained. "That man you met on Sixth Street that night—that was Abel. And by the way, that *was* Jack Kerouac with him."

A look of extreme pity overcame him, and he stepped forward and grabbed her upper arms. "Ellen, please," he begged, shaking her slightly. "It's been four years. You have to try to pull yourself together."

She bit back a sigh of frustration. "I'm perfectly sane, Simon."

"I know you are," he agreed patiently. "You're just upset about finding someone new—"

"No!" she cried. "Abel is back. That's why my house is always so cold, because that's the temperature ghosts need."

"Listen to me, Ellen," he said, pulling her closer. "I'll go back home with you, and we'll turn up the thermostat together. Ted will be there, and you'll be able to see for yourself that he's your brother, not Abel."

"But he *is* Abel!" she practically howled.

He held her rigidly and stared deep into her eyes, obviously worried. Obviously thinking that she'd lost her mind.

Then, slowly, his head tilted and his expression shifted. "Wait a second," he said, his gaze narrowing suspiciously. "You really want me to swallow this story, don't you."

"It's the truth."

"Like hell," he said disgustedly. He let go of one of her arms and raked his hand through his hair again. "Oh, I'll admit I was falling for it."

"Ted is Abel," she insisted.

"Come on, Ellen. I'm not that gullible." He rolled his eyes. "But I almost was ready to believe that you were crazy. That's what you wanted, wasn't it?"

She couldn't believe what he was saying. "No!"

He ignored her protest, backing her up against the tree trunk. "You were too afraid to tell the truth, so you were going to cook up some wild story to scare me away."

"My wild story *is* the truth." How often was he going to force her to say it?

"You actually want me to believe that Abel is alive," he said, clearly not buying it.

"Not alive. He's an angel," she corrected him staunchly. "Well, almost an angel."

"A ghost. Right." He looked at her in silence, shaking his head. "If you regretted the other evening, Ellen, you didn't have to cook up this cockamamy story."

She let out a frustrated breath. "You'll never believe me."

There was a silence again, and then he took a step forward, leaning one hand against the tree trunk at her back. His rising anger was palpable as he loomed over her. "If you want my opinion, this is all to cover up the fact that you're afraid."

Her head snapped up, and she tossed him a challenging glance. She didn't like feeling penned in. "Afraid of what?"

"Losing someone."

She narrowed her eyes. Of course—she was terrified of losing Abel. But he said he didn't believe her story about her late husband coming back to her. "Who?"

"Me," he said.

She smirked at his immodesty. "I hardly think—"

"Don't get me wrong," he interrupted. "It would have been just the same with Martin Mayhew or that bearded fellow or even Larry Lambert. The truth is that you won't allow yourself to love someone because you're afraid of losing them like you lost your husband."

She crossed her arms, becoming surprisingly angry at his words. "What do you really know about my life?"

"I've seen enough to know that you've let a lot of it pass you by. What about your career?"

She tossed her head proudly. "For your information, I'm starting law school this year."

"Terrific," he said. "When are you going to take the time to start a marriage? Or have children—I doubt a ghost can give you those."

Ellen flushed scarlet and looked away. "My biological clock still has some time ticking on it."

He shook his head. "Well I hope it hasn't run out on you by the time you finally decide to stop mincing around life."

Even if his words held truth, she couldn't help being defensive. "Who are you to tell me how to run my life?"

He looked stunned, and took a moment before answering. "I thought that was obvious. I care about you, Ellen. More deeply than I ever expected to care for any woman."

The confession suddenly chilled her anger. Inside her, there was a bitter tug-of-war going on, threatening to split her heart in two. She'd never expected to care for another man, either—but she *couldn't* love anyone as much as Abel. It just wasn't possible.

Confusion overwhelmed her. Her eyes filled with moisture—not from the weather, but tears—and she lifted her hands to her head, rubbing gently at her temples. "I can't..." Her throat went dry before she could finish the sentence.

"Can't what?" he urged, his voice concerned, but firm.

She took a deep breath and looked him in the eye. "I can't go out with you anymore."

His brown eyes widened as if she'd struck him. "I see."

"No, you don't," she told him, wishing she could make him understand, wishing she could have two things at once. Abel *and* Simon. "If I could only make you believe what I'm telling you."

He grunted in exasperation and pushed away from the tree. "I *do* see," he said disgustedly, stepping away from her, distancing himself. "You'll never let yourself care for anyone else, Ellen. You say you're living with a ghost? Sure, I believe that."

"You do?" she asked doubtfully.

"A ghost of your own making," he told her. "A security blanket you've kept wrapped around you for four years. You'd rather live with a ghost than risk loving someone again."

Her jaw dropped in shock. "You have no idea—"

"Don't I?" he asked, swaggering toward her. He pinned her between both arms this time, so that there was no escaping him. "I've been drawn to you from the first, and when we kiss, when we make love, something sparks between us. You can't deny that. We belong together."

She shook her head, trying to look away from those eyes.

"But again and again, you keep erecting that barrier." His lips twisted in a bitter frown. "Your ghost. Well, if you ever screw up the courage to live again, let me know. I might still be around."

He pushed back, dug his hands in his pockets and walked away quickly, ducking his head against the thickening mist. Ellen felt like running after him, yet she remained where she was, frozen, her feet glued to the wet ground. *This is for the best,* she told herself. This was the conversation they should have had weeks ago. Clearly, he understood nothing about loss, or grief, or longing....

Longing is exactly what she felt at that moment. She longed to run after him, longed to have him hold her again, longed to have her divided feelings reconciled.

"GESUNDHEIT."

Ellen reached for another tissue, which she waved at Abel in acknowledgement before sneezing again. She'd been holed up in bed now for three days. Three days of feeling feverish and rundown, spent watching Abel prepare manically for his birthday party on Friday. And all the while, she couldn't help moping a little over Simon and their bitter words on Sunday. Luckily, since she hadn't been to work, she hadn't been forced to see him.

What he'd said had hit a nerve. Maybe she *had* been hiding behind her grief, using it as an excuse not to get involved with anyone. But that was before Abel had returned to her. He wasn't just a ghost of her own making—he was real, and he was with her again. She couldn't turn her back on him now. Not when she finally had what she'd wanted for so long.

Except now she wasn't certain that what she wanted was all that she'd thought it would be cracked up to be. Sure, Abel was here. But now she couldn't stop pining after Simon.

And Simon probably thought she was viciously trying to get rid of him by making up stories about ghosts. If he'd cooled off enough to realize that wasn't the case, he most likely assumed that she was crazy as a loon.

Oh, why did her life get so complicated just when it should have been so simple?

Abel returned with a huge bouquet of flowers. The spray of birds of paradise was spectacular, and she wondered at once where they had come from. "Are these for your party?" she asked. Abel was more a balloon-and-streamer sort of decorator.

"No, they just came for you," he said, placing them on her bedside table.

"Who could they be from?" she wondered aloud.

"You have to ask?" Abel rolled his eyes and snorted. "How about Simon Miller, Mr. FTD himself."

She frowned at him as she opened the tiny card. "That's impossible," she said, looking down to read the signature.

Get well soon.

Love, Simon

He'd sent her flowers, after all that he'd said to her? After what she'd said to him? Perhaps he wasn't mad at her anymore. Or maybe he was just too honorable a man to turn his back on someone he thought was a clear mental case. Yet he did sign the card "love" and not "sincerely" or simply with his name. . . .

When she looked up again, Abel's brow arched knowingly.

"How did you guess?"

He shrugged. "He hasn't been around, and since you've been moping—"

"I have not!" she defended. "I've just been sick. If it weren't so cold in here all the time, I probably would be fine."

The accusation in her statement didn't escape him. "Is the temperature what's caused you to have crying jags all week?" he asked, sending her a pitying look.

She ducked her head and blushed. "I'd hardly call them jags."

Abel sat on the edge of the bed. "Are you so sure you want things the way they are?"

"Of course!" she exclaimed. Then she paused. Why was he asking? "Don't you?"

He nodded, shrugging. "Sure."

Sure? "You seem awfully nonchalant," she pointed out.

"I thought I could afford to take things a little for granted around here," Abel said. "Am I wrong?"

She shook her head. "No, I want you to feel like you can stay here always."

"You don't sound like you mean it."

Her head snapped up. "Of course I do." Why did everyone insist on questioning what she said? "If that's what *you* want."

He smiled patiently. "Okay. Hey—wait till you see the entertainment I've lined up for the party. Everybody's gonna have a blast." He looked at her, concern in his eyes. "Hope you're okay by Friday."

"I will be," she said determinedly. "I'll be dancing all night in honor of your birthday."

Abel frowned and cocked his head to the side. "You hate to dance."

Ellen froze, remembering one day recently when she had very openly enjoyed it. Simon was the perfect partner. How could she dance with anyone else again?

She couldn't, she decided. Maybe it was overly sentimental, but that was an activity she would just have to give up from now on.

"Well, I'm sure I'll enjoy the music, anyway."

And she would just make herself forget about that other time.

SIMON SAT BACK AMONG the jumble of papers and files and books on his floor and looked at his watch. Six o'clock on Friday night, and here he was still at the office, with only the sounds of an old Barry Manilow tune for company. The instrumental music was supposed to be soothing, but snatches of the stupid seventies romantic ballad kept repeating in his mind—all about aching and taking and breaking. To someone already in romantic distress, it was the musical equivalent of Chinese water torture.

He should go home, like everybody else, but he had to stick around and do all the work he couldn't keep his mind on earlier in the day. One of the chores was to clean out his office, which was due to be painted dove blue over the weekend. He'd started off great guns this morning, but at noon he'd discovered the picture of him and Ellen in San Antonio, taken at the restaurant. He could have stared at the thing for hours, looking at the joyous gleam in her eyes, how her hair spilled down her shoulders, remembering all the while how it felt to hold her. Several times he attempted to put the photo away, but there was nowhere he could hide that picture that it wouldn't draw his attention back. Finally, he stopped trying and just placed it on his desk.

He sighed, considering throwing it away. Clearly, Ellen wanted nothing to do with him. He thought about those flowers he'd sent and could have kicked himself. *You just can't give up, can you?* Ellen either wanted him to think she was crazy, or actually *was* crazy, and still he hadn't been able to leave her alone.

He muttered at himself for being a vulnerable sap and tossed some papers in a box. He had a tense, sickening feeling inside his gut, one that didn't have anything to do with the fact that he hadn't eaten since breakfast. Lovesick, Yolanda would call it. Well, he'd better get used to it. Next week Ellen would be back at work, and he would have this kicked-in-the-stomach ache every time he had to look at her. Which, if Harlan Smith had his way, would be often.

Just this afternoon Harlan had come by asking if Simon were going to some party at Ellen's house, to which half the office had received invitations. Of course, Simon had never gotten one.

What did he expect?

There was a knock on his door, and Simon looked up. A good-looking man in a white hat and coveralls surveyed his office with removed interest. "Painter," the stranger gruffly explained. "We're doing this side tomorrow morning."

Simon nodded. "I'm cleaning as fast as I can."

"Good," the man said, coming forward, deftly sidestepping the mess on the floor. He picked up Ellen's picture off his desk—and seemed almost as captivated by her likeness as Simon was. "Say..." he muttered, "isn't this Ellen Lantry?"

"Yes, the woman who works down the hall," Simon answered.

The man stared down at him, owl-eyed. "Ellen works *here?*"

Simon tilted his head. How did this man know Ellen?

On second thought, did he have to ask?

"Say," the man wondered aloud, "do you know if she ever married that guy?"

Simon stood. "Which guy?" There seemed to be a multitude to choose from.

"Oh, I don't think she ever mentioned his name."

Simon held up his hand to try to clear some things up. "Could this by any chance be something she *wrote* to you?"

"Yeah, a couple of weeks ago. We'd been corresponding for..." He scratched his head. "Well, it had to be two months or more. Then all of the sudden I got this letter telling me she'd met this other guy and that it was really serious. That was it. Two months I'd invested in this lady, more writing than I'd done since my days in Miss Longoria's comp class in high school, and she just calls it off!" He snapped his fingers in front of his face. "Goodbye letters every week, goodbye romance, goodbye, Ed."

"That's too—" Simon stopped in midsentence. "Wait. Did you say your name is *Ed?*"

"Yeah. Ed Parton." He peered curiously at Simon over Ellen's photograph. "You know Ellen well?"

Simon wasn't sure how to answer. Ed had to be the person she'd been writing the "Dear Ed" letter to the day he'd found her legal pad in the little conference room. That had been the Monday after their first date together. So was *he* the guy responsible for her calling it quits with Ed? The one she was "really serious" about?

Nah, that couldn't be.

Yet he had to be. After all, there couldn't be an infinite number of men whom Ellen was hiding. Even she had her limits.

"I know her pretty well," Simon agreed carefully.

Ed shook his head. "Then you probably got one of those weird invitations, too!"

"No, I didn't," he said, still bitter on this point.

The painter pulled a card from his pants pocket and shoved it toward Simon. "Look at that, why don't you. First she tells me it's quits, then she sends me this invitation to her brother's birthday party. Like I'd ever show up to that," he said hotly. "I never even knew she had a brother!"

Simon looked up. "Neither did I, till recently. He seems to be the black sheep of the family."

"Oh, I don't give two hoots about the brother," Ed finished, resentfulness in his tone. "I guess I'm just sore about being written off." He barked out a laugh. "Literally!"

"So did you two ever meet?" Simon asked.

"Me and Ellen? No, never." He ducked his head. "I guess you're right. Hard to get too torn up about a woman when you've only seen her picture. But she sure is a looker, huh?"

"She sure is."

Ed sighed. "Oh, well. I guess stuff like this has happened to other people before."

"You'd be surprised how many times," Simon assured him, still staring at the invitation. Ted's birthday party started at eight o'clock tonight.

"Do me a favor," Ed asked.

"What?"

"If you see Ellen, don't tell her you met me, okay?"

Simon frowned. "Why not?"

He shrugged. "I dunno. Maybe I fibbed a little when I wrote to her. You know, like, maybe I forgot somehow to tell her exactly what kind of painter I was." He tugged at his white trousers. "I mean, I'm not exactly Van Gogh here, you know what I mean?"

"I don't think she'd care about that," Simon assured him.

"Still, if it's all the same to you, I'd like to let it rest. Not that I'm heartbroken, mind you. The way I figure it, if I was really in love with the woman, I wouldn't be wandering around an office looking at paint chipping on the walls. I'd be at home, getting ready to go to that party and do my best to win her over. Know what I mean?"

A lump formed in Simon's throat. "Yeah, I know."

"I mean, the lady said it herself." He cleared his throat and quoted from memory, " 'Love is one of the conditions for happiness.' "

Actually, Albert Camus said that, Simon thought, smiling wistfully. He appeared to be the only man on Earth who hadn't received a letter from Ellen, yet he was beginning to know her writing style by the material she stole.

"So if I'm happy without her, which I am," Ed continued, "it must not be love, huh?" He didn't wait for an answer. "Well, it was nice meeting you."

Simon lifted his head, but said nothing. By the time he thought to respond, Ed was already gone, anyway. Maybe he wasn't thinking too clearly this evening. He looked back down at the invitation that was still in his hand.

It's a party! The confetti and streamers in primary colors festooning the invitation were completely at odds with how he felt. Those bright, exuberant colors seemed to have found their way into his hands from another world entirely.

And yet, he had felt a moment of celebration when he'd thought that *he* was the man Ellen had written to Ed about. Could it be true? Or maybe she'd just been making up an excuse. But it was curious timing, coming after their date....

How would he ever know?

Ask her.

He looked up again, considering the idea. Ed's words came back to him. *If I was really in love with the woman, I wouldn't be wandering around an office....*

Simon shook his head.

No. He'd already sent her flowers when she had made it clear she wanted nothing to do with him. In fact, he'd never chased after a woman for so long with so little result. And yet...

No. Definitely not, he decided, bending down again to stuff boxes with papers, working more quickly now. The party started at eight. It was just after six. That left...

No. He was not going. If Ellen wanted to change her mind, she could do it without his help. She knew where he lived. She certainly knew where he worked. He didn't care how unhappy it made him, he wasn't going to go to her house tonight.

No way.

Chapter Thirteen

Martin Mayhew was beside himself. "Celebrity City, Arizona!"

Ellen tried to shrug casually, but she had to admit, it was hard for her to take her eyes off Abel's impressive guests. Late movie stars, more garden-variety ghosts and mere mortals mixed easily. Yolanda was there, as was Harlan Smith, his stark silver hair a standout in the milling group. Both Ellen and Martin kept their eye out on Annie, who was the life of the party. She had been out in the middle of the dancing area in the streamered backyard boogying with James Dean until another familiar face had cut in. Joe, the hunk in the Volvo. Much to Ellen's discomfort, Abel had invited everyone.

She wasn't in the most festive of moods—just getting over a cold, she told herself, rationalizing her status as resident party pooper—but even she felt drawn to the festive hoard, bizarre as it was.

When the lead singer for the evening stepped up to the mike and started singing "Jailhouse Rock," she thought Martin was going to lose it. "I can't believe it's...no." Martin shook his head and pushed his glasses up the bridge of his nose, peering out in amazement at the dark-haired, swivel-hipped rocker. After a second and third look, he turned to Ellen. "I didn't know this was a costume party."

She cast him a sly glance. "Can you keep a secret, Martin?"

He nodded eagerly.

"It's not."

He shot her a edgy look, not certain whether she was kidding him or she was crazy. "I think I'll see if I can't get to Annie somehow," he muttered, walking away.

Next time she looked, the dentist was dancing with Jean Harlow, but his eyes were on Ellen's neighbor, two couples away. To Ellen's amazement, Annie and Martin exchanged syrupy gazes over the people separating them.

She couldn't believe it. Annie was dancing with the handsomest guy there—just the kind of man she'd been searching for—and Martin with one of the sexiest women to come along in a century or so, and yet they only had eyes for each other. Moments later, Martin cut in on Joe to dance a slow number with Annie.

Ellen tried not to be envious. But, implausible as it seemed, they looked so... romantic. She swayed wistfully to the music. *You don't like to dance, remember?* Not without the perfect partner.

She'd stopped berating herself for thinking about Simon too much. That, she'd discovered, was a futile task. She'd had a whole week to consider his words, his accusation that she was putting life at bay by living with a ghost. Looking around her, what better proof did she need?

At the end of the song, Annie came running over. "What a party!"

Ellen nodded. "I saw you dancing with Martin."

"I think it's love!"

Ellen couldn't believe her ears. "But what about Joe the hunk and James Dean—I mean, all the other guys?"

"Oh, I like them, too." Annie shrugged. "But you know what? Ever since I met Martin, I've been wondering if I hadn't been chasing after the wrong thing. Martin's the dependable type. And don't you just love those cute little glasses?"

Ellen smiled limply. In her own way, wasn't that what she'd been doing—wanting something that wasn't necessarily right for her? She glanced over at the jitterbugging Samuelsons, who were apparently continuing their nonstop bliss-a-thon.

"Hard to believe a month ago we were both so bored, bored, bored all the time," Annie said.

Ellen nodded. Life certainly had been calmer then.

The music changed tempos again, this time to a tremulous tango, sans Elvis. Suddenly, Martin appeared, two plastic cups in hand. Hearing the music, he immediately set them aside and grabbed Annie's arm. "Dance with me," he begged.

"He's so persuasive," Annie confided with a giggle just before she was swept away.

Ellen was left standing alone, partnerless.

She'd wondered at the restlessness she'd felt as she was laid up in bed this week, which she'd chalked up to her cold. But it was more than sneezing and sniffles. It was those flowers, and remembering Simon. And realizing, too late, that she'd fallen in love with him.

Being cooped up in the house together for a week made her see that she and Abel could never have the life they'd enjoyed before. Deep down, she wasn't even sure she wanted to. Abel had other things on his agenda. She thought about another separation from Abel, and painful as it was, it didn't frighten her like it used to. Watching him out there, host of ghosts and guests, standing beside Cliff Webber and Marilyn Monroe and Jack Kerouac, she didn't feel the void she used to. She could reach out and he would be there, forever young, forever the first man she'd ever loved. And he wasn't alone.

Maybe meeting Simon had made her realize that she wouldn't always have to be alone, either. Oh, she had no illusions that there was hope of salvaging that relationship. She could mope all she wanted and that wouldn't change the fact that he probably never wanted to lay eyes on her again, in spite of his get-well bouquet. But maybe someday she would meet someone else, under better circumstances...and next time she would know to keep her lip buttoned about ghosts.

"Next time" wasn't much of a consolation to her broken heart, though. For the second time in her life, she was deeply, irrevocably in love—but now Simon probably wanted her about as much as he would want the bubonic plague.

Ellen turned, walking toward the back of the yard, where there was a small iron table and a lawn chair set up by a rose bush. When she was certain she was out of earshot, she took out a Kleenex and blew her nose, then rubbed her eyes with the back of her hand.

"Silly," she said to herself. Here everyone was dancing and drinking and celebrating, and all she could do was collapse onto the lawn furniture in a weepy heap.

"The party isn't working, is it."

Ellen looked up and saw Abel standing in front of her, his hands in his jeans pockets. "It's a wonderful party, Abel," she said, dabbing at a tear. "Everyone's having such a good time, even my boss. Seeing him dance up a storm, you'd never guess how sick he was just months ago."

Abel smiled patiently. "Some of them react that way." He sighed, then flopped down in the grass next to her just as another tear spilled down her cheek. "Oh, man. I've really screwed things up, haven't I. No wonder I'm a loser angel.''

"No, you're not!" Ellen insisted. "It's not your fault I'm unhappy. You came all the way from heaven to help me—not many people get that kind of assistance."

"Yeah, but it didn't work."

She shrugged. "I guess I'm just a tough case."

"You're just in love," he corrected her.

She opened her mouth to contradict him, but clamped it shut again. What was the point in denying it? She nodded miserably.

"Man, this is my fault," Abel confessed, running his fingers through his thick hair. "I saw right away how you felt about Simon, but I sabotaged you."

"I'm to blame, too. I never intended to go through with the original bargain. I wanted you. And then I wanted to have you and Simon both."

Abel shook his head. "You understand now, don't you? It's cheating life to live in the past. And you've got a lot of life ahead of you."

"I do?" she asked, surprised. He seemed very definite about this point.

He smiled. "I want to make things right for you, Ellen. If there's anything I can do, or say to him—"

She shook her head. "No, I'm afraid I really bungled it. It would take more than a miracle to change his mind now." Which meant more lonely days ahead. She bit her lip worriedly. "You can't leave now, can you?"

He hesitated.

"I feel guilty," Ellen said. "All this time you've been worrying over me, when you should have been tending to your good deeds."

Abel looked at her, his expression suddenly thoughtful, as if an idea had just occurred to him. "It wasn't wasted time, Ellen. A good deed might come of it yet."

"What do you mean?"

He shrugged. "Never mind," he said, getting up. "Don't you want to come meet some of my friends? Herman's here."

She shook her head slowly. "I don't know...I might feel a little out place talking to Herman Melville. But I wouldn't mind something cool and bubbly to drink," she said, straightening up.

Abel reached out and took her hand. "Stay where you are, babe. One cold and bubbly, coming right up."

He squeezed her hand and was about to let go when she stopped him. "Abel..." She took a breath, leaned forward and kissed his cheek. "Thanks."

"For what?"

"For coming back. I needed you."

"No problem." The smile he shot her was his old, reassuring grin. "Everybody needs an angel sometime."

He let go of her hand and backed away slowly, almost reluctantly, though he was only heading off to the snack table. Finally, he turned and started strolling away, his head bobbing to the music, his blond hair spilling down his back. Ellen watched him go until his flannel shirt disappeared into the crowd in her yard.

She leaned back in the chair and closed her eyes. For the first time in weeks, she felt relaxed. Maybe it was because of the warm summer air, or the gentle music. That familiar voice was singing one of her all-time favorites, "As Time Goes By," which made her smile. Anachronism notwithstanding, it wasn't a bad rendition. As she listened, she stretched like a cat and felt a surprisingly cool refreshing night breeze wash over her body.

She couldn't imagine what was causing the sleepy, content feeling she had. She'd been off cold medicine for a few days now, and she hadn't had anything to drink so far tonight. Yet it seemed the very air had a buzz to it suddenly, and she simply lay back, enjoying it, bathing herself in moonlight and the soft receding sounds of music. And then it sounded as if all the sounds of the party were becoming distant—the voices, the laughter, the clinking of ice cubes against cups and glasses. For a moment, she thought Abel had come back to her, bearing the promised glass, but her vision of him became fuzzy, and then he was gone altogether. Another light breeze cooled her skin, and she listened for the sounds of people around her.

Strangely, there was only silence, except for one word, whispered, heartfelt, carried on the wind. Goodbye.

FROM A DISTANCE, Abel watched her sleeping and smiled, filled with equal parts sadness and satisfaction. He'd had few successes in his life, but his marriage to Ellen had been a definite high point. Now, summoning up the will to leave, was another.

He'd been selfish to stand in her way, to cling to her in any manner he could. He'd just assumed that, coming from where he did, his motives would remain aboveboard. Though angels didn't age, he discovered they still sometimes had plenty of growing up to do.

The solution to their quandaries was deceptively simple. After months of straining to devise ways to make Ellen happy and even out his good deed debit, the answer to both problems came to him in stunning clarity. Sometimes the best deed was simply to let go.

"ELLEN, ARE YOU AWAKE?"

She wasn't certain how long she had lain sprawled out in

her chair, but the voice that awoke her certainly wasn't the one she'd been expecting. Her eyes popped open, and she immediately sat up, disoriented.

"Simon!" she said. She was so glad, so shocked, to see him standing there in his jeans and polo shirt that she was certain that her whole face lit up as much as his did. She lunged forward and gave him a huge hug.

He returned it full force. "You seem to have made a full recovery," he said.

"Now that you're here, I feel much better." She looked up, checking to make sure this was him, that this wasn't another part of that odd dream she'd been having. "Oh, Simon, I've been wanting to apologize all week for the horrible way I acted last Sunday."

"Then you don't mind that I crashed your shindig?" he asked.

"Not a bit!" she said emphatically. Only... her shindig, so recently in full swing, was now apparently over. The yard was empty, the air shockingly silent. She gasped, pushing away from Simon's chest.

"Where is everybody?"

He looked around the lawn, now eerily deserted except for the snack table piled with empty plastic cups and cans.

"Looks like the party picked up and moved elsewhere," he said.

"But..." Ellen blinked, unable to believe her eyes. She ran across the lawn, completely confused. What happened to Abel and Annie, and Martin, and Elvis? The food was gone, too, and the ice chests of soda and beer. "They cleaned us out!"

Simon walked up behind her, surveying the damage. "I wouldn't call this clean, exactly."

She laughed, then turned. For the first time, she noticed Simon was carrying something in his hands—a champagne bottle.

He held it up for her to inspect and smiled. "I guess it's a good thing I brought this. It's the one I bought for your birthday, remember? I told you it would keep."

One cold and bubbly, coming right up. Ellen stood stunned, suddenly understanding what had happened. Abel was fulfilling her request...with an added bonus. She looked into Simon's heartbreaking brown eyes and felt her chest constrict painfully, felt tears building again. Had Abel rounded up Simon especially for her...or had he simply gotten out of their way?

Maybe they would never know.

"Being the last guest, and an uninvited one at that," Simon continued helpfully, obviously in a clearer frame of mind than she was, "I certainly don't mind doing cleanup detail. If you've got the garbage bags, I've got the time."

She took the champagne from him. She had the suspicion she was going to need it. "Since you brought the bubbly, how can I refuse?"

They made short work of doing away with the party refuse, folding up the tables on the back patio, and setting everything to rights again. A half hour later, the champagne was popped open by the combined yellow glow of bug light and moon.

Ellen held up her glass. "To party crashers."

Simon's eyes sparkled as he clinked his plastic cup against hers. "To absent guests."

Ellen nodded. She had one absent guest in particular to toast, and she did so silently, taking a sip and sending up a silent prayer for his safe return.

"And to the most beautiful hostess a man could ask for," Simon continued. "Now, if only we had some music."

"We do!" Ellen said. She turned and found the boom box she had set up in the corner as an emergency measure, before she'd realized that no one was likely to have any complaints about the band Abel had put together. Next to it were a few tapes. "Any requests?"

"Anything—as long as it has a good beat and you can dance to it."

She tossed him a saucy glance. "Who do I look like, Dick Clark?"

He shook his head, giving her a head-to-toe once-over that made her shiver. "Not a bit."

She popped in her favorite old standby Frank Sinatra tape and joined him. Simon took the glass out of her hand, placed it at her feet with his and pulled her into his arms. "Frank?" he asked, twirling her playfully to the tune of "Witchcraft." "Seems like you have something in common with Mr. Samuelson."

What would Simon have said if she told him that Mr. Samuelson and his angelic wife were two of her guests tonight? Ellen decided not to test him. He'd apparently forgiven her for seeing ghosts once, and she was now too experienced in the fragile nature of second chances to blow this one. She looped her arms lightly around his neck and smiled.

"More than you know," she assured him.

"It's a good thing I'm not prone to jealousy," he told her, adding, "that's just another of my good qualities."

"What are the others?"

"Well . . ." He dipped her low, then brought her back up with a dizzying spin. "I suppose charm would be up there on the list. And intelligence, of course. Did I ever tell you I was second in my class at law school?"

She laughed. "Don't leave out modesty."

"That was the next thing I was going to mention." His expression sobered. "But maybe we should be discussing my bad qualities, instead."

She tilted him a doubtful glance. "Bad qualities? You?"

"Admit it. I've annoyed you."

"Persistence is usually considered a good quality," she informed him.

"Then how about the way I acted last Sunday—lashing out at you when you were so obviously on the brink of a serious illness." He shook his head. "I was kicking myself all week."

"I didn't behave too well myself."

"Yeah, but—"

She stopped his worrying by placing two fingers against his lips. "I think we should make a pledge. What's past is past. I want to start concentrating on the future."

He kissed her fingers, then reached up and took her hand. Their dance came to a standstill. "That's a pledge I'd be happy to take, as long as I figure into your vision of the future."

To answer, she rose up onto her toes and pressed her lips against his. "I think that could be arranged," she assured him.

He pulled her close, a broad grin spreading across his lips. He looked so handsome, so irresistible. How wonderful life was going to be now that she didn't have to resist him!

The strains of "As Time Goes By" started up, and they began swaying to the gentle rhythm of the old tune. Once the song had brought tears to her eyes, reminding her of all she'd lost. Now she clung to Simon, her thoughts racing forward, not to the past. Time was such a precious commodity.

"I have so many plans now," she said, "so much to do in the days ahead."

"How about the years ahead?" Simon asked her.

"Oh." Ellen swallowed, looking up at him. "I hadn't really thought *that* far in advance."

"Looking at you," he told her, "I feel as though I could map out a lifetime or two." He pulled her close against him and looked directly into her eyes. "I love you, Ellen. I've loved you ever since I met you." He laughed lightly. "Maybe even before."

Maybe that wasn't as impossible as it sounded. She heard the words and felt her heart soar with happiness. "I love you, too," she said.

"For a lifetime?"

"Forever," she said, just as he lifted her into his arms for a last dizzying twirl before carrying her inside.

Epilogue

Four months later...

Simon took Ellen's hand. "This is it," he told her.

"Are you sure you want to be saddled with me for the rest of your life?" Ellen asked him, a little worried crease appearing across her brow.

He kissed it away and couldn't help but laugh. Saddled with Ellen? He couldn't think of a happier fate awaiting any man. "Just get me in front of that judge so I can prove it to you!"

"All right, then, but you won't be able to say later that I didn't give you every opportunity to change your mind."

"That's not an opportunity I'll need," he promised as they walked into the chambers of Judge Clint Jergens.

After months of trying to plan out when to arrange a church wedding between Simon's work and Ellen's new law school schedule and including both their families—as well as trying to round up Ellen's brother, who had suddenly picked up and moved to Alaska—they'd finally decided that it would be much more romantic to ditch everything for a week and elope. After making a quick stop in front of an Austin judge, they would drive to Louisiana and have a whole week to relax and explore that beautiful state, culminating in a few days in New Orleans.

They walked into the paneled room decked from floor to ceiling with books, and Simon felt an immediate hint of regret. It was all so familiar—like getting married at work! The clerk introduced them to Judge Jergens, a handsome man of medium height with a carefully tended full beard. His dignified demeanor as he stood to greet them pacified Simon somewhat...until the judge got a close look at Ellen.

"Ellen?" his honor asked, a smile of amazement spreading across his face. His whole expression brightened. "Ellen Lantry?"

Her head tilted dubiously, and the few sprigs of baby's breath that she'd braided into her hair drooped to one side. "Y-yes...?"

"I can't believe it's you!" the judge exclaimed. "Don't you remember me? It's me, Clint!"

Simon felt his stomach turn in dread.

"Oh..." Ellen, with her summer bouquet held in a white-knuckled grip, began to back up, tugging Simon with her. "I don't quite..."

"You look just like your picture," Clint assured her. "Only older. Look, I still have it!" He ran back to his desk and pulled open the top drawer.

Ellen sent a silent but desperate, pleading glance to Simon.

"I'm sorry, Ellen," Simon announced. "I've changed my mind."

Ellen gasped again, and he sent her a sly wink.

The judge stopped and looked up before he could produce an eight-by-ten glossy photo of Ellen. "Oh, dear," he said. "I hope I haven't—"

Simon held up his free hand. The other hand kept a firm hold on Ellen's as they continued in a backward lockstep toward the door. "That's all right. Please don't feel responsible."

"But if it's about our correspondence, let me assure you it was all innocence. She even signed her letters with 'Sincerely.'"

Ellen stopped, frowning. "I did?"

Simon rolled his eyes. "Come on, Ellen, I think we have some discussing to do."

He pulled her out the door and she stumbled after him, down the tile hallways of the old office building. He stopped at a pay phone.

"I'm sorry, Simon," Ellen said, casting her eyes down to the pavement at her feet. "I had no idea.... Who are you calling?"

"Harlan."

"Our boss?" Ellen asked. "What for?"

"I thought he might know of another judge who would marry us." He looked at her as he dialed. "Harlan's done more to engineer our relationship than you realize. First, he brought me to Austin—and do you know he talked about you from the very first? He was the one who told me about your birthday. And then he arranged for that day in San Antonio—" Simon stopped abruptly. Ellen's face was as white as a sheet.

"'Some of them react that way,'" she muttered vaguely. "Oh, dear. He's one, too—and I thought I was so good at spotting them!"

"One what?" Simon frowned. She seemed agitated by the old man's interference. "He was only trying to help, Ellen. Don't you believe in guardian angels?"

She tilted her head and shot him a wry look. "Boy, do I." She placed her hand over his, hung up the phone, then tugged him out toward the glass doors that led out to the bright, sun-drenched pavement in front of the courthouse. "Can't we just find a judge on the way to Louisiana?"

"All right, if you'll answer me this," Simon said, stopping her. "Say we stopped to get married along the way, would we be likely to run into another one of your mystery men?"

"I swear, that was absolutely the last one," she vowed as they walked to where the Jeep was parallel-parked by the curb. "Absolutely."

Simon smiled as he got in and started up the vehicle. "Good." It was nice to know that no more men would be popping out of the woodwork proclaiming to be eternally devoted to his wife. Though he could certainly understand the feeling.

"At least," Ellen added underneath her breath, "he was the last one that I know of..."

He nearly plowed into a Buick as they pulled into traffic. "How could you not know?"

She shrugged sheepishly. "It's sort of a long story."

"I'd like to hear it."

"You won't believe it," she warned.

"Try me."

She crossed her arms and leaned back, a secretive smile pulling at her lips. "You just keep driving, Simon. I'll tell you all about everything—*after* we're married."

DRIFTING ON A FLUFFY white cloud high above, Abel looked down at the Jeep speeding toward the Louisiana border and grinned. Finally! Seeing Ellen so blissfully happy made him happy, too. And more than that, he felt a huge load had been taken off his immortal shoulders. Now all he had to do was figure out what to do with all this time stretching before him.

But he'd always been a guy who appreciated spare time. Besides, he might not have suitors to write to anymore, but there was one ruse he would have to keep up for a long, long time. He sat up, leaned back on one of those new wings of his, and began to write.

Dear Sis,
Alaska is about the coolest place you could ever imagine. . . .

BRIDE'S BAY RESORT

UNLOCK THE DOOR TO GREAT ROMANCE AT BRIDE'S BAY RESORT

Join Harlequin's new across-the-lines series, set in an exclusive hotel on an island off the coast of South Carolina.

Seven of your favorite authors will bring you exciting stories about fascinating heroes and heroines discovering love at Bride's Bay Resort.

Look for these fabulous stories coming to a store near you beginning in January 1996.

Harlequin American Romance #613 in January
Matchmaking Baby by Cathy Gillen Thacker

Harlequin Presents #1794 in February
Indiscretions by Robyn Donald

Harlequin Intrigue #362 in March
Love and Lies by Dawn Stewardson

Harlequin Romance #3404 in April
Make Believe Engagement by Day Leclaire

Harlequin Temptation #588 in May
Stranger in the Night by Roseanne Williams

Harlequin Superromance #695 in June
Married to a Stranger by Connie Bennett

Harlequin Historicals #324 in July
Dulcie's Gift by Ruth Langan

Visit Bride's Bay Resort each month wherever Harlequin books are sold.

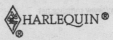

HARLEQUIN ®

BBAYG

HARLEQUIN®
AMERICAN ◆ ROMANCE®
®

Maybe This Time...

Maybe this time...they'll get what they really wanted all those years ago. Whether it's the man who got away, a baby, or a new lease on life, these four women will get a second chance at a once-in-a-lifetime opportunity!

Four top-selling authors have come together to make you believe that in the world of American Romance anything is possible:

#642 ONE HUSBAND TOO MANY
Jacqueline Diamond
August

#646 WHEN A MAN LOVES A WOMAN
Bonnie K. Winn
September

#650 HEAVEN CAN WAIT
Emily Dalton
October

#654 THE COMEBACK MOM
Muriel Jensen
November

Look us up on-line at: http://www.romance.net

MTTG

HARLEQUIN®

Don't miss these Harlequin favorites by some of our most
distinguished authors!
And now, you can receive a discount by ordering two or more titles!

HT #25663	THE LAWMAN by Vicki Lewis Thompson	$3.25 U.S. ☐/$3.75 CAN. ☐
HP #11788	THE SISTER SWAP by Susan Napier	$3.25 U.S. ☐/$3.75 CAN. ☐
HR #03293	THE MAN WHO CAME FOR CHRISTMAS by Bethany Campbell	$2.99 U.S. ☐/$3.50 CAN. ☐
HS #70667	FATHERS & OTHER STRANGERS by Evelyn Crowe	$3.75 U.S. ☐/$4.25 CAN. ☐
HI #22198	MURDER BY THE BOOK by Margaret St. George	$2.89 ☐
HAR #16520	THE ADVENTURESS by M.J. Rodgers	$3.50 U.S. ☐/$3.99 CAN. ☐
HH #28885	DESERT ROGUE by Erin Yorke	$4.50 U.S. ☐/$4.99 CAN. ☐

(limited quantities available on certain titles)

	AMOUNT	$
DEDUCT:	10% DISCOUNT FOR 2+ BOOKS	$
ADD:	POSTAGE & HANDLING	$
	($1.00 for one book, 50¢ for each additional)	
	APPLICABLE TAXES**	$_____
	TOTAL PAYABLE	$_____
	(check or money order—please do not send cash)	

To order, complete this form and send it, along with a check or money order for the
total above, payable to Harlequin Books, to: **In the U.S.:** 3010 Walden Avenue,
P.O. Box 9047, Buffalo, NY 14269-9047; **In Canada:** P.O. Box 613, Fort Erie, Ontario,
L2A 5X3.

Name: _____

Address: _____ City: _____

State/Prov.: _____ Zip/Postal Code: _____

**New York residents remit applicable sales taxes.
  Canadian residents remit applicable GST and provincial taxes.   HBACK-JS3

Look us up on-line at: http://www.romance.net